BANJO
BOY

BANJO

VINCE KOHLER

BOY

ST. MARTIN'S PRESS   NEW YORK

Design by Judith A. Stagnitto

Library of Congress Cataloging-in-Publication Data

Kohler, Vincent.
    Banjo boy / Vince Kohler.
        p.   cm.
    ISBN 0-312-11475-3
    1. Journalists—Oregon—Fiction. I. Title.
PS3561.0358B36   1994
813'.54—dc20   94-18216
                                                         CIP

First Edition: September 1994
10 9 8 7 6 5 4 3 2 1

AUTHOR'S NOTE

Banjo Boy is a novel. Like its predecessors, *Rainy North Woods* and *Rising Dog,* it is about imaginary people and their adventures on a fictitious stretch of the southern Oregon coast.

The story is set in an isolated American town just before the start of the Reagan-Bush years. Thus, some of the characters express social and sexual attitudes unacceptable today. None of the characters, places, or events have counterparts in the real world. Any references to reality are fictitious.

for
Marie Steuerwald
and
Marguerite Lonergan

ACKNOWLEDGMENTS

Many people helped make *Banjo Boy* a reality. They include my wife and manuscript editor, Mary Joan O'Connell; Steve Perry, author of the "Matador" novels; and Brian McCullough, Bridget Madill, and Daniel Haché, who assisted with Eldon's French. Others who stuck in useful oars include Jerry Baron, Foster Church, Paul Duchene, Jim Lane, Paul Menconi, Rod Patterson, and Phillip M. Margolin, author of *Gone, But Not Forgotten* and other thrillers.

Special thanks go to Charley Stough for revealing the secrets of topiary and to David Rosenak for his invaluable advice on playing poker. Any errors are entirely mine.

As usual, I owe a debt to Sharon Jarvis, my agent; and to Michael Denneny, Keith Kahla, John Clark, and John Hall of St. Martin's Press, New York.

The citations from Arthur Rimbaud are from *A Season in Hell & The Drunken Boat,* translated by Louise Varèse (New York: New Directions Books, 1961). The citations from Paul Verlaine are from *Two Volumes of Erotic Poems: "Lovers" and "Women,"* translated by Maurice Gloser (Los Angeles: Avanti Art Editions, 1972).

most of these rats here are just rats
but this rat is like me he has a human soul in him
he used to be a poet himself

—DON MARQUIS,
The Lives and Times of Archy and Mehitabel

Show your cards all players. Pay it all pay it all
pay it all back.

—WILLIAM S. BURROUGHS,
Nova Express

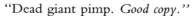

1

"Dead giant pimp. *Good copy.*"

The words resonated in the telephone receiver that Eldon Larkin pressed to his ear. It was Jimbo Fiske, calling from the newsroom of the *South Coast Sun.*

"Dead giant pimp," the editor repeated. "Dee-de-dee!" Fiske sounded as if he were gasping with excitement.

"Where?" Eldon asked.

"In Scoquel. Down among the tulips in south county. Body in a house, blown to bits. Scanner says the sheriff is rolling. Good thing you told me where you were headed."

"I'm on my way."

"You don't have a car—"

"I do now." Eldon slammed down the receiver and turned to the used-car salesman. "Gimme those keys."

The salesman looked like the victim of some wasting disease who was still healthy enough to plan larceny. His bright green leisure suit hung on a scrawny frame. "So you're gonna buy—"

"Take it on a test drive." Eldon snatched the keys, grabbed his notebook and battered Nikkormat camera and charged out of the mobile home that was the car lot's office.

The car was an old Isetta, parked beneath a sagging line of red and blue plastic pennants among rundown pickups and autos a decade old. It looked like a dented egg: white and pale blue, glistening with droplets from the recent early summer rain. Head-lights stuck out on either side like Mickey Mouse ears.

"It's a three-wheeler—" Eldon tried to find the door.

"Naw, it's not," the salesman said. "The back wheels are just real close together. The front opens up." He shambled down the mobile home's redwood steps, twisted a handle on the car, and pulled; the front swung out on squeaky hinges.

Eldon scrambled inside. The seat was little more than an upholstered board. "How does it start?"

"You gotta leave a credit card as security."

"I'm Eldon Larkin from the *Sun*. You know where to find me."

The salesman shrugged. "Starter's on the right. Go easy on the turns—"

"Right."

The salesman slammed the hatch. Eldon squared his floppy jungle hat on his head, taking care not to catch his fingers on the fishing flies decorating it. He turned the key and was elated when the engine caught immediately.

The gearshift stuck out of the left-hand wall. Eldon fumbled the lever into the wrong gear—third was where he expected first to be—and nearly killed the engine.

"It's a reverse-H pattern!" the salesman yelled. "Shift backwards!"

Eldon yanked the lever toward his stomach, got the car into first gear, and hit the gas. The Isetta lurched forward. He twisted the wheel and headed out onto Bayside Drive, rolling south through shabby, rain-swept Port Jerome, Oregon. *Good copy* lay ahead. He began to think it wouldn't be too bad a day.

All I need now is to meet a nice woman, Eldon thought.

He depressed the accelerator. The car picked up speed, vibrating as he drove through town. Port Jerome's core was a collection of bars, stores, and gas stations along the edge of Nekaemas Bay, where a couple of rusty cargo ships added to the vacant, desolate effect. Back from the highway, weathered Victorian houses, stucco cottages, and clapboard dwellings faded into a deep-green forest of pine and Douglas fir. Blowing mist made the forest seem to be in slow flight; the treetops appeared to drift like sails in the gray sea of the sky.

2

Eldon avoided looking in the rearview mirror as he drove. He knew all too well what he would see if he adjusted the mirror—a fair, fleshy face with sandy hair and a walrus moustache: an innocent face with a choir boy's blue eyes and plump cheeks. But his eyes were tired and filled with disillusion; his hair was starting to recede. God, it was already 1979. Already he was thirty-three.

He watched instead the people on the street—obese women in polyester, their hairstyles years out of date, teenagers with empty, insolent expressions driving pickups, and ferret-eyed, rangy men in dirty jeans and baseball caps splashing indifferently through puddles in their logger boots. *Dawn of the Dead* was the first-run movie at the theater—something about people trying to escape from man-eating zombies. Eldon had started amusing himself by imagining South Coast residents as cannibals, trying to decide which ones would enjoy munching which parts of their victims. He was beginning to scare himself with his own joke.

What could Fiske be talking about?

Eldon drove past the skeletal smokestacks and great derelict log pile of the abandoned Wapello Head Mill at the edge of town, past the bridge that led to the village of Regret, where he lived, and headed south on U.S. 101. He'd covered nearly every murder and fatal accident here in Nekaemas County, Oregon, since 1973. Six years of violent death. But it had provided *good copy*. That and the fishing made up for a lot.

Eldon stopped thinking about whatever story lay ahead—there would be plenty of time for that—and concentrated on the Isetta's performance. There was a giddy sense of speed; since the Isetta had no hood, he was looking through the front window directly onto the road. The highway widened to four lanes for a short stretch, and Eldon took the opportunity to carefully change lanes. The steering wheel twitched under his hands and then settled down. So far, so good. His luck with cars was no better than his luck with women, but this ridiculous little import just might do if he could keep it running.

What about parts? How do I get them? Can I afford them? Eldon wondered. Where can I find an Isetta mechanic? The most recent woman in his life had been a mechanic, but she was out of the question. She had nearly gotten him killed. . . .

Eldon steered down the wet highway as it turned inland. The road wound through the lush dairy country of the Nekaemas Valley, where coastal fir and pine gave way to pastures and deciduous growth. He passed through Preacher's Hole, the run-down county seat, and reached the turnoff for Scoquel a few miles later. Eldon slowed and made the turn. The wheel twitched again. The Isetta tottered. Eldon's heart lurched. It would be awfully easy to roll this thing, he thought.

A car going the other way flashed by. Eldon had a momentary impression of the driver's smiling, white-bearded face and fluorescent bow tie—Dr. Rosenak, the county medical examiner, returning from the crime scene.

They'll have the stiff in the ambulance and gone before I even get there, Eldon thought.

He stepped on the gas. The Isetta vibrated.

The two-lane spur road ran downhill into the little Scoquel Valley. The sun had broken through the clouds, and the valley floor was bright with row upon row of irises: yellow, purple, and white. They sparkled from the rain. Eldon envisioned a shootout between two commercial flower growers, bullets and flower petals flying. But Fiske had said "dead giant pimp." The words were clear enough—but made no sense.

Eldon spotted flashing blue lights ahead, just off the road. Sheriff's cars. But no ambulance. Maybe I'm in luck, he thought. Deputies stood around a gingerbread cottage decorated with flower boxes and Teutonic floral designs. It looked like something out of the Brothers Grimm. Irises brightened the path to the door. In the doorway was Detective Art Nola.

I'd like to beat Art to the crime scene just once, Eldon thought as he drove up and parked the Isetta. He shoved open the door and had just enough time to inhale the damp mold smell of the air outside before the deputies began heckling.

"Hey, Eldon, what the hell's that?"

"Yee-ooo—Larkin's gone sporty on us!"

"Hey, Art, check this out! Eldon's drivin' an Easter egg!"

Nola sauntered down the walk, hands thrust in the pockets of his raincoat. His graying russet hair was awry. His long, lined features were creased in a characteristic lupine smile. Eldon got ready for the usual argument—not an argument, exactly, but a psychological waltz in which Nola asserted his authority over the crime scene and Eldon asserted his First Amendment prerogatives as a representative of the press. After decent debate, in which Nola took entirely too much pleasure, Eldon usually got what he needed for a story. Might as well start dickering, he thought. "Hiya, Art. Dead giant pimp, eh?"

Nola eyed the car. "That thing got current plates?"

"It did when I left the car lot. It's an Isetta."

"This is worse than that Citroën you used to have. It doesn't even look like a car."

That's why I'm going to buy it, Eldon decided. To stay out of step with all you rednecks. "It rolls right along. And the price is right. Now, what's this about a murder?"

"News travels fast, as usual," Art said.

"Who got killed in there? Hansel and Gretel?"

To Eldon's surprise, Nola grinned. "Come in and see. He's in the kitchen."

Nola led Eldon into the cottage. The living room decor was Black Forest kitsch. Eldon caught his breath at the terrible taste. The colors, the cheap furniture, the overdone Mitteleuropa flower motifs—all contributed to a flavor of nasty decadence. If Little Red Riding Hood was sold into a brothel, this is where she'd wind up, he thought.

But there was a good stereo system, and a finely carved European cuckoo clock hung on the wall. Sweet-faced little porcelain figurines stood on tables and on the mantelpiece—milkmaids, shepherd lads, and couples wearing eighteenth-century styles. Eldon looked closer and saw that some of the figurines were of couples copulating.

"The G-rated ones are authentic Hummels," Nola said drily.

Eldon remembered that Art collected fine porcelain.

The detective waved Eldon through the kitchen doorway. "Archie Loris—*this is your life!*"

Eldon stepped into the kitchen and stood astonished. Then the sense of distance that he felt at scenes of violence settled over him, and he began examining the spectacle.

Squeezed behind the table in the tiny kitchen, sitting on a heavy stool wedged against the wall, was an enormous dead man in lederhosen. Four hundred pounds if he's an ounce, Eldon decided.

The man had been shotgunned point-blank in the chest over a meal of spaghetti and meatballs. He still gripped fork and spoon. Spaghetti was strung between the utensils and balled around the fork. The center of his chest was punched in like soggy red cardboard. Blood and pellet holes and tiny bits of greenery spattered the wall behind him, as well as the table, cabinets, and stove.

A bottle of Henry Weinhard's beer had tipped over and spilled out across the checkered tablecloth. The smell of stale beer and an acrid gunpowder stink hung in the room. Eldon's stomach lurched as he stared at the food. That's not all tomato sauce, he realized, and forced himself to study the dead man's face.

The brown eyes stared . . . not back at Eldon, not at anything. A strand of pasta hung from the half-open mouth, plastered to the unshaven chin. Bits of what looked like parsley flecked the waxy skin. Eldon scoffed at the notion that corpses had any expression at all, but this one looked . . . mean—pettish that anyone would dare interrupt his meal to commit this ultimate lese majesty. The frozen eyes were narrow and too close together; they watched nothing with none-too-latent cruelty. Death had made them glassy, like a shark's. The jaw was like a shovel. High cheeks suggested heavy bones under the pillows of fat. The nose had been broken more than once. The man alive had been physically powerful. Eldon sensed that he had wielded his power like a vicious, jaded Roman emperor.

"What are these green bits? Parsley?"

Art shrugged. "Maybe his lunch exploded. Meet Archie Loris, pimp, pornographer, and general scumbag."

Eldon pulled out his notebook and pen. "D.O.B.? Middle initial?"

"Archibald Loris. That's *L-O-R-I-S*. Born one-six-forty-one and burning in hell at last. Isn't he a beaut? Take some pictures. Be my guest."

"You always give me hell about body shots. What gives?"

"I like to see you put good news in the paper," Nola said.

"Not your favorite guy, eh?"

"Archie had an arrest record back East that you could've wrapped around his middle, though us hicks never managed to pin him for anything serious. Now someone's solved the problem, and the South Coast is cleaner."

"You're usually more objective than this."

"Not about this bastard. Every cop knows someone like Archie, some particular brass-bottomed asshole that he just can't sink."

Why haven't I heard of this guy before? Eldon wondered. But that was the rainy North Woods—things were always sliding out from under the wet rocks. "I'm impressed. Not many slip through your fingers."

"Archie wasn't smart but he was shrewd. As you might imagine from his size, he didn't get out much. He did business from this house, so you didn't see him much on the streets. He ran girls to service the merchant ships. He also dabbled in drugs."

Eldon jotted notes. "So?"

"So he was brutal to his whores. We know he beat one to death in Brookings and maimed a couple more. Those women have as much right to go on pushing air in and out as you and me."

"Maybe a whore or her boyfriend, then, settling accounts?"

"Or one of the minors in Archie's porno films."

Eldon's skin crawled. Murder was one thing, but now he was getting into *good copy*.

"Archie's specialty was runaway teenage girls," Art continued. "And oh, yeah, he liked to do crossword puzzles. The girls he'd pick up and add to his stable—mostly they were girls, anyway. His crossword puzzle books are in a basket in front of the VCR, mixed in with the porno mags."

"Hm." Eldon noticed several clear plastic evidence bags on the counter by the sink. One contained a worn brown wallet, the others cards and money. "That stuff his?"

"Yeah." Nola passed over a bag containing Oregon and Illinois driver's licenses. "The wallet was lying on the floor with stuff spilling out of it."

Eldon read the licenses. The Oregon license was current. It gave Loris's weight as four hundred fifty-two pounds. The Illinois license was long expired; it showed a Chicago address and a younger, thinner Archie. "It's him, all right. He had his wallet out while he was eating?"

"Might've been uncomfortable to sit on it." Art held up a plastic bag full of twenty-dollar bills. "There was more than five hundred bucks in it. A pimp's idea of pocket money."

"So the motive wasn't robbery."

"Guess not."

"We're on the record, y'know."

"No problem. Free ride for you today, Eldon. Well, make it 'an undisclosed amount of money' for now, will you? But the motive wasn't robbery." Art picked up another bag and handed it to Eldon. It contained something shiny.

It was an old clipping from the *South Coast Sun,* preserved with clear tape—a story about a forgotten Port Jerome High School football victory. A photo of a young football player accompanied the story. Eldon recognized the mean little eyes. "Jeez. It's Loris."

"Almost two decades younger and two hundred pounds lighter," Nola said.

Eldon nodded. "How'd he get so fat?"

"Steroids. Probably started 'em in high school. Too dumb to quit."

"There are drunks with clippings about themselves sitting in bars all over Port Jerome."

"The back of his head is what fascinated me," Art said with a smirk. "When he was alive, it actually rippled. It looked like another face was trying to emerge. I often get that feeling about fat heads."

8

Eldon didn't want to look at the back of Archie's head. He turned his attention to another clipping in the bag, also preserved with tape. It was about a high school talent contest. Archie had placed fourth for playing the banjo. That part of the story was underlined in ballpoint pen.

"I guess Archie never got over missing the gold," Nola said, with a nod at the clipping. "So in his dim way, he set out to make something of himself. This is what it got him."

"When was he killed?"

"At lunchtime, obviously," Nola said. "No more than a few hours ago. Rigor's set in. And the food on the table is still fresh, and you can still smell the gunpowder."

"And the beer."

"And the beer."

"He was killed with a shotgun?"

"I'd say a sawed-off 12-gauge or 10-gauge. Sure hope it hurt."

Eldon focused his Nikkormat and banged off a few exposures. There was plenty of light in the kitchen and he was shooting Tri-X film. Even if Fiske didn't use the photos, he could sell a few to the wire service for twenty-five dollars apiece. "Good story, Art. Thanks."

Something powered by a diesel engine rolled up outside.

A red-haired deputy carrying a crowbar walked into the kitchen. He had rolled up his sleeves to expose enormous tattooed arms. "Art, the crane's here."

"The crane?" Eldon asked.

Nola grinned and started outside. "You want a real picture, stick around."

Eldon hurried after him.

A flatbed truck and a motorized crane emblazoned with DALE NOLA CONSTRUCTION—PREACHER'S HOLE had pulled up in the driveway. Metal cables swung from the crane's stout ironwork lattice. The crane driver waved from the square yellow cab and threw the crane into gear. He guided it carefully past the patrol cars and Eldon's Isetta, around the cottage and into the backyard.

The cops followed. The deputy with the crowbar stepped forward as his comrades lined up with pry bars. They wore heavy work gloves; some had pulled on coveralls. They radiated enthusiasm.

"Good send-off for Archie," the red-haired deputy said. He stepped up to the corner of the cottage, thrust the crowbar into the juncture of the rear and side walls, and pulled. Nails came away with a groan. The other deputies stepped in with their pry bars and went to work.

Eldon started snapping pictures. "What the hell are they doing, Art?"

"We've got to get the body out, don't we? It's too fat to get through the kitchen door on a gurney. So my Uncle Dale loaned us his truck and crane. Save your film. The best is yet to come."

The gingerbread cottage was stoutly built. The deputies' grins became determined grimaces as each nail had to be prized from the wood. They swiftly worked up a sweat. Eldon was going for close-ups of scowls and white knuckles when he heard another car drive up. The engine shut off and a door opened and closed.

"Hey, hey, Melissa!" someone said.

"Sure enough, got the right tool for the right job—"

"Bring it here, sweetie!"

Eldon lowered his camera to see a pretty auburn-haired young woman in a tailored tan business suit come around the side of the house. She smiled, acknowledging the accolades. She carried a chainsaw. Eldon's heart fluttered, for her appearance was uncharacteristic of the South Coast.

The woman stepped carefully up to Art Nola, her high heels sinking slightly into the wet ground. Eldon watched her hands as she handed Nola the chainsaw. They were short-fingered, manicured . . . light-colored nail polish . . . and *there was no ring* on the third finger of her left hand. . . .

Eldon bustled over. "I'll bet this is someone I should meet."

Art smiled. "Probably so. Eldon Larkin of the *Sun,* meet Melissa Lafky, the county's newest deputy district attorney."

"Hello," Melissa said. Her voice was curiously husky, almost froggy.

They shook hands. Melissa's grip was firm. Eldon studied her appreciatively. She was no more than thirty, with a round, pleasant face. Her heavy-lidded green eyes held a sharp, sensuous intelligence. Her hair was collar-length, stylishly done. She was of medium build, with a nice bust and legs, and impeccably groomed. Eldon saw that a small golden cross hung around her neck; then he noticed how calm her eyes were—calm and tired. A warning bell rang in his mind. But Melissa was a combination of professionalism and femininity he found irresistible.

"N-nice to—to meet you." Of course, I swallow my tongue, Eldon thought. He felt frowsy in his shabby clothes and eccentric hat. He fumbled with his notebook, trying to recover his self-possession. He looked up; Melissa was watching with a smile. She's not fooled, Eldon thought desolately. I'm making an ass of myself.

"Come take a look around the scene before we pull 'er down," Art said.

Art passed the chainsaw to the red-haired deputy and escorted Melissa into the house. Eldon scurried after them. Light was coming into the kitchen from the new rents in the wall.

"Oh, my," Melissa said when she saw the stupendous corpse. "They said you'd need the chainsaw to get him out, but I never imagined this." She put the back of a finger to the corpse's cheek. "Cooling down."

She glanced down at the food and then at Eldon. "No Italian recipes for a while, eh?"

Melissa strolled from the kitchen, Eldon and Nola following along. She gave Eldon an amused wink when she discovered the obscene figurines and then wandered into the bedroom. It contained a king-size waterbed with a leather-upholstered rosewood frame and black satin sheets.

"Mmm, kinky." Melissa glanced around. "Has this room been checked?"

"Yeah, it's clear," Art said.

Melissa picked up a boxed deck of playing cards from the night-stand and slid the cards into her left hand. LUCKY POKE SALOON—PORT JEROME, OREGON, the box read. She did a rapid one-handed shuffle, then swept the cards into double fans, collapsed them, shuffled them again, and fanned them out once more in her manicured fingers. "Pick a card, Eldon. Don't show it to me."

"You're left-handed."

"Yeah. Wired backward. Don't worry, I won't drop them."

Eldon flushed, took a card, looked at it. The six of spades. "Where'd you learn that?"

"Got started in Girl Scouts. I like magic tricks."

The chainsaw motor started outside. Melissa dropped the cards on the bed and hurried from the room. Eldon tossed the six of spades down and followed. They got back to the kitchen just as the saw's whirling chain-blade punched through a corner with an explosion of sound. They stood back with their fingers in their ears as the saw chewed its way down the wall, spraying sawdust. The saw withdrew; in a few moments it burst through the room's other corner and carved through the studs.

The house trembled. Then the wall toppled outward and fell flat to the ground. Deputies stepped inside dragging a chain. They began wrapping Loris's huge body, which was still seated upright clutching fork and spoon.

Eldon saw that the chain ran out to the crane. He readied his camera as the deputies lifted the table out of the way.

The crane motor snorted and the chain was taken up. Eldon started snapping pictures. Loris's chair tilted back, skidding. The chair's legs cracked. The dead pimp left the house with a lurch, rocking back and forth on his throne. The crane hauled upward and then Archie was airborne, swinging just above the ground like a monstrous clock-weight as the deputies jeered.

"Bon voyage, Archie!"

"Oh, you swinger, you!"

Eldon, Melissa, and Art stepped out into the yard.

"He made one enemy too many," Art said.

"I don't think this was a vengeance killing," Melissa said. "This was a professional hit."

Eldon sidled up quickly. "You sound pretty sure of that."

"He didn't go after the face," Melissa said.

Nola interposed before she could say more. "She means that when you see a murder victim's face assaulted, that often means it's personal. The murderer knew the victim and wanted to get them."

Melissa glanced at Nola, carefully picked a bit of greenery off her coat, and held it up between manicured nails. "Singed."

"What is it?" Eldon asked.

"It looks like moss. Something like that. And there's a bit of what looks like wire in it."

"Wire? Inside *moss?*" Eldon scribbled a note.

"He'll have this in tomorrow's paper," Nola said.

"It's okay," Melissa said. "Who'd we be fooling?"

The crane pivoted, carrying Archie slowly through the air toward the flatbed truck.

"I need to take a picture of you," Eldon told Melissa. "For our files." Anything to keep the conversation going.

"Okay. Can I have a copy? To send to my mother?"

"Absolutely! I'm a good photographer—"

They headed for the front yard. The pimp's body hovered over the flatbed truck. Melissa asked, "Oh, is that your car?"

"It's an Isetta. I'm fixing it up." Please don't laugh, Eldon thought.

"It's cute."

"I'll—take you for a ride in it."

"That would be fun. Maybe at lunch sometime."

"I'll come to the courthouse." Eldon banged off one, two, three exposures of Melissa's face. "That's a nice smile. Now we'll do a straight-faced one, for the serious stories."

Melissa complied. The crane began to lower the dead giant pimp. Eldon turned and shot pictures as Archie's stool touched down on the truck. The stool collapsed and Archie rolled onto his back. The deputies started lashing him in place.

Eldon let his camera swing around his neck by the strap and began picking irises. He rapidly collected a bouquet of bright flowers and brought it to Melissa with a bow.

"Why, thank you, Eldon!" she said. "I never got flowers at a murder scene before."

"I never gave anyone flowers at a murder scene before."

"They're beautiful. But we need another yellow one for balance—" Melissa reached out and plucked a yellow iris from behind Eldon's ear. And then the six of spades. She handed Eldon the card with a dazzling, practiced smile.

Love and death, it's all here, Eldon thought with happy astonishment as the deputies covered Archie Loris with a tarp. He slipped the six of spades into his jacket pocket.

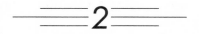

Fiske was wandering around the newsroom rubbing his little belly when Eldon hurried through the side door.

"Jimbo's stomach's growlin'," the editor declared. "The pounds are leaking off."

Eldon pulled off his coat. "It was a dead giant pimp, all right. I got some great shots."

Fiske picked up a spring-grip hand exerciser and started flexing it. "What—hap—pened—out—there?"

"A murder. Great stuff. . . . What *is* that thing?"

"I'm losing weight, shaping up."

"Since when?"

"Since this morning. Since you went lookin' for a new car."

"Aw, you look all right."

"Not right enough to be worthy of my new girlfriend."

Eldon stared. Fiske had been married for decades. His wife was active in the Lutheran church. Eldon gathered that she wasn't active enough in other ways. "You and your wife have broken up?"

Fiske put his free hand paternally upon Eldon's shoulder. He kept squeezing the hand exerciser with the other. "You're kind of young to understand this, Eldon, but my wife *is* my new girlfriend."

"That's really nice, Jimbo."

"She's lost twenty-five pounds and—does—she—look—*good!*"

"You've fallen in love all over again."

"That's right!" Jimbo pumped the grip exerciser. "And I'm—shap—in'—up—too! Losin' weight. Mic-ro-bi-otic-ally."

"You mean macrobiotic," Eldon said. "You have to watch that stuff. You can die of malnutrition."

"It's worth the risk," Fiske said. "My wife and I walked past the Timber Topper bar last night and someone whistled at her. I've got to make m'self worthy of her, Eldon."

"But a macrobiotic diet—"

"Cures flatulence. And cancer." Fiske waved a magazine. "Tells all about it right here."

Eldon sighed. It was the new issue of *Sasquatch and UFO*. The journal's irregular arrival in the mail inflamed Fiske's imagination in amazing ways.

"Special issue on New Age wisdom," Fiske explained.

"They've dropped lost continents? No more flying saucers? No more Bigfoot stories?"

"The article says Bigfoot eats microbiotically." Fiske's eyes glowed and he pumped faster on the hand exerciser. "Bigfoot eats exactly right. That's why even a little sasquatch is four hundred fifty pounds of natural muscle and sinew. That kind of fitness is my goal."

"The dead pimp weighed four-fifty-two," Eldon said.

"That's big for a pimp, isn't it?"

"Wait'll you see these body shots. And it's a mob killing—that's official."

"Soup that film, dee-de-dee. I'll re-dummy tomorrow's Page One."

Eldon went into the darkroom and pulled the sliding door shut. He developed the negatives promptly and then wished that he had dawdled. The presses wouldn't roll for the *Sun*'s next issue until noon the next day. Fiske still had not replaced the paper's most recent photographer, who had gone on to better things months ago. She had left Eldon her richly upholstered van and taken a piece of his heart with her. Now the van was gone, too.

But Eldon brightened as he examined the negatives.

I got some good shots of Loris, he thought. And some great pictures of Melissa. She sure is cute. And she's a lawyer—really cultivated. No Oregon forest bimbo here. I can't ask her out while I'm covering this story, but we could have lunch to discuss the case. And to go for a ride.

Fiske banged on the door. "Eldon! Time's a-wastin'! I wanta get home to my wife!"

"Right." Eldon slid the door aside.

Fiske grabbed the negatives and peered at them through a plastic viewing lens. "Dee-de-dee! Eldon strikes again! What's that—a crane?"

"They had to haul him out of there with a crane."

"You don't say? Run these and we'll get calls about 'bad taste' for sure."

"Maybe we should become a 'good taste' newspaper, like the *Oregonian,*" Eldon said.

"Aw, what's the fun in that?" Fiske demanded with a homely grin. "Half of journalism is body shots. You say gangsters offed this fat pimp?"

"He got it with a shotgun."

"Put that part up high."

"You should run this mug shot, too."

"Nice-lookin' gal. She kill him?"

"Melissa Lafky. She's the deputy D.A. on the case."

"And you're in love. I know how it is."

"She's an important source. She says it was a gangland killing."

"Actual gangland? Not just 'gangland-style'? Haven't had one of those since the blowtorch murder back in—"

Eldon hurried to his desk before Fiske could launch into the well-worn story. Fiske had a million newspaper war stories, all interminable; Fiske's journalism career had been a very long war. Eldon rolled a sheet of newsprint into his battered gray Royal 440 typewriter and rested his fingers for a moment on the worn white keys. The feeling came over him as it always did: He felt ethereal, powerful, relaxed yet resonating with energy. Free of care. Ready to grind it out for the greater glory of journalism. Ready to write.

By Eldon Larkin
Sun *Staff Writer*

SCOQUEL—A 452-pound pimp was killed Monday with a shotgun in his rural house, in what a spokeswoman for the Nekaemas County district attorney's office said was a gangland slaying.

Melissa Lafky, deputy district attorney, said the murder of Archibald "Archie" Loris had hallmarks of a mob assassination. Sheriff's deputies said Loris, 38, had a long record of arrests in Chicago for his involvement in prostitution, stolen goods, and pornography.

Detective Art Nola said that Loris, who once was a Port Jerome High School football star, was killed by a shotgun blast to the chest about noon, as he sat in his kitchen eating spaghetti.

Deputies used a crane to pull Loris's huge body from his house on Scoquel Road. . . .

Fiske poked Eldon's shoulder with a finger. "Take 'pimp' out of the lead. 'Bad taste.' "

"It's what he was." Eldon stared at the finger. "Where's your pipe? You usually poke me with your pipe."

"Make it 'alleged pimp,' " Fiske said. "Change it somehow. I've stopped smoking."

"That's great." Eldon typed a row of X's across "pimp" in the lead sentence, then typed "former high school football star" above the X's. He turned to see whether Fiske approved but the editor had wandered back to the news desk and was looking mournfully at his pipe.

Eldon turned back to the story, chuckling as he wrote about Archie's body being hauled around by the crane. He described the gingerbread house and put in Nola's comments on Loris's arrest record. He did not mention that the deputies had mocked the pimp's corpse. He had to work constantly with them, and there was no sense in throwing up obstacles.

Let's see, he thought, I want to get some of Melissa's comments in here—

"Good copy, I hear," someone said.

Eldon looked up to see young Frank Juliano, pushing his glasses up his long nose. He held Eldon's negatives. Frank, who covered the Nekaemas County government for the *Sun,* looked like a boyish, earnest basketball player. He had a far-flung network of news sources and an equally widespread network of girlfriends.

Eldon envied both. But today he had a scoop. "Dead giant pimp. A real bad-taste job."

"Fiske told me. He said to make some prints while you write. Which shots d'you want?"

"Fiske didn't say?"

"He said to pick some. He's busy talking to his pipe."

"He's quitting smoking. He's saying good-bye." Eldon glanced toward the news desk. Fiske had cradled the briar in his palms and was crooning to it. Eldon shuddered and turned back to the negatives. "Print number ten. And number twenty-one. Make an extra print of twenty-one, will you?"

Frank examined the frames with a loupe. "Ah, ha—I know number twenty-one. A tasty item."

"How well do you know her?"

"We haven't gone out or anything, if that's what you mean."

"I mean, how good is she?"

"At her job? Very good. Very sharp. One of those lawyers who always has a card up her sleeve."

"I've got a few cards myself," Eldon said. "Such as you."

"Oh?"

"Loris had some Chicago connections. Could you rattle around and find out what that might mean?"

"Sure. Melissa has broken a few hearts around the courthouse, you know. One of 'em might sing."

Eldon burned with irrational jealousy. He turned back to his story, telling himself not to be a fool. You can't get involved with a news source, he thought. You've learned that the hard way.

I could turn the story over to Frank, Eldon thought. Then dating her wouldn't be a conflict. But no way. This story is too good.

The telephone rang. Eldon went on writing, hoping someone else would answer it. The phone kept ringing. Eldon looked around. Frank had gone into the darkroom. Fiske was fixated on his pipe. No one else was near. Eldon picked up the phone. *"South Coast Sun.* Larkin."

"Where's the money?" a nasty voice demanded.

"Pardon?"

"We don't let people drive off with cars without paying."

"Oh—the Isetta. I took it on a test drive—"

"Far as I'm concerned, you've bought it."

"It drove okay, I guess. Uh, how much?"

"Eight hundred dollars."

"That's outrageous!"

"That's cheap. It's a rare 600 Series. A collector's item."

Eldon thought fast. "I'll give you five hundred."

"Eight hundred. You should've dickered before you stole the car."

" 'Stole!' You can have your damn car back. It's right here on the *Sun* lot."

"Bring it back."

"Come and get it," Eldon said.

"I'll send a deputy sheriff."

"They don't do repossession."

"Repossession!" the salesman screamed. "I'm talking *criminal charges!* You took that car and you won't pay—"

"I said I'd pay you!" Eldon's heart raced; he told himself that this was a typical South Coast–style sales pitch. God, people around here were mean to one another. He had never gotten used to it.

"Eight hundred," the salesman said.

"Eldon, where's the copy?" Fiske called.

Eldon waved Jimbo off. "Seven hundred. Or come and take the car. Go see the D.A. if you want. I write stories about him all the time. You really think he's going to charge *me?*"

There was silence for a moment. Eldon knew the bluff had worked. A significant minority of newspaper readers regarded reporters, public officials, enemy neighbors, and indeed anyone they perceived as having a wider range of options than they as not only corrupt but in cahoots. It was an idiotic notion but common enough to be worth invoking.

"All right, seven-fifty," the salesman said. "Cash."

Eldon's mind raced. He had barely that much in his savings account. "Seven and a quarter. Half now, half on time."

"Now you're talkin'," the salesman said with a greedy chuckle. Eldon knew the man was calculating the extra cost in interest.

"Eldon!" Fiske insisted.

"Deal." Eldon hung up with the sinking feeling that he had been taken to the cleaners. Seven hundred twenty-five dollars seemed like all the money in the world. In the hole and no way out—it was the story of his life in Port Jerome.

Frank emerged from the darkroom with four photographs. He put two on the news desk, which mollified Fiske, and brought copies to Eldon. "You've got a great scoop and met a beautiful woman. What's wrong?"

Eldon snatched the photos. "I got cheated on a car."

"That Isetta in the parking lot? I wondered where that came

from. BMW used to make them. Are they street-legal in Oregon?"

"It's a rare 600 Series—a collector's item." Eldon examined the photos and felt better. The photo of Loris swinging from the crane was a strong lead shot. The snapshot of Melissa was sharp. There was an air of mischief about her—it's the look in her eyes, Eldon thought.

"I'd take that car back if I were you," Frank said. "Isetta parts are hard to come by. This could be as bad a lemon as your Citroën. You should get a pickup."

"What would I carry in it? Wood? I don't want to be like the rest of them. I'll swap the Isetta for your '65 Chevelle."

"Ha!" Frank jabbed thumbs down. "Tell me more about Loris."

"Like I said—pimping, stolen goods, porno. It's in my story."

"Well, there certainly should be some dirt around the courthouse on Archie."

"They never managed to convict him of much," Eldon said.

"Probably there's a lot of off-the-record stuff, then," Frank said.

"I need stuff I can use."

He turned back to the typewriter. But the ethereal feeling refused to return as he finished the story.

Eldon took his copy over to Fiske. "News hole's full, Jimbo."

"I knew I could rely on you, Eldon, dee-de-dee."

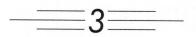

3

The Isetta ran smoothly on the way home from work. Eldon drew three hundred fifty dollars out of the bank, virtually murdering his savings account, and took it to the car salesman. The man grabbed it like a skinny rat snatching cheese.

Eldon left the car lot quickly. Now the damn car will quit working, he thought.

Things seemed to break down when Eldon became committed

to them. Look at Bernice, he thought, with bitterness as sharp as the day he'd realized her "one-year art fellowship in Australia" was permanent and that their marriage was over. By then he was marooned in Port Jerome, moldering in the rain. He moldered still.

He hadn't heard from his ex-wife in some time—postcards now and then, a Christmas card a while back. Eldon suspected she'd met someone else. Well, the divorce had been final for three years.

Eldon drove across the bridge to Regret, named for a nineteenth-century French-Canadian trapper. The ruined mill's smokestacks dominated the landscape. He drove north on the pitted road that skirted the bay shore, readying himself for the day's biggest challenge—getting the Isetta to his house.

Eldon lived atop Windy Ridge, eight hundred feet above the bay. The street running straight up the slope from the flats ascended those eight hundred feet in a half-mile. Eldon came to the foot of the hill, lined up the Isetta, shifted into low gear and depressed the accelerator.

The Isetta's wheels spun a bit on the wet asphalt. Then the car trundled up the grade, engine chugging like a disturbed stomach. Eldon held his breath as the egg picked up speed. He shifted into second and fed gas; the Isetta vibrated madly as acceleration increased. He shifted into third. The Isetta bounded up the hill, past the weatherbeaten houses and rusty trailers that clung to the slope. It was almost like being airborne. He reached the grassy, tree-spotted ridgetop with a sigh of relief.

Eldon's house was across a muddy gravel street from the Regret municipal tennis courts. The courts were vacant as usual, nets sagging, puddles on the asphalt.

His house faced north, with a view through alder and birches of the bay and the forested ridge on the bay's northern shore. Port Jerome and the mill stacks weren't visible from this angle. Someone had once told Eldon admiringly that this was the end of the world. He didn't mind living here on the edge. But his new car needed a talisman.

Eldon parked and entered his house. All was as he'd left it that morning—the living room with its bricks-and-boards shelves filled with books, enlargements of his news photos of traffic accidents and county fair queens on the walls, the worn easy chair before the black Franklin stove.

Eldon went to his fly-tying bench in the corner and rooted through the clutter. At last he found an eight-ball with a threaded socket hole in its base—a gearshift knob. It was the only surviving shred of his previous vehicle, the van that had come to a spectacular end. Eldon went back outside and climbed into the Isetta. He worked the handle free of the gearshift and threaded the eight-ball onto the shaft. It's a little loose but it fits, he thought.

He returned to the house and went into the kitchen. He opened the refrigerator's freezer compartment, pulled out a tub of French vanilla ice cream and spooned a generous helping into a bowl. He got down the green bottle of Courvoisier V.S.O.P., laced the ice cream with cognac and went back into the front room. "I don't feel like cooking tonight," he muttered. "It's been quite a day."

Eldon set the bowl on the arm of his easy chair and went to the bookshelf. He usually passed his evenings reading and sipping cognac or tying fishing flies while he listened to music. Sometimes he talked to himself. He was doing that more and more. Comes of living alone, he thought.

But there was no way to socialize in Port Jerome except to go to church or drink in the horrible bars. Eldon was a lapsed Catholic, and he avoided the bars.

He ran his finger along the books. Faulkner, Hemingway, Stanislaw Lem. Molière in French. Ralph Ellison and André Malreaux. He had hundreds of books. Let's see . . .

Eldon fingered the spine of a French-language paperback he'd found at a Berkeley garage sale. Arthur Rimbaud's *Illuminations, The Drunken Boat,* and *A Season in Hell* in one volume, carted around for years unread. Definitely non–redneck, he thought, and I've got to keep up my French. *Une saison en enfer,* that's for me. He went back to the armchair with the book, took a big spoonful of ice cream and gazed out the window at the forest across the choppy bay. I ought to lose some weight, he thought.

His French was good. He began to read.

Once, if I remember well, my life was a feast where all hearts opened and all wines flowed. . . .

The telephone rang. Of course, Eldon thought. Now that I'm comfortable, I have to go cover a traffic accident.

One evening I seated Beauty on my knees. And found her bitter. And I cursed her. . . .

He picked up the telephone.

It was Frank. "Hi, Eldon. I was afraid you weren't home."

"Where is there to go?"

"I got the word on Loris."

"At the courthouse?"

"No, I called a friend on one of the Chicago papers. He checked their files. He says I owe him a beer, because of the two-hour time difference."

"You could've waited until tomorrow."

"Hey, how about some gratitude?"

"What've you got?"

"Loris was a small-time hood in Chicago."

Eldon sat up. "You didn't tell your source Archie got killed, did you?"

"Sure. Why not?"

"I don't want to get scooped by the Chicago papers. Christ, if they come out here, it'll be like the Normandy invasion—"

"Archie's demise rates two paragraphs in Chicago. Have some perspective, Eldon. Keep your wits about you."

"Right. So give."

"Archie had a rap sheet back there, all right; starting with car theft—he arrived in Chicago in a stolen car. He got involved with the mob, worked his way up to bagman and finally into prostitution and porno. Gambling, too. A couple of assault raps. Archie came home to Oregon a few years ago." Frank snickered. "His last arrest in Chicago was for trying to beat a prostitute to death with a banjo."

"Huh? Why?"

"She held out money on him."

"I mean, why the banjo?"

"Part of her gig was playing the banjo in the nude."

"That sounds like something that would happen in Idaho," Eldon said.

"The case got dropped and Archie left town," Frank said. "My friend says that was part of a deal with the D.A.'s office. Archie was to leave Chicago forever. So much for his life of big-time crime."

"But then he turns up back in business here. You know, I'll bet the mob set him up in business."

"And finally rubbed him out," Frank said. "I wonder what the beef was?"

"Maybe the godfather liked banjo music," Eldon said. "Thanks."

"Sure. What now?"

"I'll look around for some of Archie's enemies. Might make for interesting interviews."

"If they're willing to talk." Frank sounded distracted. "I gotta go. Got company."

Eldon heard a feminine giggle in the background. He hung up the phone and sighed. How did Frank manage it? Women went crazy over his boyish looks and gawky sincerity. Ain't I sincere? Eldon wondered.

A bite of ice cream renewed his spirits. A mob killing, right here in Port Jerome! The story was real, and since it was real, he could get hold of it. What an angle! Killing on the South Coast customarily was an impetuous act, an existential flowering of human spirits beaten down too long by rain, poverty, and isolation. Guns, knives, axes, even four-wheel-drive trucks were the murder weapons of choice.

The shotgun is the only thing that fits the pattern, Eldon thought. But someone didn't care much about covering his tracks, making it look like a passion killing. Why should he? A professional hit man would have already left town. He's probably back in Chicago eating pork chops right now, Eldon thought. Hog Butcher to the World.

Eldon ate faster. I like that perverted local-boy-makes-good angle, he thought. I'll tie the story into the South Coast's depressed economy—the only prosperous people in Nekaemas County are criminals. . . .

But who would talk to him about it?

People glad to see Archie dead—that's who, Eldon thought.

His gaze went to his fly-tying table. His fishing rods rested in a rack above the table. This is going to be like fishing, Eldon thought. Archie had plenty of enemies, but I need the right kind of lure to troll them in.

Then it came to him. Deputy District Attorney Melissa Lafky could point him toward the bottom-dwellers. She may know card tricks, but I've got some cards up my sleeve now, too, thanks to Frank. We can trade information.

The thought filled Eldon with lustful resolve.

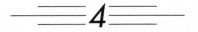

Fiske was full of resolve of his own when Eldon got to work the next morning.

"Food's the key," the editor announced.

"Still eating right, Jimbo?"

"Now, forever, and always," Fiske said. "I miss my pipe."

"The newsroom isn't the same without it," Eldon replied and added maliciously, "It's better."

Fiske grabbed the hand exerciser and started pumping. "When I started in newspapers, everybody did business with a bottle of beer on his desk. It was normal. Journalism is gradually phasing out the corrupting pleasures. That's good."

"Good?"

"Better diet means better news. Look at this dead giant pimp. If he'd eaten right, no telling where he'd have wound up."

"They sure wouldn't have had to use a crane to—"

"He's on Page One today. There'll be calls about 'bad taste' after this edition hits the streets, dee-de-dee."

"I don't want to deal with them. I don't have time."

"You're right. You don't," Fiske said. "We're looking at an important story. I'll handle the calls."

"Good. I want to talk to Melissa Lafky and see if—"

Fiske thrust a news release at Eldon. "Oats in the Bowl."

"What?"

"Oats in the Bowl. That hippie restaurant. I want a business feature."

"Jimbo! I'm busy. Can't Frank do it?"

"He has to cover the Board of Commissioners."

"Then have Marsha do it."

"She's allergic to wheat germ."

"It's a veggie place. She can order a salad."

Fiske leaned close, his free hand cupped around an imaginary pipe bowl. *"Their menu is microbiotic."*

"Macrobiotic," Eldon corrected desperately.

"I want you to try the Ohsawa Salad. It's on special this week."

Eldon studied the press release. " 'Three kinds of wholesome grain, organic lettuce, and Oriental tea—food found along the path to humility, enlightenment, and physical health.' "

"Test that salad out, see if it rebalances your ying-yang," Fiske said.

"Ugh! Go test it yourself. Macrobiotics is drivel. I went to Berkeley."

"That's why you'll know if this is the real McCoy. A consumer-protection story. I need to know for my self-improvement program." Fiske pumped the hand exerciser. I liked his pipe better, Eldon thought gloomily.

Fiske looked over Eldon's shoulder toward the front of the office. "You've got company, Eldon. It's the mug-shot lady."

Eldon turned. Melissa stood waving at the front counter. Today she wore a blue blazer and a gray skirt. Eldon rushed to escort her across the orange industrial carpet. "Hi!"

"I'm up from Preacher's Hole on business," Melissa said as

Eldon brought her to his desk. "I wanted to thank you again for the flowers."

"Courtesy of Archie Loris," Eldon said.

"Could I see my picture? If it's not too much trouble?"

"No trouble at all!" Eldon found the extra print that Frank had made the day before. "Take this one."

"Oh, this is fine." Melissa studied her photograph happily.

"That'll be in today's paper," Eldon said. "You're a celebrity."

"Can I buy some extra copies of the paper, too?"

"You can have some for free. The press runs at noon."

"I'll come back then."

"No, stick around. Maybe . . . we could have lunch."

"I'd love to," Melissa said.

"Great! Wow—" Eldon grabbed the extra print of Loris's body swinging from the crane. "Here. Take this, too."

Melissa stifled a laugh. "God, how gross."

"You kept a straight face."

"With all those cops watching? You bet I did. Is this going in the paper, too? Oh, wait 'til Mother sees this."

Eldon admired her as she studied the picture. Melissa was so trim and well turned out that he felt unkempt. He looked self-consciously at his fishing hat, lying on his desk, and grabbed it to hide in a drawer. Then he remembered the six of spades, still in his pocket, and handed it to Melissa. "This is yours."

Melissa reached across the desk; the card vanished. With her other hand, she plucked something from Eldon's ear and handed it to him—the six of spades.

Eldon turned the card over. "How the hell did you do that?"

"Magic."

Fiske ambled over, still flexing the exerciser. "Guess I'll meet the mug-shot lady."

"Melissa Lafky, this is James O. Fiske, editor of the *Sun,*" Eldon said.

"Jimbo," Fiske said. "I always like to meet those prominent in the news."

"I've never seen a newspaper office before," Melissa said.

"I'll show you the press room," Eldon said.

"Better yet, show her how a reporter covers a story," Fiske said.

"I've seen him do that already," Melissa said.

Fiske nodded. "Eldon's good on murders. But he's good on consumer-protection stories, too."

"Jimbo—" Eldon stopped. Oats in the Bowl didn't sound very appealing, but he could take Melissa to lunch there.

"Seems to me I overheard the word 'lunch,' " Fiske went on. "Eldon's going to write about lunch today, isn't that right, Eldon?"

"Yeah, right."

"I knew I could depend on you, Eldon—you're my best reporter. You should take along a guest. Get another point of view. Bring back the receipt. The *Sun* will pick up the tab." Fiske regarded Melissa as he stood pumping the hand exerciser and grinning with his ugly, gold-backed teeth. "Not a conflict of interest for you, I hope."

"I think the D.A. will overlook it," Melissa said. Her green eyes glittered with interest.

Eldon caught his breath. She thinks I've got a romantic occupation, he thought. "Let's go now. We'll take my Isetta."

Oats in the Bowl lay near the Nekaemas Bay boat basin, where the fishing boats put out to sea and unemployed loggers and fishermen punched out one another's lights in the bars during the long, rainy winters. I won't have to deal with any of that today, Eldon thought happily as he and Melissa bounced down the chuckholed road in the Isetta. "Stayin' Alive" was on the car radio, and they were wedged together in the seat with promising closeness as clouds rushed across the sky.

"I feel as if I'm going on a picnic in Mr. Toad's car," Melissa said.

"Fun, isn't it? Lots of places we could go." The hell with Jaguars and vintage Thunderbirds, Eldon thought, it's the Isettas that get the girls.

"That eight ball kind of sets the tone."

Eldon rubbed the shift knob. "Souvenir of a great adventure. I'll tell you about it sometime."

He waited for Melissa to press him for details but instead she took out the photo of Archie Loris and studied it. "What a picture. I can't believe you're putting it in the paper."

"We're in the information business," Eldon said.

"Sells newspapers, I suppose."

"Actually, most of them are sold before they're ever written. Subscriptions. And I'm not in the censorship business. That's the way Thomas Jefferson wanted it—" Eldon forced himself to stop chattering.

"My mother will like your photo of me," Melissa said.

"Where does she live?"

"In Eugene."

"Were you a lawyer there?"

"In private practice. It was hard to make ends meet, in more ways than one. So it's the public sector for me."

"As a prosecutor."

"I had a lot of trouble defending people I knew were guilty."

"Everybody's got a right to a lawyer."

"Even people like Archie. 'Thomas Jefferson wanted it that way.' But I don't have to be the lawyer. . . . I guess I just like putting people away."

"Remind me not to do any crimes," Eldon said. "How'd you come here, particularly?"

"It's where the job was."

"Same for me."

"When I got divorced this seemed like a good place to come."

Eldon clutched the wheel and the car jerked left. Another refugee! A comely one! I could be in on the rebound, he thought, if I don't flip this damn car. Carefully he said, "I'm divorced, too."

"Was it recent?" Melissa asked.

"It was six years ago."

"My husband's a good man," Melissa said. "Also a lawyer. But we didn't have that much in common. We didn't see eye to eye on that defense thing, for instance."

"Don't worry. You'll get over it." Eldon mentally licked his chops.

"I wonder if you ever do," Melissa said. "I feel like I've got to make up for something now."

"Oh, that's natural at first," Eldon said.

"You don't feel that way now?"

"Naw, I've got my work and the fishing's good. Hey—here's Oats in the Bowl."

The restaurant was in a low, dark-shingled old house with a covered porch where wind chimes tinkled in the light breeze. Bright stained-glass pieces hung in the windows—a smiling sun, dancing dolphins, a rainbow. Just like Berkeley, Eldon thought as he drove into the parking lot. They probably have sand candles on the tables.

He held open the building's heavy wooden door for Melissa. The place had more light in it than Eldon had expected. There were heavy wooden chairs and tables. Sure enough, there were sand candles on the tables. The pleasant smell of sandalwood incense was in the air. Eldon and Melissa were the only customers in the place.

A short, balding man in his late thirties sat in the corner playing an upright piano. Eldon looked at him with interest—you didn't run into much live classical music on the South Coast. Mozart, Eldon thought as he and Melissa took a table. At least he's not playing a sitar.

The piano player nodded to them as his square, meaty hands moved precisely over the keyboard. He had a round face and small blue eyes. He wore tan slacks, an open-collared shirt, and a gray cardigan. He looked like a lightweight wrestler who had turned to chamber music. A big brandy snifter sat atop the piano, a couple of dollar bills crimped over the lip.

Melissa picked up a menu. "Are you going to tell them you're from the newspaper?"

"Shhh. No special treatment. We're under cover."

"Do you do that sort of thing a lot?"

"Now and then I commit sins of omission." Eldon started perspiring. Suddenly it was as if he were on his first date again, in high school. It was always this way. He studied his own menu to hide his nervousness. "Fiske wants me to try the Ohsawa Salad."

"I'll order something different and you can try some of that, too," Melissa said. "Isn't that the best way to do a review? Compare points of view?"

"My point of view about macrobiotic food got pretty well set in Berkeley," Eldon said.

"You're a meat-and-potatoes man," Melissa said.

Eldon squirmed. Was she looking at his waistline? "I'm a shipwrecked hippie."

"You should give yourself more credit," Melissa said. "I'll have the lentil-and-black-bean soup."

They gave their orders to a waiter who wore a pony tail and a tie-dyed shirt. Thinking of Berkeley inevitably made Eldon think of Bernice. Well, Bernice is gone and Melissa is here, he thought. "Anything new on the Loris investigation?"

"I thought we were doing a restaurant review," Melissa said.

"News never sleeps."

"Well, no, there isn't anything new. We're waiting for the autopsy."

"Archie is one of the most colorful specimens I've encountered," Eldon said. "He'd have made a good feature if he'd lived."

"Oh, dear! You mean as a local businessman?"

"That would be an angle. But I was thinking of doing something about how to lose weight. No, better yet—Archie the movie genius."

Melissa laughed. "You heard about the porno movies."

"Yeah—"

"I suppose you want to see them."

Eldon shrugged.

"They're popular at the sheriff's office," Melissa said in an informative tone. "All that kind of stuff gets thoroughly screened."

"I've never been invited to a screening."

"Well, you have to be part of the club."

"Have you seen them?"

"I'm in the club."

"Are they—ah—any good?"

"Amateur stuff. Archie's the star. He had an extensive collection. He was going in for videotaping in a big way when he died."

Eldon whistled. "That new technology is expensive."

"Archie had dough. If you eliminate the ones starring kids, some of them are funny."

Eldon's heart speeded up. This was an encouraging sign, although he never could understand women who found pornography "funny."

"There's said to be one called *The Fat Man Pumps Good Gas,*" Melissa continued. "Archie runs a gas station. He 'hoses' the customers. Alas, we never found it—"

"Why didn't you indict him for child pornography?"

"We couldn't identify the kids. All runaways."

"Maybe I'd see something in the tapes that everyone else has missed—oh, never mind. I can't party with my sources."

"It must be a lonely life," Melissa said.

"Sometimes."

"Me, too."

"Pardon?"

"I'm lonely, too." Melissa said it matter-of-factly.

The food arrived. Eldon wrinkled his nose at the Ohsawa Salad, arranged with tasteful sparsity on his plate. He'd make up for this later with a chili burger.

"How did you do that card trick at Archie's house?" he asked. "I put the six of spades on the bed—after you left the room."

"Never watch the hand you think you should, Eldon. Always watch the other hand."

"Which hand's that?"

"It changes. That's the secret. I'm ambidextrous. Here, taste my soup." Melissa ladled up a spoonful and held it out to him. The suggestion of intimacy pleased Eldon. He leaned across the table, blew on the soup, and tasted it. It was rather bland, but at least it had some body. "You got the better of this meal."

"Want to trade?"

"That's okay. Tell me some more about Archie."

"You know about as much as I do."

"I may know a little more." Eldon outlined what Frank had told him about Loris's past.

Melissa's eyebrows rose. "I'm impressed. You know some sleight-of-hand of your own."

"It's useful information, then?"

"We'd have gotten it. But you got it faster."

"Deadlines, you know."

"Are you going to put it in the paper?"

"Eventually." Eldon picked at his salad. "The killer has no doubt left town. You'll probably never find him."

"That's what I'm afraid of." Melissa stirred her soup. "But suppose he *hasn't* left town?"

"What makes you say that?"

"Just a thought I had."

"And why do you say 'he'? It could've been a woman, couldn't it?"

"A 12-gauge shotgun seems like a pretty heavy weapon for a woman," Melissa said.

"Around here? You'd be surprised."

"Maybe. But it's not what I'd pick." Melissa's eyes flashed. "A nice little automatic pistol. That's my pick."

"That's just what Archie would've been on the lookout for."

"He'd have noticed a shotgun even faster."

"Not if it looked like something else—like moss."

"That's good. Go on."

"You're baiting me."

"Just having a little fun, Eldon. You're doing fine."

"The shotgun was wrapped up in moss, somehow." Eldon

waited for Melissa to laugh; she didn't. "The wire must've held the wrapping together. Moss was spattered all over that room. You said it was singed. Someone fired a shotgun through the moss."

"Good thinking."

"So he was murdered by a gardener?"

"Eldon, I can't give out details of the investigation."

"Off the record."

"Absolutely not. Eat your salad."

"You know, I'm just as good at my job as you are at yours."

"No doubt."

"You might as well tell me—"

"Nope."

"—because I'll get the information sooner or later." Eldon waited for Melissa to change her mind and talk, but she merely returned to her soup. Eldon was irritated at her aplomb. Get a grip on yourself, he thought. Don't drive this one off. He cast around desperately for something to say as the classical piano piece ended. His eye met the piano player's. "Say, there, can you play, ah, 'Norwegian Wood'?"

"No," the musician said with scorn.

"How about some more Mozart, then? Sonata No. 15 in C, K. 545."

The pianist looked startled. "Sure." He started playing.

Eldon turned back to Melissa. Was she regarding him with new respect?

"You know music," she said. "What's 'K. 545'?"

"I know what I like," Eldon said. "K. 545 is the Mozart catalogue number. That *is* the piece I asked him to play, by the way."

"I wouldn't know."

"Trust me. I speak French, too."

"Yes? Good French?"

"Comes in handy sometimes. I've gotten some good stories because I spoke French."

"Really? How?"

"Come to my place for dinner," Eldon said. "I'll tell you over dinner. I cook a lot better than they do in this restaurant. Real food. You ought to try my Cornish game hen stuffed with wild rice. My specialty." Eldon realized that he was speaking a little too intently. But he plunged ahead. "Gourmet Seduction Dinner Number One. . . . That's just a figure of speech, of course."

"Of course." Melissa rested her elbows on the table and cupped her chin in her hands. "I rather think you'd like to sleep with me, Eldon."

"Ah. Er." Eldon stuffed some lettuce into his mouth and swallowed it the wrong way.

Melissa waited until he was finished choking and thumping his breastbone with his fist. "Well?"

"Yes. . . . I would like to sleep with you."

"No chance."

"Oh, don't patronize me. You asked."

"Except . . . " Melissa waited.

"Except what?"

"I really do think you're as good at your job as I am at mine, Eldon—maybe better, because you've been at yours longer. So I'll tell you what . . . " Again the pause.

"Well, what? Going to pull a joker out of my ear?"

"I'll do a lot more than that—if you can find out who killed Archie Loris."

"Solving the case is what *you* get paid to do," Eldon said.

"No, it's what the sheriff gets paid to do," Melissa said with sudden anger. "I'm pissed at the sheriff."

"Why?"

"They've got a goddamn lackadaisical attitude about this case. The cops don't give a shit who killed Loris."

Eldon was startled by Melissa's swearing. "It's a murder."

" 'Other priorities.' Look who's the victim. They're just glad he's dead. And I think they're in over their heads."

"Art Nola's on the case. Don't sell Br'er Fox short."

"I don't. I think you might be able to solve it faster—with the right incentive."

"And the incentive is—you?"

"Uh huh."

"You'll go to bed with me?"

"You bet your ass."

"You're kidding."

"No," Melissa said.

"What do you take me for?"

"Don't tell me you're not that kind of boy!"

"It's hard to believe—"

"Trust me."

"You really want to solve this crime. Why?"

"Professional pride. I'll show those damn cops that they can't pat
me on the head."

"Or on the ass?" Eldon smiled to show that he was kidding but
that he nevertheless knew about the broken hearts in the sheriff's
office. Before Melissa could respond he asked, "What constitutes
'solving the case'?"

"An arrest. A conviction."

"I can't guarantee that. I'm a reporter, not a lawyer."

"So what can you guarantee?"

"Maybe a story leading to an arrest. The conviction's your
problem."

"Just get the scoop, then. That's the term, isn't it? The 'scoop'?"

"It is in old movies."

"I'll handle the conviction," Melissa said. She returned his gaze
with a wide-eyed one of her own. "I never made a bet like this
before. Have you?"

"No."

"I think it's fun, don't you? Finish your salad."

Eldon stared at the salad and was filled with resentment against
Fiske. Jimbo makes me eat dreck in front of beautiful women,
Eldon thought. Makes me do his dirty work. I'll show him. I'll get
the girl *and* the story.

He realized that he was more afraid of missing the Loris story
than of missing a chance to get laid. If he didn't get laid he would

merely still be horny. But if he lost the bet he wouldn't be a crackerjack reporter anymore. He'd be just another redneck fly-fisherman who happened to make his living on a newspaper. "You're on."

"Oh, good!" Melissa clapped her hands.

"When we get down to it—anything goes?" Eldon asked.

"Anything goes. I hope you're not thinking about whips."

"Not at all."

"Remember, you've got to solve the case before we do."

"I'm used to deadlines."

Melissa leaned toward him a little, looking into his eyes as she moistened her lips with light touches of her tongue. "Which one do you think you are, Eldon? Bernstein or Woodward?"

"This is my town," Eldon retorted. "I'll get the scoop."

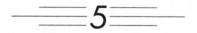

Marsha Cox was alone in the newsroom when Eldon returned from lunch. She looked over her typewriter and gave a thin smile as he swaggered across the carpet. Marsha wore a blouse with a Peter Pan collar and a ribbon tie.

Her smirk did not dampen Eldon's heady enthusiasm over the bet with Melissa, especially with the press now running off the day's edition. Eldon could feel its rhythmic thudding through the floor. The story of Archie's murder was launched out into the world. Eldon was committed. He was in this to win.

Marsha was not bad-looking, in a prim, birdlike way, he reflected, but of course she couldn't compare with Melissa. "Where's Fiske?" Eldon asked.

"Taking a *long* lunch." Marsha gave a disapproving sniff. Her trademark.

"He and his wife are having an affair, you know."

"You took a *long* lunch, too."

"I was on assignment."

"Calls are coming in about 'bad taste.' They started as soon as the edition hit the streets, and I've had to handle them. That photo was *awful.*"

Marsha thrust out a sheaf of goldenrod-colored telephone message slips. Eldon took the slips and went to his desk. The callers objected to Eldon's description of Loris as a "former Port Jerome High School football star." They said he had slandered the school. Marsha had written down each complaint in careful, tiny cursive, using red ink. The gripes were of course anonymous—from "Irate Subscriber," "Lifelong South Coast Resident," "Port Jerome High Forever," and so forth. One message asserted that Eldon was a Communist.

Do they think we'll cancel their subscriptions if we know their names? he wondered, annoyed. One message was brief and bore a name: "Congratulations—Stephanie." Who was Stephanie? Was the message sarcastic? "Is this for me?"

"She asked for you," Marsha said.

"Beats me," Eldon said. "It must be one of Frank's girls. Where is Frank, anyway?"

"I don't know. I heard you bought a silly-looking car."

"Connoisseurs know better."

"I was a stringer for *Cosmopolitan,*" Marsha retorted, as if that settled everything.

"Well, I'm a restaurant critic now." Eldon returned to his desk and rolled paper into his typewriter. The restaurant review would be a warm-up for pursuing his bet with Melissa. He was full of good will toward Oats in the Bowl, despite the meager lunch.

That meal was a landmark, Eldon thought. Pinning Loris's killer could lead to more than just a roll in the hay. I might get a better job.

Eldon smiled at the thought of working on a metro daily. More money. The big city. Plenty of classy women.

He started writing:

PORT JEROME—New Age eating has come to the South Coast at Oats in the Bowl, a restaurant dedicated to Oriental cuisine with a special philosophy. And the piano player knows Mozart. . . .

Fiske came slowly through the front door, gazing down at something Eldon couldn't see because of the counter. Fiske moved as if he carried a great yet fragile burden. As Fiske rounded the counter, Eldon saw that the editor tenderly held a brown paper bag.

"You okay, Jimbo?" Eldon asked.

Fiske returned a mournful stare and went to the news desk. He opened the bag and took out a block of Lucite. His pipe was imbedded within like a fly in amber. "I'm thinking about mortality."

Ceci n'est pas une pipe, Eldon thought.

"I had it done during lunch," Fiske said, "to please my wife."

"Jimbo! I'm proud of you!" Marsha cried.

Fiske scowled at her. "I need copy. If I can't have a smoke, I want copy."

Marsha threw the news brief she had been working on into the copy basket and fled.

Fiske stared at Eldon. "What about you?"

"I went to the restaurant—"

"It better have been good," Fiske said. "I'll need microbiotics to get through this."

"Oh, it was great."

"The Ohsawa Salad?"

"The best, Jimbo. Lots of roughage."

"That's good."

"I'm writing the review right now," Eldon said. "Then I want to start chasing the Loris story."

"And that cute deputy D.A.?" Fiske smiled, his mood seeming to right itself. "Dee-de-dee. Gimme a good restaurant feature and you can go to it."

Eldon jumped back to his typewriter and resumed pounding the keys. The blarney flowed out—the subtle wisdom of the Orient, the mysterious herbs and flavors, the soothing ambiance. Then some gobbledygook about macrobiotics, half-remembered from Berkeley. And fine dining music . . .

That stopped him. He didn't have the piano player's name.

The phone rang. Fiske looked up from reading wire copy to answer and began alternately talking and grunting. Eldon knew he was dealing with a complaint.

Fiske hung up the phone. "Eldon. Get out of the office."

"Huh?"

"You're gonna be picketed."

"Huh?"

"That was Ambrose McFee, our illustrious sports editor. The Port Jerome High School football team, its cheerleaders, and its many fans are on their way down here. Gonna picket the *Sun.*"

"Because of the body shot?"

"Because you slandered the high school."

"About Loris? Balls! It's true."

"They say I should fire you. Get scarce. It'll be easier to handle 'em if you're not around."

"What're you gonna say?"

" 'Dee-de-dee,' of course. Ambrose will cover the picketing."

"I'm not done with the restaurant review—"

"It'll have to hold, anyway. This Jimmy Carter story just came over the wire. . . . Say, are peanuts microbiotic?"

"Sasquatch and UFO didn't say?"

Fiske cupped his hand absently, as if holding his pipe. "My wife craves peanuts. This whole situation reminds me of the time I did a feature on this retired carny over in Josephine County; claimed he was the only man in the world who could breathe through one lung at a time—"

Eldon hurried out the side door, climbed into his Isetta, and started it up. Idiots, he thought. I give them hot news and this is the thanks I get. I'll show 'em—I'll keep Archie on Page One every day for weeks. For as long as it takes to win my bet.

Archie was into prostitution and porno, he thought as he pulled out of the parking lot. How can I find out more about him?

Why, talk to a whore, obviously.

Eldon snickered, then shook his head. He knew where to find prostitutes from a previous assignment. A corps of girls serviced the freighters that came from Asia to pick up wood chips from the mills. They were part of a marginal subculture of thieves, pushers, pimps, and hangers-on that served the merchant marine's darker appetites. Eldon shivered. That crowd was bad news.

But it's broad daylight, he thought. I should be safe.

He headed for the waterfront.

6

The wharf shared the air of abandonment common to Port Jerome's desolate industrial sites. A huge golden mountain of wood chips from the mills rose into the sky at the waterline. Eldon saw as he climbed from his car that one of the freighters in the bay had tied up to take on chips for shipment to the Orient. The smell of wet shavings hung on the breeze. A few gulls turned against the pale cloudy sky.

Eldon strolled along the pier's rough dark boards, listening to the lap of water on pilings and watching the freighter's crew swing long, pleated canvas conduits over her side. Linked to compressors in the ship's hold, the hoses would gradually suck the wood chips aboard. Meanwhile, the ship would draw the girls.

Eldon walked to a weedy graveled area where buoys, crab pots, spools of cable, anchors, rolls of fishing net, and other pieces of nautical equipment too heavy or too commonplace to steal were stockpiled. He leaned against a cable spool and waited. Shortly, a car pulled up at the lot's far edge, a battered red sedan so old it had tail fins. The body was mostly dents and rust.

A man and a woman were in the car. The man was behind the steering wheel. A prostitute and her pimp, Eldon thought hopefully. But how to approach them? Hi, I'm Eldon Larkin from the *Sun*. I'm not buying any sex today, but I wonder if you knew Archie Loris. . . .

He pretended to watch the chip-loading operation as the woman got out of the car and came toward the pier, walking head down as she picked her way around puddles. Her long, dark hair blew in the breeze. She was young and rather rangy, clad in pink slacks and a big, bunchy white sweater with a Christmas motif woven into it. She swung a white plastic purse by a long strap as she walked. Eldon couldn't see her face clearly because of her blowing hair.

Maybe I can get a conversation started, he thought.

But it was the hooker who spoke first. "Hey, Eldon! You reporters sure work fast. How'd you know where to find me? Never mind—you can't reveal your sources."

Eldon realized with shock that he knew her. "You're—uh—"

"Stephanie Hosfelder. You covered my wedding on the *Orient Star* last year."

"And nearly got killed. How's the groom? Is that him over in the car?"

"Ahmed's at sea," Stephanie said, pouting a little. "Immigration got on his ass."

"I didn't think that was him." The car was too far away for Eldon to see the man clearly. He looked at Stephanie and thought, Christ, what cement-mixer have you been rolling around in?

Far worse than the passage of several months' time had ravaged Stephanie's face. Its bright, teenage plumpness had faded. Her face was pale and puffy. Her skin looked clammy.

She's lost a lot of weight—that's why I didn't recognize her, Eldon thought. Stephanie's figure had been lush. Now she was ropy-looking. Stephanie brushed her hair back, and Eldon saw that her hands were gaunt and trembled slightly. The predatory glitter he remembered in her eyes had dulled.

"Sorry I drew a blank on your name," Eldon said.

Stephanie laughed. "How could you forget? Hey, just kidding—you must meet a lot of people. Congratulations, like I said. That was a great picture of that son-of-a-bitch Archie."

"You called me today!"

"Yeah. You were out. A lady took the message."

"You should've left a phone number."

Stephanie shrugged. "Pay phone."

"Thanks anyway. People are pissed off because I slandered the high school."

Stephanie wiped her nose with the heel of her hand. "Stupid shits. That's why I quit."

"Oh."

"I liked French class, though. And English, too. I used to write, like you. Poetry. In a book." Stephanie hauled her purse up by its long strap and pulled out a slim, cloth-covered journal. "See?"

"Keep it up."

"I don't write much anymore." She put the book away.

"I'm writing about Archie," Eldon said.

"Yeah? Like what a piece of shit he was?"

"Basically. Want to help?"

Emotions crossed Stephanie's face like overlapping streaks of light—keen interest, elation, then anger and fear. "I can't."

"I won't put you in the paper. I just need some clues."

The car's horn blew. Twice.

Stephanie looked hastily over her shoulder. "Look, I gotta get to work. Or my friend's gonna be mad. He gets awfully mad."

"Tell him I was too cheap to meet your price."

"You'd have to be pretty cheap. You'll leave me out of the story? You just want to do a job on Archie?"

"I want to find out who killed him, if I can."

"Christ, you don't want to do *that.*"

"Let me worry about that."

"Nothing stops a reporter, does it?" Stephanie said with admiration.

"I know that Archie was into pimping. And drugs."

"And porn."

"I've heard all about Archie's hobbies," Eldon said. "But I need people who can fill me in."

"Well, they're gonna have to be braver than most." Stephanie watched the sailors aboard the chip ship. "You left out Archie's biggest hobby."

"What's that?"

"Gambling. Play cards?"

"No."

"You know the Lucky Poke Saloon? Go hang out there."

That pack of cards in Archie's bedroom had the Lucky Poke's label, Eldon thought. Bingo. "So Archie was a gambler?"

"A supplier," Stephanie said. "Cards, tables, dealers. Even hookers. The works."

"So *that's* how he made his money."

"A regular John D. Rockefeller. It was easier than drugs. Safer, too. The cops can't do shit."

"I guess not. The gaming law's a mess."

"It kept Archie in videotapes. He had this new-fangled camera he was really proud of." Stephanie eyed him. "You haven't seen those tapes of his, have you?"

"No. The cops took 'em."

"Oh, well. I was going to ask you how you liked mine."

"Haven't seen it. Sorry." Eldon felt gooseflesh.

"Archie had a lot of enemies," Stephanie continued, matter-of-factly. "But it's funny—his getting killed caught everyone by surprise. Like inheriting money."

"Did he owe anyone money?"

"Eldon, I gotta go." Stephanie wiped her nose again.

"You . . . worked for Archie?"

"For a while. When he quit dealing, I switched. Had to. Hey . . . do you have ten bucks to spare?"

Eldon knew about panhandlers from Berkeley. Never take out your wallet, he thought. He fished in his pocket, handed over a crumpled one-dollar bill and three pennies.

"Hey, thanks a lot, Eldon. This is great."

"Don't mention it."

Stephanie sidled closer. "You're cute. A dollar-three won't getcha much, but—"

"Thanks. I've got a girlfriend," Eldon said, more abruptly than he had intended.

"Oh. I bet she takes good care of you."

"Yeah. Now, who should I talk to at the Lucky Poke?"

The car's horn blew again. Stephanie glanced back furtively as she stuffed her loot into her purse. "Mr. G—well, just ask . . . the first person you see when you get there."

Eldon sighed. "Okay. Thanks. And good luck."

"Always glad to help a fellow writer." Stephanie gave a wan grin and headed for the ship, swinging her purse.

Eldon clambered into his Isetta and drove away, giving the pimp's car a wide berth.

Melissa must've known about Archie and the gambling—but she didn't mention it, he thought. She's not playing fair. . . . But then all's fair in love and war.

Eldon knew little about how to play cards, but the idea was exciting. It carried overtones of the illicit. Oregon's gambling law was bizarre. It was legal to play cards in a bar or tavern, the intent being to allow penny-ante games among friends; the house could not profit from such gaming. But in practice, the statute could not be enforced. Card rooms flourished. Typically, the house would rent floor space to gambling barons such as Archie who supplied everything—cards, chips, roulette wheels, and dealers, often ones who had been banned from Nevada's casinos. Ostensibly, the house didn't earn a cent. In fact, the house made out handsomely selling drinks to the gamblers and skimming gaming profits, not to mention floor-space rent. Some proprietors collected kickbacks from prostitution and drugs, as well.

All of which pointed to a wonderful story—maybe to an award-winning series.

And to something else.

I might get lucky at cards, Eldon thought. If I could win, I could pay off the Isetta. I'd be out from under.

Eldon imagined himself a Mississippi riverboat gambler, in bro-cade vest and broad-brimmed hat, grinning as he pulled in the chips across a green felt table. Melissa, clad in a low-cut strapless dress, leaned upon his arm. The daydream kindled a warm excitement akin to that of anticipated sex, or fly-fishing.

I'll have to weasel my way in at the Lucky Poke, he thought. Build up my skill. But what if they cheat? How can I tell?

Then came another thought: They won't cheat me, because I'll get Melissa to teach me how to gamble.

Eldon heard band music as he neared the *Sun* office. He slowed the car, thinking, I forgot about the pickets.

The crowd was bigger than he'd expected—adults as well as high school students. Maybe fifty people. Kids with band instru-ments milled in the street playing rally music as cheerleaders pranced with insulting signs. The musicians were in civvies but wore the tall, plumed shakos of the Port Jerome High School marching band. The garish, archaic headgear made them look like toy soldiers who had somehow invaded an Oregon lumber town. Eldon wondered where to park.

He wasn't worried about the students. The sullen adults on the crowd's fringes were the danger. High school sports shared status with religion on the South Coast. Disputation could grow violent, even over intramurals. Adults attending a children's demonstration at this time of day most likely were unemployed mill workers. They had nothing better to do than argue about sports in the bars. They might decide to relieve their frustrated idleness by putting lumps on Eldon's head.

Traffic backed up as cars inched through the crowd. Students waved picket signs at the motorists, who honked encouragement. Eldon read the signs as the Isetta crept along. FIRE LARRKIN. Get a copy editor, he thought. RESPECT OUR SCHOOL, said another. Eldon nodded and honked vigorously.

Snare drums rolled. A pole with a rope threaded through a pulley at its top swung into the air. The rope was pulled, the pulley turned and a featherless rubber chicken, painted bright green, was hauled to the top of the pole. A sign attached to the chicken read ELDON LARKIN.

They spelled it right that time, Eldon thought.

Someone set a copy of the *Sun* afire and waved it under the chicken. Eldon decided it would be rash to pull into the *Sun's* parking lot. He drove a half-block past the office, parked at the curb, and walked back. He would slip into the building through the rear loading dock. A cheerleader saw him and hurried over. Two huge boys in letter sweaters swaggered after her. The boys had the nasty, self-important grins of sociopathic adolescent jocks everywhere. Eldon was about to turn and run when the girl said, "Sign our petition, mister?"

"Sure! Give it here."

"You want to know what it's about?" the girl asked.

"He knows what it's about," one of the boys said. "The whole town knows what it's about."

"That reporter guy," the other boy said.

"Eldon Larkin," Eldon said.

"Is that his name?" the cheerleader asked.

Eldon nodded. "He's a hack. I've hated him for years."

"Right on!" the cheerleader said.

"He's really biased," the second letterman said. "He oughta be fired. Hey, it's our school."

"That's right," Eldon said.

He scanned the petition. It demanded a front-page apology from him and the *Sun* for slandering the good name of Port Jerome High and that of one of its football heroes, "Archy Lorris." It demanded that Eldon leave town forever. The petition bore several signatures. Eldon took out his pen and signed, "A. Lincoln, Springfield, Illinois," in mock nineteenth-century cursive.

"Here you go." He handed the petition back.

"Thanks, Mr. Lincoln!" the cheerleader said.

Eldon tipped his hat and strolled on. No one who hadn't met him had the slightest idea who he was. He was tempted to join the demonstration and shout slogans against himself but decided not to push his luck.

Circulation crews were at work on the loading dock, throwing wire-bound bales of the day's edition into idling pickups; deadlines and deliveries waited on nothing—certainly not on demonstrations. Eldon hoisted himself over the dock's edge and walked into the warehouse, where huge squat rolls of blank newsprint were stacked to the ceiling, ready to feed the press. From the warehouse, he entered the press room. The day's run was finished. Pressmen were cleaning the fifty-foot-long Goss offset press.

A siren blared outside, muffled through the pressroom's cinderblock walls. A sheriff's car had arrived to clear the crowded street. Eldon took a deep breath, filling his head with the tangy smell of printer's ink. He felt pleasantly on the run as he opened the door to the newsroom.

A red balloon with a Frowny Face on it floated through. Eldon saw that someone had released a cloud of balloons in the main office, each emblazoned with the Frowny Face.

Frank sat behind his typewriter batting drifting balloons with a pica stick. Marsha was not present. Fiske had his feet up on the news desk, hands behind his head, and a telephone receiver in each ear. Balloons drifted across the news desk.

Ambrose McFee was interviewing a deputation, taking notes on his typewriter. McFee's greasy purple baseball cap with the yellow Q sat on his head, so Eldon knew it was serious business.

McFee, who was five feet tall and shaped like a tree stump, had cranked his swivel chair up as high as it would go so that he could comfortably reach the typewriter keyboard. He sat in the chair crosslegged, rotating slightly to the right.

Eldon ambled to his desk. No one paid him any attention. He strained to hear what the deputation was telling McFee. They were a sleazy-looking lot and not a student among them. The men had oiled cowboy hair and wore leisure suits, the cuffs turned back to reveal faded tattoos. They wore rings so big they could double as brass knuckles. The women's hair was piled up, and they wore too much makeup and jewelry. All the faces were hard, the skin grainy. They looked as if they had been preserved for years under yellowing glassine, like the old news clipping in Archie Loris's wallet.

Snippets of the discussion with McFee drifted to Eldon. "—bad for business—" . . . "—why don't you like us—?" And McFee's affable reply: " 'Like' doesn't have anything to do with it."

Eldon dialed Frank's extension. "What gives?"

"Ah, Prince Kropotkin. Good of you to drop in."

"They don't know who I am."

"They know you're a malignant force," Frank said.

"They're Port Jerome High School alumni?"

"They're card-room owners. They want the Legislature to establish a casino zone here on the South Coast." Frank reached up a long arm and batted a balloon. "They supplied the balloons. They don't like what you said about Archie."

"It was true. Tough shit if it's bad for business."

"Archie was part of the casino-zone lobbying effort," Frank said. "Threw a good deal of money at it. They say our coverage of his murder is in bad taste—unjust to their cause."

"They're mainly worried because Archie was their under-the-table gaming supplier," Eldon said.

"Ah! You've been busy since lunchtime."

"Nothing concrete, but I know where the story is going," Eldon said. "I plan to visit the Lucky Poke Saloon."

"That's a rough place," Frank said. "You might get your teeth kicked in."

"That can happen in any bar around here."

"Why the Lucky Poke, particularly?"

"There was a deck of cards from the Lucky Poke in Archie Loris's bedroom."

"That's thin, Eldon."

"Not if what you say is true." Eldon told Frank about his conversation with Stephanie Hosfelder.

"God, I'd forgotten all about her," Frank said.

"She looked bad. Doing drugs. Archie spoiled everything he touched."

"What's this crusading tone?"

Eldon laughed. "I've hit the jackpot, thanks to Archie. Melissa Lafky and I discussed much more than macrobiotic food at lunch today."

"Yeah?"

"We made a bet. All I need to do is figure out who killed Archie, which I was going to do anyway."

"And . . . ?"

"And Melissa will sleep with me."

Eldon saw Frank push his glasses up his nose and look over at him with an expression of awe. "That's unprecedented. It's also sleeping with a source."

"Well, we won't do it until after I've published the story." Eldon couldn't help grinning. He batted a balloon toward Frank. He felt like drumming the desk with his fists.

The card-room owners were leaving. Eldon hung up his phone and watched them pump McFee's hand, slap him on the shoulder. Ambrose escorted them to the front door like a little sheepdog herding cattle through a meadow of drifting balloons.

Ambrose returned, dusting off his hands. "Just a few over-wrought football fans. Nothing to get excited about."

"What did you tell them?" Eldon asked.

"I said I'd write a story about it."

"Are you going to denounce me?"

McFee merely winked one of his enormous blue eyes.

Fiske strolled up. "Thought you'd made yourself scarce, Eldon."

"Scarce enough. I even signed a petition against myself."

"Dee-de-dee," Fiske said. "This casino stuff deserves an editorial."

"Hit 'em hard," Eldon said. "Casinos would wreck the coast. Who wants to live in a honky-tonk?"

"That's right," Fiske said. "Enough bad food around here now." He pulled a balloon from the air and regarded its frowning face like Hamlet regarding Yorick's skull. "Hamburgers with fries in congealing grease. Stale popcorn. Twinkies. *Corn dogs*. The card rooms are the worst offenders. The South Coast's ying-yang is so far out of balance, it's no wonder we've got problems."

"That's 'yin' and 'yang,' Jimbo," Eldon said.

"Huh?" Frank said.

"Read my restaurant story," Eldon told him.

"Microbiotic casinos," Fiske said. "Craps players eating blue seaweed. Think of what it could do for this town!"

Eldon didn't reply.

The mob wants casinos in Oregon, he thought as he returned to his desk. Maybe Archie got in the way of that somehow and paid for it with his life. Maybe he tried to set himself up as an independent. Or maybe he was killed by someone who *didn't* want casinos. . . .

Melissa and I must talk, he thought. Over dinner.

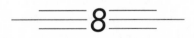

Eldon called the D.A.'s office. When the secretary put him through to Melissa, he said, "Hi—this is Eldon."

"Hello!"

"Just wanted to say hi. Busy day?"

"A couple of drunk-driving cases and a child abuser. You?"

"I got picketed," Eldon said.

"Really? Why?"

"People got upset at my Archie story. And the picture."

"What? They were *great*, Eldon."

"Thanks."

"Nothing like that happens to lawyers."

"Or to reporters, usually. It was instructive."

"How?" Melissa asked.

"The picketing was instigated by a bunch of card-room owners who want a legal casino zone. Ring a bell?"

"I suppose I've heard of them."

"I thought you might be looking into their activities—"

"Well, there's not much we can do about the card rooms."

"—because of Archie's gambling connections. Archie was bank-rolling the lobbying. And now he's been murdered."

"Yes." Melissa sounded wary, as if sensing a trap in a routine cross-examination.

"You know about the connection? You didn't mention it."

"Eldon, I can't talk about a pending investigation."

"You can make some pretty tall bets, though."

"I thought you wanted to!"

"I do. But I want to get the story, too. And you want to solve the case, right?"

"Right." The word was clipped off.

"Good." Eldon began perspiring. His chances with Melissa seemed about to fall through. But he had to press on. "I know how to deal with sources who stonewall me, Melissa."

"Oh! How?" Her voice was very hard and precise now. Very lady-lawyer, Eldon thought.

"I invite them to dinner," he said.

Melissa giggled. "Do you always?"

"Just special ones. Will you come? Tomorrow night."

"I don't think we should socialize—"

"Oh, come on! We've got a bet! And there's no point in du-plicating efforts. Do you want the case solved or not? I'd be calling you for comment even if we'd never had lunch."

"I don't know—"

"I'm a good cook."

"Eldon, I don't think it's wise."

"I could write a story right now on what I know. Alert every-one. That wouldn't help your investigation."

"And this'd be the last help you got out of this office."

"I won't write it if you come to dinner," Eldon said lightly.

Melissa laughed. "Eldon, you do have balls, you know that? Sure, I'll come."

"Great. Tomorrow at six. Is there anything you don't eat?"

"Nope. Am I getting Gourmet Seduction Dinner Number One?"

"Passé. We're doing Gourmet Seduction Dinner Number Two. Fresh fish, caught and cooked by yours truly."

"Delicious!"

"There's a catch. You have to teach me to play poker."

"Poker?"

"The key to this case is the card rooms. I'm going to hang around the Lucky Poke."

"Will anyone there talk to you?"

"We'll see. I might win some money."

"Forget about breaking the bank, Eldon. They'll break you."

"It's worth it when I think about the stakes," Eldon said.

Melissa chuckled. "Okay, I'll bring a deck of cards."

Eldon gave her his address and tossed the phone receiver into its cradle with glee. Melissa made him feel competent, even suave.

A little voice of warning spoke in the back of his mind: Maybe that's the way she *wants* you to feel.

Oh, the hell with it, Eldon thought. Go for broke. The stakes are on the table now.

Eldon was ready to go at five the next morning. The rising summer sun cast golden beams through the trees as he took his fishing equipment to the car. No rain today, he thought cheerfully and turned to the first challenge: fitting a fishing rod into an Isetta. But he found that the car's interior volume was greater than it looked. He could set the pole at a slant with the butt in the passenger's corner and just make it. His tackle box, creel, and hip waders went onto the shelf behind the seat.

Eldon adjusted his fishing vest, squared his jungle hat on his head, and climbed into the Isetta. It's like shutting myself in a refrigerator, he thought as he hauled the door shut. He adjusted the choke and switched on the ignition. The single-piston engine started promptly. Eldon fumbled with the gearshift. The left-handed shift and reverse-H pattern still confused him. Finally he pinpointed reverse and backed into the street.

He aimed downhill on the graveled back road that led to the flats and hit the gas. The Isetta plunged. Gravel rattled on the car's underside. Eldon gripped the wheel and treadled the brake, fighting off the feeling that he was about to roll head-over-heels down the slope. He had a special, secret destination this morning; if he crashed, the secret would die with him.

He was heading for Sackett Lake, a secluded pond rich with trout. Eldon had never met another soul there or heard any other fisherman talk about it. He felt as if he owned the place.

Every fisherman had such fishing holes, their locations jealously guarded. Eldon glanced in the rearview mirror to make sure he was not being followed; such tricks were common among fishermen where secret fishing holes were concerned. He had bought some line in a tackle store last night, a place where he was known. Someone might have guessed the significance of his purchase. . . .

The rearview mirror was empty. Eldon had to smile. The fact was, he enjoyed being paranoid about his fishing holes. Every fisherman did. It was part of the fun.

He reached the bottom of the hill, the car skidding a little as Eldon reduced speed. He turned right onto the road skirting Neka-emas Bay's shady eastern shore, where lush forest growth spread back from the mud flats and up into the hills. Maple and alder flourished there amid Oregon grape and bracken ferns. Huge pale mushrooms grew on sodden logs. The slopes on the northern shore were sunnier and more open, the domain of Douglas fir. But Eldon wasn't going that far today. Shortly, he turned off on a track that ducked behind dairy farms and wound up into the shadowed forest. It was an unmapped shortcut to Sackett Lake.

The bay's briny smell faded as Eldon drove along the green-shaded tunnel formed by the trees. His mouth watered with the thought of eating fresh trout. Of course, he had to catch them first, but with his skill that was no problem. He speeded up as he turned his mind to a critical question—which fly to use? Eldon tied his own flies, and that was half the art. The other half was choosing which flies to use when. Fish caught with an artistically appropriate fly always tasted better. His lucky hat was studded with flies because he liked carrying them next to his brain.

The Grasshopper . . . the Woolly Worm . . . the Code Three that had been given him by a Portland cop. . . . Fishing flies twinkled in Eldon's imagination like Christmas tree ornaments. He toyed with options as he steered along the twisting track, deliciously putting off a decision until he reached the lake. Then he topped a rise and caught sight of the water, serene and greenish, surrounded by trees. The morning sun cast a shimmering stripe across the dark water. A perfect morning for fishing!

Eldon started down the slope—then boggled at the sight of a blue Ford pickup. And standing in the shallows was a fisherman! Fishing Eldon's lake! A lanky guy in a cowboy hat!

Torque ripped the steering wheel from Eldon's hands. The Isetta skidded on a wet rock and rolled sideways. Eldon yelled in terror and curled into a ball as the car made a half-roll and slid upside-down to a gentle stop near the pickup, engine still puttering. Eldon's tackle box hit the Isetta's ceiling with a clank.

He gasped for breath and tried to untangle himself. How to get the door open? Was his fishing rod broken? Were his bones broken? Everything seemed intact—

"I say, are you okay?"

The voice was British. Eldon twisted to see the invader at the side window, holding a rod in one hand and a string of rainbow trout in the other. He was about forty, with horn-rimmed glasses and neat fringe whiskers decorating a head shaped like a wedge. The man wore an enormous white Stetson and a garish orange Western shirt with overall waders. Eldon squatted on the ceiling and slid open the side window. "Yeah, I'm okay—"

"This happens with Isettas," the fisherman said cheerfully. "Did it myself once, in London."

"We've got to get the door open. Get a crowbar—"

"You don't need a crowbar. We'll get you sorted out. But turn off the engine first."

Eldon found the ignition and turned it off. He felt as if he were groping through a crashed space capsule.

"I'm Simon Blood," the fisherman said.

"Eldon Larkin. I'll shake hands when I get out of this. You're English?"

"Long a citizen of these United States and of this fine South Coast, thank you. This happens with Isettas," Blood repeated. "In fact, you can't really consider yourself an Isetta owner until it *has* happened to you. Had it long?"

"No—"

"Doesn't look as if you've hurt it. That's good. It's a rare 600 Series."

"Yeah—"

"Looks like a '58. How much did you pay for it, if you don't mind my asking?"

"Seven-twenty-five—"

"Oh, that's rather a lot!"

"I didn't have much choice—"

"I rolled an Isetta in London, as I said. Tried to change lanes too quickly, flipped and skidded right along the pavement upside down. Fortunately, it was a Saturday morning."

"—but I'd like to get out now!"

"Oh! Right!" Blood waved his string of trout. "What you've got to do is face forward and stand up—well, crouch if you like— and spread your feet. Now rock back and forth until she turns right side up again. Go ahead, she weighs less than eight hundred pounds. I'll give you the cue—"

Eldon braced his feet and gingerly shifted his weight from foot to foot, building up a rocking motion. Then Blood called, "Now!" Eldon threw his weight onto his right foot. The car rolled and popped neatly upright, tumbling him into the seat.

"Good show." Blood set down his rod and opened the door. Eldon staggered out. "Thanks."

"It's a good thing to know," Blood said as they shook hands. "Great little cars, aren't they? You just have to get used to their center of gravity."

Eldon peered at him. "How'd you find this place? Did you hear about it in England?"

"I've been fishing here for ten years." Blood squinted back. "How did *you* find it?"

Eldon didn't answer. He realized that they had fished this spot for years on different days. They probably even got here by different routes. And Blood was senior fisherman at Sackett Lake. At least the lake's secret would stay between the two of them. Finally Eldon said, "Looks like good fishing this morning."

"You bet. Got my limit. I was just about to head off."

"I'd better get out on the water," Eldon said. "I've only got an hour or so before I go to work."

Blood pulled a cooler from the back of his pickup and put his fish inside. He began stripping off his waders. "Wait a minute. 'Eldon Larkin.' You work for the newspaper."

"Uh, yeah." Eldon hoped Blood didn't follow high school football. "Maybe you've read my stories."

"I know Ambrose McFee. He's mentioned you. Ambrose is a fellow rugby fan. Tell him I said hello."

"I will." Eldon wondered why Blood followed rugby instead of rodeos. Beneath his waders, the Englishman wore pipestem blue jeans and a wide leather belt tooled with Native American designs. The buckle was in the shape of a huge Indian-head nickel.

"Thanks for helping me out," Eldon said.

"Don't mention it. I admire anyone who'd buy an Isetta in this day and age—the cost of parts is out of this world."

"It's running okay so far."

"Have it checked," Blood commanded. "Especially the drive couplers—they're made of rubber, in six pieces. Is there a rattle?"

"I don't think so."

"The drive couplers rattle when the bolts start loosening up. If they break, you stop." Blood got a pair of cowboy boots from the cab of his truck, pulled them on and, with a wave to Eldon, got in his truck and drove away.

Eldon sighed. It looked as if he was in way over his head when it came to cars—as usual. But he wasn't hurt and he was ready to go fishing. Optimism bloomed as he thought of dinner with Melissa.

He retrieved his equipment and sat down on a rock by the water. He moved stiffly, pulling on thick woolen socks and then his waders. I'll have to soak in a hot bath tonight, he thought.

Eldon opened the tackle box. Most of the bright flies were still in their staggered trays despite the rollover. Eldon pondered them. None would do. He removed his hat and considered the flies hooked into the green fabric. The obvious choice was the Bucktail Coachman.

He admired the fly as he worked it free of the cloth. It had a bright red body and red hackle and a special white wing he'd made from polar bear hair. The hair had been a lucky find, in that dirty little tackle shop in Reedsport.

He measured off ten feet of leader, tied the fly to the leader and the leader to the line. A long leader was best. He surveyed the lake and stepped carefully into the water, treading out to stand with the breeze at his back. He could feel the cold water even through his socks and waders. Trout would be near the shore, seeking cover amid the weeds and protruding mossy stumps.

Eldon brought the rod upright, stripping line from the reel with his free hand as he judged his first cast. That half-sunken log was a fine place to start. It was a long cast but that would save energy. He swept the rod back. The line ran out behind him. He flicked the rod forward, enjoying the springy feel. A good cast was like uncoiling a punch. The Bucktail Coachman sailed through the morning sky like a red spark.

On target! The first cast of the day! Even though his secret fishing hole was compromised. Even though he had just rolled his car.

He let the fly sink, counting to fifteen, then made a slow, steady retrieve and cast again. And again, falling into the rhythm of it, the repetition soothing his tense muscles.

With the rhythm came the sense of stability that was at the heart of Eldon's devotion to fishing. Eternal verities—the sky, the water, the fish. A fresh fish dinner had to impress Melissa. The ancient lure of machismo.

Indigenous rainbows weighed as much as a pound apiece. Five or six would do nicely. Catching that many was no sweat. Retrieve . . . cast . . . retrieve and cast again. . . .

The strike was a solid tug on his line. His rod bowed and the line weaved and flashed in the sun. This was no trout.

Eldon worked the reel to tire the fish out. Light raced up and down the line. At last he reeled in the prize—a big black bass. His mouth watered; he could already taste the sweet white meat.

It must weigh three pounds, he thought as he unhooked the fish and slipped it into his creel. Not bad for a guy who just rolled his car.

Eldon savored a wry feeling of triumph over Simon Blood. The Englishman might know Sackett Lake, but he'd missed this granddaddy bass.

Eldon glanced at his watch. His blood was up, but he had a fine fish for dinner. He could always come back. He started for the shore. He'd prepare curried bass—fillet out the meat and cut it into bite-size chunks, marinate it for about an hour before cooking it in lemon and lime juice with a little crushed red chili pepper. He'd make a sauce with onions and garlic. Red potatoes and a salad on the side. And lay on the wine.

Eldon felt so good by the time he reached the shore that he plucked some hanging moss from a tree and used a fly hook to hang it on his hat for luck.

9

Eldon's luck held. The day's work was routine. Assignments were easily handled by telephone. Fiske was undemanding, preoccupied with his entombed pipe. Eldon thought about the finer things.

He modified his dinner menu several times, returning at last to his original plan with the addition of some crisp French bread. And he decided to use a canned sauce, to save time. Should he serve French wine? That would show class. But he decided on an Oregon Riesling. The state made good wines. He couldn't go wrong serving Oregon wine to an Oregon native. Besides, it was cheaper.

He finished his review of Oats in the Bowl, not bothering about the piano player's name. Fiske accepted the story with doleful gratitude. Eldon prayed there wouldn't be a major traffic accident or murder late in the afternoon. Whether through divine mercy or thanks to the lucky sprig of moss in his hat, the police scanner remained quiet. He left early to shop.

The day remained sunny and warm. The vegetables in the supermarket were fresh, the prices good, the checkout line short. Eldon got home in plenty of time.

He mixed the marinade, cut up the fish, immersed it, and put it in the refrigerator. He cleaned house, with special attention to the bedroom. He dusted off his books and made sure his photos hung straight on the walls. He tidied his fly-tying bench, too. Then he set up the card table in the living room to take advantage of the view. He covered the table with a white tablecloth and carefully set out silverware and dishes.

He put a rare Modern Jazz Quartet album on the stereo and got busy in the kitchen. He was finishing dinner preparations to the tinkle of vibes when Melissa knocked promptly at 6 P.M. Eldon threw open the door and bowed her into the house. *"Entrez-vous, madam.* The view is in your honor. The meal is cooking."

Melissa sniffed the air. "Smells great. . . . And you've got quite a view up here."

Eldon saw that Melissa carried a briefcase. "Let me take that. Did you just come from work?"

"What a day! Drunken drivers, a dog-control case, and similar rubbish."

"Let me get you a drink."

"Bourbon, rocks," Melissa said.

Eldon hurried for the Jack Daniels and the ice. He wondered whether Melissa had really "just come from the office." She wore a severe blue suit, but with a lace-trimmed white blouse with a deep neckline that revealed a hint of cleavage. Not quite the thing for court.

Melissa put down her briefcase and slipped off her suit coat. The long-sleeved blouse had lacy cuffs. Classy strip-tease, Eldon thought as he poured bourbon for both of them.

"I've had quite a day myself," he said.

"You've solved the Loris case? Thanks."

"No, I rolled my car."

"Eldon! Are you all right?"

"Nothing to it. Isettas are great little cars, but you have to get used to their center of gravity. In fact, you can't really consider yourself an Isetta owner until you've rolled one. They're just the thing for going fishing."

"You did it while you were fishing?"

"Caught a nice black bass for dinner."

"But you're okay?" Melissa's eyes were large.

"My right shoulder's a little sore—"

"Sit down. I give a pretty good massage."

Oh, boy, Eldon thought and sat in his easy chair.

Melissa stepped behind the chair and began massaging his shoulder with strong fingers. "Got to make sure you're up to playing cards. I'll show you the basics after dinner."

"Are you going to cheat?" Eldon asked playfully.

"I will not. You couldn't spot a good cheat anyway."

"Ahh, that feels good. Do they cheat at the Lucky Poke?"

"They might."

"A little higher," Eldon said. "That's great. . . . Only 'might' be cheating? I thought Archie used banned dealers?"

"Mostly to keep the overhead down. Straight or crooked, the house always takes its percentage. Keep that in mind, Eldon."

"I just want information. I don't care if I win."

"The hell you don't." Melissa leaned down to speak in his ear. "You're a wagering man."

Eldon turned to kiss her but Melissa straightened, still working his shoulder. "Your muscles aren't all that tight."

"Luckily I can still cook."

Melissa gave his shoulder a final squeeze. "That's why I don't want you too relaxed. . . . What's that pretty album? The Modern Jazz Quartet?"

"Right. *Concert in Japan '66.* I hunted for it for years."

"That's a find—they only released that one in Japan."

"I found it in Berkeley." She was leading me on at Oats in the Bowl, pretending that she didn't know music, Eldon thought. Well, let's see who out-bluffs whom tonight. "It's time to get back to the stove."

Melissa followed him into the kitchen and watched as Eldon readied the sauce, first sautéing the onions and garlic in bouillon. As he worked, Eldon told stories about his Berkeley student days. He carefully played down his marriage in favor of amusing tales of Vietnam-era draft-dodging.

"I have to admit it was my teeth and not my principles that finally got me off the hook," Eldon concluded. "Caps." He tapped his front teeth.

"Caps got you out of the draft?"

"It surprised me, too. A lot of things about Vietnam didn't add up. . . . Of course, the Loris case doesn't add up, either."

"Oh, my—back to business."

"You're still certain it was a mob killing?"

"Are you interviewing me, Eldon?"

"I warned you."

"Maybe that's why I wore my lawyer suit. But I hoped we were off duty."

"We are. This isn't for print. But I've got this bet with a beautiful woman—"

"Okay." Melissa smiled. "It's a professional hit that doesn't look like one. The pros don't usually use a shotgun. It's too messy, attracts too much attention. This isn't the movies."

"So what do the pros use?"

"Art Nola says a .22 pistol is popular. The bullet is so small that it goes in but doesn't come out—it bounces around inside. You walk up behind the target on the street, pump one into the back of the head and walk on past. Almost no noise. The body keeps walking, too, for a few seconds—until it realizes it's dead."

"We don't get a lot of that around here." Eldon added the fish to the sauce.

"No."

Eldon turned up the heat under the pan and began stirring. "So why do you think it was a professional hit?"

"Because I was looking into social gaming when Archie was killed. That's why I was assigned the murder. We'd heard the rather surprising rumor that the card rooms were crooked. Archie was a major supplier. There must be a connection."

"You were surprised?"

"They don't need to be crooked. That just brings heat. I told you, the house always takes its percentage. That's the way a gaming operation stays in business. Not by cheating. And of course there's the ancillary vice."

"So what doesn't add up?" Eldon pulled the fish off the stove. "Dinner's ready. Tell or you don't eat."

"If the mob wants casinos on the South Coast, and Archie's bankrolling the campaign to get them, why kill him?"

"Like you said—for skimming profits."

"But why should they care as long as they get their cut? No, there's something else here, Eldon, something hard to get at. They killed Archie the way they did to throw us off track, make it look like less than it was."

Eldon led the way to the table, carrying the main course before him.

"There's another thing that doesn't make sense," Melissa said.

"What?"

"All that moss spattered around the kitchen. It's just . . . moss. And tiny bits of wire."

"Some kind of sadistic shotgun load? An Italian thing?"

"It wasn't fired from the gun. And they aren't all Italians."

"Then obviously, the shotgun was wrapped up for camouflage."

"I thought of that. But *moss?* What kind of nutty thing is that?"

"Beats me." Eldon spooned red potatoes onto Melissa's plate and made a mental note to contact nurseries around town.

Talk of Archie evaporated as they attacked the food. Dinner was a triumph. Eldon had to admit he'd seldom cooked a better fish. Melissa ate with gusto and was delighted with the wine. They drained the bottle as the sun set.

"This is so much fun," Melissa said. Her face was pleasantly flushed. "I'd expected to be raked over the coals in exchange for some fried food."

"Like hell. Ready for cognac?"

Melissa blotted her lips with her napkin. "Let's relax a little first." She flipped the napkin away to reveal a deck of cards in her hand. "How much do you know about cards?"

"A lot less than you do, obviously!"

"Not tricks—games."

"Not a lot. Solitaire. And I played twenty-one for pennies, when I was a kid."

"Nothing else? No strip poker in college?"

"Sadly not! I guess I know about simple draw poker."

"Clear away these plates."

"Even as you speak, madam."

Melissa slid the cards from the box and swept them across the table face-up in a fan, swept the deck back together, and shuffled it. "At least you don't have any bad habits. No, wait—where do you stick when you're playing blackjack?"

"Sixteen."

"Always stick at twelve," Melissa said. "I'm going to teach you the rudiments of poker, Eldon. You don't have to be any good, but you don't want to make a fool of yourself, either—that'd attract attention."

"Maybe you should come with me. Pose as a dealer looking for work."

"Not likely."

"They'll take me to the cleaners."

"Probably. How much money is the *Sun* prepared to lose?"

Fiske won't put up a cent, Eldon thought. "A hundred bucks?"

"That's plenty," Melissa said. "The Lucky Poke is full of lousy card players. But they *try*. You have to know how to try. If you win a little, so much the better." She began dealing. "Poker is the science of deception. There's no such thing as luck. Got any poker chips?"

"No—"

"A jar of pennies? Buttons?" The cards kept falling.

"Just a second." Eldon went to his fly-tying bench and got his tackle box. "Fishing flies. Tied most of 'em myself."

Melissa laughed. "Ever the sportsman."

"We'll make the white ones worth a dollar," Eldon said, doling them out. "And the green ones, like this Grasshopper and these Spruce flies, five dollars. These red ones, the Bucktail Coachman and the Red Ant, will be worth ten. Watch the hooks."

"What's this cute fuzzy brown one?"

"That's a Woolly Worm. That's worth fifty bucks."

"We're going to need a lot more than just these."

"Oh. Just a minute." Eldon went to his bench and returned with a shoe box. He put the box on the table and removed the lid. It was filled with fishing flies.

"You tied *all* of these?" Melissa asked.

"I don't have much to do evenings," Eldon said shyly.

"This will be plenty," Melissa said. "And this is a deck of cards. It can be worth a lot of money, if you know how to use it. There are nearly two-point-six million five-card combinations. . . ."

She walked Eldon through a few trial hands as she explained the rules for five-card stud: two cards apiece at first, one face down, one face up. Then a bet. Then one card apiece, face up, three times, each followed by another bet. Winning hands—high card, pair, two pair, three of a kind, straight, flush, full house, four of a kind, straight flush; and when to call, when to raise, when to stay. . . .

"We'll play draw poker, too," Melissa said.

They started playing. There was a lot to remember, but Eldon was undaunted. Betting with his own flies made him feel lucky despite Melissa's warning. What served him well on Oregon's waters should profit him at its poker tables.

Several disastrous hands later, he realized that remembering the winning combinations was easy; finding them in the deck was hard. Melissa had won all the flies on the table. Eldon was amazed at how quickly he had lost them.

"Let's play some more," he said.

"Glutton for punishment, huh?" Melissa said.

Eldon pulled more flies from the box. "I want to *win*."

"I said you were a betting man. I'll have that cognac now."

"Right!" Eldon brought the bottle and poured two snifters of brandy.

"You've got to bet more conservatively. Be careful with your money." Melissa swirled her glass under her nose before drinking. "Ah. This tops off a really wonderful meal, Eldon. You're a terrific cook."

"Thanks. I wish my talents included cards."

"You'll improve. But you must *never* try to fill an inside straight. The odds are too long."

"Let's get on with it!"

Melissa regarded him over her snifter. "You like this?"

"Yeah!"

"We could make it more interesting. Up the ante."

"How?"

"I mentioned strip poker."

Eldon's stomach flipped. He could only nod. It's my cooking, he thought. Fix 'em a good dinner, top it off with cognac—works every time. He put aside the fact that this had never happened to him before.

Melissa shuffled the cards. "Five-card draw, buster."

If I win tonight, I won't need to solve the Loris case, Eldon thought.

"Ante up." Melissa dropped a white fly on the table.

Eldon anted. He was dealt a pair of sixes. That was okay. He drew three cards and suppressed a chortle—a pair of fours! He bet two Red Ants.

Melissa took a single card, matched the bet with four green flies. "Call."

"Two pair." Eldon showed his cards.

Melissa tossed down her cards.

"What did you have?" Eldon asked.

Instead of answering, Melissa drew up a stockinged leg and slipped off a black shoe with a medium heel. Her skirt slid back as she brought up her knee and Eldon glimpsed what looked like a black garter belt. He almost fell out of his chair as Melissa, smiling, readjusted her skirt. A woman who wore a *garter belt* in this day and age! In 1979! Oh, man . . .

Melissa kept her eyes on Eldon's as she dropped the shoe.

Eldon tried to contain his excitement. "Want to bet your deputy D.A. badge?"

"Strip poker does not extend to the contents of a lady's briefcase." Melissa took a sip of brandy.

"Attorney-client privilege, eh?" Eldon drank as she dealt the cards. "Just remember, no tricks."

"I do not need to cheat."

Honestly or not, Melissa dealt Eldon a handful of trash. He

remembered what she had said about playing conservatively and quickly folded. Melissa offered the deck but Eldon waved it away. "I like to watch you deal."

Melissa dealt another hand. Trash again for Eldon. He bet and Melissa matched him. Eldon drew three cards, netting a pair of threes, while Melissa discarded one card. The bright flies piled up.

At last, Eldon said, "Call."

Melissa showed a pair of deuces.

Eldon showed his hand. "Let's have that other shoe!"

Melissa removed the other shoe.

"We're rolling now." Eldon scooped up the deck and dealt himself a good hand—three jacks. Melissa studied her hand, drank more brandy, took two cards, carefully bet a Zaddack and a Code Three, two mostly green flies. She seemed a little unsteady.

Wine plus brandy, mighty handy, Eldon thought. I can't wait to get her out of that blouse. He raised.

Melissa raised.

"I call, little lady," Eldon said. "Three jacks."

"Full house, buster."

"Shit." Eldon pulled off a shoe.

Melissa smiled and rolled back a lacy cuff. "Nothing up my sleeve . . ."

"You won't be able to do that much longer," Eldon said.

"Do what?" Melissa started dealing the next hand.

"Roll up your sleeves—if you get my drift."

"Oh, my. Then I'd better roll up the other one." Melissa turned back the other cuff.

Eldon was delighted—even more so when he saw his hand: the ace of hearts and the ace of spades, and two of the three other cards hearts. The last was the five of diamonds. I could try for three of a kind and still have the pair of aces, he thought, and bet two more Red Ants.

"Well, you're pretty impressed with yourself," Melissa said. "I'll see you."

Eldon glowered and discarded the five of diamonds. He picked up its replacement with a quick prayer. The six of spades. Damn, he thought and bet one Spruce fly.

"Backpedaling—tsk, tsk," Melissa said. "I'll raise you. But only ten—I'll be kind." Melissa dropped Grasshoppers on the table.

She's bluffing, Eldon decided, and matched the bet. "Call."

He laid out his pair of aces.

Melissa caught her breath slightly and revealed her cards: a pair of sevens. She looked wide-eyed and bit her lip as Eldon stared. After a long moment, her fingers began creeping down the front of her blouse, slowly undoing the buttons.

Eldon's heart pounded, a caveman rhythm that filled his ears. I like poker, he decided as Melissa slipped off her blouse and tossed it aside. Beneath, she wore a lace-trimmed white chemise.

"Deal," Eldon commanded, his eyes fixed on Melissa's ample bust. The cards fell—and abruptly Eldon lost another shoe. Well, he thought nervously, I still have a lot of clothes to go.

Shortly, he discovered that he did not wear so many clothes after all. He lost his socks and belt. It was as if the good cards had flown away somewhere. Or had gone up the dealer's sleeve. . . .

Eldon was praying for something to back up a lonely ace when he lost his shirt. He had nothing left to bet but the Woolly Worm. And his pants.

"Want to quit?" Melissa asked.

"No!" Eldon defiantly held up his Woolly Worm. "Gimme some change."

"Okay." Melissa gave him lesser flies in exchange for the Woolly Worm, then shuffled the deck and started to deal.

The fresh pile of flies renewed Eldon's confidence. I'm going to think this through like a poker player, he decided. I can beat her yet.

He got an ace up, Melissa a five. Eldon looked at his down card—a four. The ace may lead to something, he thought, and bet.

The next cards fell—an eight for Eldon, a five for Melissa. Now she had a pair of fives showing. She upped the ante.

Eldon peeked at his four again and saw her bet.

A ten for Eldon. Melissa drew a nine. She immediately bet the same amount as before.

She didn't improve on that pair of fives, Eldon thought. Or she doesn't want me to know that she *did* improve on them. He felt panicky, checked his down card again. What to do?

Then a light went on in his mind.

I've got three cards showing and they're all higher than five, he thought. I'll convince her that I've got a higher pair and bluff the pants off her. Eldon glanced at his four for reassurance and matched Melissa's bet.

Melissa's brow wrinkled slightly. "Last card."

"Deal 'em, honey."

A jack for Eldon. A queen for Melissa. Eldon took a last look at his down card—it's still a four, he thought, with a weird sense of security—and raised everything he had left.

Melissa instantly matched the bet and flipped over her down card: a six.

"Damn!" Eldon cried.

"Let's see that last card of yours, Eldon," Melissa said. "Let's see what kind of shorts you're wearing, too."

"No!"

"You play, you pay," Melissa said. "If you've got something that beats my pair—" She reached across the table and turned up his four—"I'll strip right now. . . . No? I guess *you* will."

Eldon stood and wrestled off his pants. He tried to be jaunty about it but he was burning with embarrassment. He was down to pin-striped boxer shorts. He had been hooked with his own fishing flies.

Melissa beamed, quite sober. "Another hand? Double or nothing?"

Eldon shook his head miserably, hands clasped in his lap. I've got to lose weight, he thought. "You cheated!"

"No, I didn't. I just saw through your ploy."

"How did you know I didn't have—?"

"You kept looking at your down card, even after the last card was dealt. You'd have remembered what it was if it had been any good. You're too greedy." Melissa raised a finger. "A smart poker player knows when to quit. Not that you were ever ahead."

"I had to try—"

"You didn't try. You just jumped in and sank. . . . Those boxer shorts are cute."

"Yeah, okay, I get the picture!"

"Calm down. If you're not careful, you'll go broke so fast at the Lucky Poke, you'll have no excuse to hang around."

"Maybe I—I should stick to blackjack."

"It's far easier to be cheated at blackjack than at poker."

"I thought you were drunk," Eldon said stubbornly.

"An amateur magician gets a lot of experience in school theatricals." Melissa took on a pleasantly befuddled expression—tipsy lass at the New Year's party. Her next words came with care: "My tricks are nothing compared to what you might run up against."

"Why did you even make the Loris bet? So you can gloat over me?"

Melissa rose and slipped into her blouse, then leaned close. "Maybe I want to lose." Her lips brushed his lightly; the tip of her tongue flicked his teeth. Eldon reached for her but she stepped back, sober again. "I've got to go. Thanks for a wonderful meal—a wonderful evening." She put on her jacket.

Eldon fumbled with his pants. "Maybe we can have dinner again—without the cards."

"No, dinner *with* cards. You'll get better with practice." Melissa picked up her briefcase and winked. "Luckier."

=10=

"I like it," Fiske declared the next morning, smiling and cupping his hand around an imaginary pipe bowl. "Dee-de-dee."

He's in a good mood again, Eldon thought. "The Lucky Poke will make a good feature, if nothing else."

" 'The Shadowland of Social Gaming,' " Fiske said. "After the blowtorch murder, I did a story on house painters, because the blowtorch was played back and forth across the victim's face like a paintbrush—"

"I know. I need a hundred bucks poker money—"

"I talked to six or eight painters, but they never caught the killer. That's a lot of money, Eldon."

"Not if we solve the Loris murder."

"Solve the murder?" Fiske rested a hand on the Lucite cube containing his pipe, now a paperweight for curling strips of wire–service copy. "What've you got?"

"Nothing yet."

"You're getting pretty hot under the collar about a dead giant pimp. Why not let the cops do their job and then report on it?"

"Because it's good copy."

"Could it be that you're trying to impress a certain well-dressed young lady?"

"Oh, that's not it at all, Jimbo—"

"You're dressing better yourself lately," Fiske observed.

Eldon looked down. He usually wore whatever came to hand in the morning—often flannel shirts and threadbare corduroys—but today he had on a nice plaid sport shirt and his second-best slacks: Maybe Melissa would show up.

"You look too good for the Lucky Poke," Fiske said.

"I'll change."

"Suit yourself. I'm in a *good* mood. It's been a while since we ran a juicy exposé."

Eldon nodded. "The angle is the push to establish a casino zone. We tell what the card-room owners said about Archie's lobbying—and then trot out his criminal record."

Fiske chuckled. "Did ya see their complexions? They obviously eat nothing but fried food. Casinos and microbiotics can't mix. Those people burned a rubber chicken right out there on the street."

"The students burned the chicken," Eldon said.

"Just goes to show—setting a bad example for their elders," Fiske said. "Young junk-food eaters. . . . I got to thinking about the blowtorch murder because I remembered the argument with my wife years later about the ugly wallpaper she put up in the kitchen. It reminded me of the murder."

"You've said so, many times—"

"I thought about it because my wife and I don't argue anymore. Far from it! Dee-de-dee!" Fiske seized his hand exerciser and pumped away, grinning.

"I've wanted to write about social gaming for a long time," Eldon said.

"So get on with it. Frank can handle your beat, make the morning cop checks and so forth, since you'll be working nights. I'm not paying overtime, though."

"Comp time's fine. I'll go fishing."

"Bring Jimbo trout? Fish are microbiotic."

"Sure. Now, about the hundred—"

"Keep receipts. The *Sun* will reimburse you."

"I can't ask for receipts in a poker game."

"Company policy, Eldon. What would the bookkeepers say?"

"So if I use my own money, I can keep whatever I win."

"Hm . . . that's a point. Tell Frank what you're up to while I mull this."

Eldon went to Frank's desk and filled him in.

"You get all the good assignments," Frank said.

"You get all the women," Eldon said.

"A hundred bucks could buy a lot of beer. Let's have a party."

"Well, I haven't got it yet."

"Don't let him make you use your own money."

Marsha Cox came in the side door and stalked toward her desk, glaring at Eldon as usual. He winked at her. Marsha was about to retort when Fiske called her over.

The editor beckoned Marsha close and began whispering. Marsha glanced at Eldon and whispered earnestly in reply. Fiske worked the hand exerciser more slowly. "C'mere, Eldon," Fiske said.

Eldon plodded over, staring daggers—no, nuclear missiles—at Marsha. She returned a serene smirk.

"I've put your plan to Marsha here," Fiske said.

"You wanta come along?" Eldon asked her. "Pretend you're a barfly?"

Marsha sniffed.

"I told her about your new lady friend—" Fiske began.

"Any woman who's been to law school ought to be smart enough not to go out with *you,*" Marsha said.

"I'm dressing better," Eldon replied, trying to keep his tone light. "Jimbo says so."

Fiske beamed. "I asked Marsha how she would feel if the man of her dreams—her boyfriend Beamish, the Coast Guard lieutenant, let's say—were to tell her he was setting out to wager all to win her heart *and then asked for company money to do it?"*

"It would be a cheap, degrading trick," Marsha said.

"So what?" Eldon said. "Would Beamish do it?"

"Louis and I aren't seeing each other anymore," Marsha replied with hauteur.

So that's it, Eldon thought. She's broken up with her boyfriend and she's taking it out on me. She's probably ruined everything.

"Marsha says not to give you a cent." Fiske was enjoying himself. "But as editor, I have to apply microbiotic principles, steer the middle course. The ying-yang has to balance."

Eldon sighed. "That's 'yin,' Jimbo."

"Right, ying. Anyway, we compromised. I'll front you fifty bucks—"

"I need a hundred!"

"You can draw more, up to a hundred, as you need it. *If* you need it. When you lose the hundred, that's it. But if you win, you play on with the winnings. Build on it. And turn in anything you win."

It was a prudent plan. But Eldon was damned if he'd admit that in front of Marsha. "You don't trust me."

"It'll keep the auditors out of our face," Fiske said. "You know how the company is."

"I bet they don't have to put up with this kind of crap at the *Oregonian!*"

"Well, when you get hired there, you can tell us," Marsha said and sauntered off.

Eldon lowered his voice. "Since when does she call the shots around here?"

"She doesn't, Eldon—she just had a good idea."

"I'll show her!"

Fiske nodded. "Incentive to win."

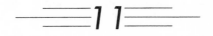

The Lucky Poke Saloon was a low-slung, windowless building that Eldon had passed many times, its ugly illuminated sign registering on some secondary level of his brain—aces and eights and dollar signs stamped on a yellow plastic sheet with lights behind it. He felt intimidated tonight as he halted his car in the gravel parking lot. The lot was full of pickups. The Isetta was a kiddy-cart among tanks.

He parked and headed for the saloon. A sallow-faced young man sat on the front steps, grinning disagreeably while he smoked a cigarette and chewed gum. He looked like an underfed shark. He bit hungrily at his gum with his little teeth, as if he were working gristle. He was smallish and skinny, dressed in low-slung blue jeans and an oddly dressy long-sleeved white shirt that led Eldon to guess he was a dealer.

The man's features looked as though they had been stretched over his skull without any meat beneath. He was Caucasian, but his skin had a coppery-olive cast, almost green in the glow of the sign. His hair and eyes were deep brown, and his eyebrows grew together. The eyes held a nasty glitter. They looked unwaveringly into Eldon's.

"Well, shit." The sneer didn't change. "That car rocks a little."

"Yeah," Eldon said, juggling his keys in his hand. "Inexperienced drivers have to be careful."

" 'Pregnant roller skate.' "

"That's what they call 'em."

The man glared. "Listen, Skate, I know my cars."

Eldon realized that he had scored a point, for some reason. "Sure you do. But my game is cards."

"This is the place. See ya after I'm off break. I deal blackjack with the best of 'em. I can get ya things, too."

The man waited, as if for a reply. Eldon tried to return the unwavering stare and dropped his keys. The dealer snatched them up. Eldon held out his hand.

The dealer twirled the keys around his finger. His grin remained fixed. Then a pair of beery loggers emerged from the Lucky Poke. One nearly tripped over the dealer. "Hey, outa the way—"

The dealer threw Eldon his keys and scrambled awkwardly aside. Eldon noticed that he wore big, floppy loafers perhaps a half-size too big.

Eldon ducked through the door and stood blinking inside the Lucky Poke, memorizing the scene as his eyes adjusted to the bright light.

He was in a small, crowded room with red velour wallpaper that suggested an outer circle of hell. Cigarette smoke hung like petrified haze. There was an ornate old bar of rich, dark wood, out of place in the cheesy surroundings. Men and women crouched around two crescent-shaped blackjack tables as dealers tossed out cards. A poker game was under way at a round table in the corner. Waitresses wearily pushed drinks. Things looked fuzzy under the blazing lights. Probably the damn smoke, Eldon thought, eyes smarting.

Everybody looked so tough. . . . He made for the bar, on the lookout for members of the delegation that had confronted McFee. He didn't recognize anyone.

But wait. A man sat playing decent honky-tonk on an upright piano wedged against the wall. His back was to the room but Eldon recognized him as the pianist from Oats in the Bowl. The same big clear goblet stood atop the piano, decorated with dollar bills. Eldon was only mildly surprised. There were only so many places to go in isolated Port Jerome, and people often stumbled over one another.

I'll have to talk to him, Eldon thought. But for now, I'll just mind my own business, lose a little money, get known. He stepped to the bar and ordered a draft beer from a thin woman who was wiping the bartop. He winced when she told him the price: three bucks. The fleecing process had already begun.

Eldon paid and got his change in silver dollars. He sipped his beer, trying to relax. "Is this bar an antique?" he asked.

The woman slowly wiped the bar. She had bleached blonde hair underscored by white eye shadow. Her face was as weathered as the shingles on an old roof. "They say it came around the Horn in the Gold Rush," she said without interest.

"Let's see—1979 minus 1849," Eldon said. "One hundred twenty years old."

"One-thirty." The woman wiped around Eldon's elbows.

"Oh. Yeah. . . . What kind of wood is it?"

"How should I know?"

"How'd it get here?"

"I said—on a ship."

"I mean, how'd it get in here—in the Lucky Poke."

"It was here when I came."

"Worked here long?"

She shook her head. "I'm from Nevada."

"I'm from Berkeley. I used to knock around Reno and Stateline, between quarters."

The woman returned a flat stare, and Eldon realized that he had said the wrong thing. "Did you work in the casinos down there?" he asked.

"You learn your subtraction in college?" she asked.

"Uh, what's a guy do to get into a game around here?"

"Just step to a table, bub."

Eldon turned and leaned back against the bar to watch the play. Blackjack might be his speed, but poker was the game of kings. He wanted to recoup his embarrassing defeat by Melissa. He wanted to walk into her office with a copy of the *Sun* edition busting open the Loris case in one hand and a sack of poker winnings in the other and command, "Take off your clothes."

"I can get you lots better than her, Skate."

Eldon turned. The skinny dealer looked straight back into his eyes. He had slipped up silently. His skin really is green, Eldon thought.

"The beer is expensive," the man continued. "A girl's a better buy. Got a teenage fox for you, Skate."

Eldon didn't respond. The dealer nudged him. "Anybody drives a car like yours is looking for something special."

Eldon's skin crawled. There was something familiar about the dealer. But certainly they had never met before.

The bartender slapped the dealer's elbow with her wet towel. "Don't bug the customers, Chump. You're supposed to be dealing."

Chump pulled away. "Fuck off, I'm takin' a break."

The bartender shook her head. "You're goofing off. If the boss finds out—"

Big grin. "Baby Huey's dead—remember?"

"It's your ass, Chump." The bartender returned to wiping.

"What happened to the boss?" Eldon asked.

"Somebody rubbed him out," Chump said with relish.

"No shit? What happened?"

"Read the papers, Skate. You could learn things."

"I heard something about it," Eldon said. "Archie somebody. Big fat son-of-a-bitch, right?"

"Archie Loris. Right on both counts."

"Who did it? Did they catch him?"

Chump gave a patronizing chuckle. "No way, Skate."

"You know what a 'chump' is, Chump?"

"The full moniker is Chump-Change. Don't forget it."

"Chump-Change?"

"Counta that's how much I'll kill ya for!"

He said it with such zest that Eldon felt sure Chump-Change had never killed anybody—certainly not Archie Loris. "Really? You kill a lot of people?"

Again the sneer. "Shit."

"Do they pay by the bullet? Per body or what? Do you have to get rid of the body or can you just leave it lie?"

Chump-Change drew himself up. "I'm a professional. I'm drawing *per diem.*"

"I think I'll hit that poker game."

"I'll help you invest your winnings wisely, Skate."

That's it, he reminds me of Billy Vogel, Eldon thought as he picked up his beer and crossed the room. I should've gone ahead and pushed Billy down the stairs in grade school; he wouldn't have punched out my teeth.

Eldon ran his tongue over his capped front teeth as he reviewed what Melissa had taught him about poker. It was a little late to think about revenge on Billy, and he was late for the poker game as well. The seats at the table obviously would be full for some time. In the ghastly light the unmoving players looked like giant figures hacked from soap.

The piano player began another rag. Eldon walked over and

dropped a silver dollar into the goblet atop the piano. "Do you like this upright as well as the one in the restaurant?"

The musician recognized Eldon after a moment and nodded. "Thanks. They keep it tuned."

"I'd have expected a jukebox loaded with shitkicker music."

"Port Jerome can be a surprising town," the musician said. "You're the one who asked for Mozart over at the Oats. After you asked for 'Norwegian Wood.' You were with a woman. What's a nice guy like you doing in a place like this?"

"I was going to ask you the same thing," Eldon said.

"You play music where you can."

"I'm playing cards."

"Poker?"

"Waiting for a seat."

"Don't hold your breath. Those hard-core sharks are nailed to those chairs."

"Looks like," Eldon admitted.

"You don't look like a poker player," the pianist said.

"Everyone has a secret life."

"Don't I know it. I'm Gordon, by the way."

"Eldon."

"Hi, Eldon. What would you like to hear?"

"You're doing fine."

"I know 'Norwegian Wood.' I just didn't want to play it at the Oats. I like to keep it classical over there." Gordon worked a few bars of the Beatles' song into the honky-tonk, regarding Eldon as he played. "Stand you a fresh beer?"

"This one'll hold me, thanks," Eldon said. "You play pretty well—I was telling my girlfriend at lunch."

Gordon started to reply but then looked quickly away.

Eldon turned. It was Chump-Change again, almost breathing down his neck. "Whatcha talkin' to him for?" Chump-Change asked. "You don't look like his type."

"You want to adopt me or something?" Eldon brushed past him and went to the nearest blackjack table. The dealer was a scrawny old woman who looked like an ancient pixie hooked on smack. Her knuckles were big arthritic knobs. Eldon took a stool next to an obese yet towering millworker wearing a Cat Tractor baseball cap pulled low over his eyes. Eldon threw down a pair of silver dollars and got two cards in return, six of diamonds up. He peeked at his second card; hey, okay—ten of spades. He remembered Melissa's orders and said, "Stay."

Other players signaled for cards. The dealer torpidly obliged and then busted, hitting twenty-three with her own hand. Eldon had won two dollars. He felt better. He would get back to Gordon later.

Right now, let's see how long I can make ten bucks last, Eldon thought. I've made it twelve bucks already.

But the dealer put down her cards and left the table. Chump-Change clopped up in his oversized shoes and took her place. "Hey, Skate, feeling lucky?" He was still chewing gum.

His break's over, Eldon thought. And I had to pick his table.

Chump-Change turned his rigid sneer on the millworker and the other players. The millworker glowered and made slow clutching motions with his huge fingers.

Chump-Change fanned the cards across the table and collected them about as gracefully as if they were roofing tiles. He's almost as inept as I am, Eldon thought. Melissa could take him to the cleaners.

Nevertheless, Chump-Change had interview potential. A perhaps all-too-typical Lucky Poke dealer. I'd interview the Devil himself if it meant a good story, Eldon thought, and tossed out two silver dollars.

He drew twelve. He bet three dollars more, took another card— and lost; it was a ten of clubs, giving him twenty-two. Melissa was right about sticking at twelve, Eldon thought.

Chump-Change swept up the money. His insolent stare made the action seem like a personal insult. Chump-Change constantly swiveled his head, looking at each player in turn while chomping his gum. It was ridiculous—except that it reminded Eldon of a snake hypnotizing its prey.

Is he cheating? Eldon wondered. He watched Chump's skinny hands but of course detected nothing. He forced himself to settle into the simple rhythm of play. Ante, get one card up and one card down, hit or stay, bet, win or lose. He lost a few dollars more, then recouped, was back up to ten dollars. You could sit here all night, he thought. There was something riveting in the cadence of play. Eldon began to enjoy the endless unfolding of the card patterns, the little thrill of having money riding on each outcome. The bigger the money, the more the fun, he thought, eagerly forking out more.

It was then that he began to lose. The steady stream of bets drained his cash. Well, it's the company's money, he told himself. He checked his resources. Ten dollars left. He had brought fifty. He'd tap Fiske in the morning. . . .

I'm betting too heavily, Eldon thought. I've got to pull back, do it the way Melissa said. Just one more hand, though; just two more dollars. I know I can win. And then I'll quit for tonight.

Eldon stuck his hand in his pocket for money. The millworker stood up without a word. Eldon thought he was quitting the game. But the man reached across the blackjack table with both hands, seized Chump's shirt and yanked Chump-Change across the table.

The millworker shifted his grasp—one hand clamped the neck, the other the crotch. Chump's gum flew out of his mouth as he croaked air. The millworker upended Chump-Change and silver dollars showered from the dealer's oversized shoes, pelting the customers, the table, and the floor.

The shoes flew. One bounced off Eldon's shoulder. The millworker dropped Chump-Change on his head and calmly started picking up silver dollars, one at a time. Chump-Change lay doubled up on the floor gasping, hands in his crotch.

"Stay put," the millworker told Chump. He looked at Eldon: "Sorry about that shoe."

"That's okay."

"He owes me sixty-eight dollars. Better get yours back while you can."

Eldon looked around for a bouncer but there didn't seem to be one. His fellow players were grabbing silver. Other patrons snatched up dollars that had rolled out of range. The piano music had stopped; Eldon saw Gordon looking on with a grin.

"What happened?" Eldon asked the millworker.

"Scammin'," the man said. "Palmin' cards every few hands and pitchin' dollars into those oversized penny-loafers when he won."

"I'll be damned." Eldon grabbed the few dollars left on the table.

The bartender strolled over, smoking a cigarette. "You're outa here, Chump."

Chump-Change spat weakly and crawled after his loafers. The millworker kicked Chump in the ribs, not too hard. "Forget the shoes," he said.

"Owww . . . ! " Chump-Change got up and staggered out the door in his stocking feet, clutching his groin and his ribs. The customers jeered as the door slammed.

Eldon counted his take—he'd recovered a lousy thirteen dollars. I should've moved faster, he thought. He was angry that Chump-Change had spoiled his fun. He felt surprisingly bitter.

Serves you right, you little bastard, Eldon thought. Good story color, too.

This place is nothing but a factory for cheating honest working people, Eldon thought. And now they want to build casinos where scumbags like Chump-Change can flourish. Over my dead body. I'll expose them. Cheat me, will they? I'll put a stop to it personally.

It would be good copy. And he had to extinguish the appetite he had discovered in himself.

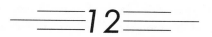

=12=

Art Nola scowled at the row of figurines on his desk, each with its evidence tag. "Obscene Hummels. Great."

His corner desk in the sheriff's office over the county jail in Port Jerome was otherwise bare as usual. On the wall were a community college diploma, a typed work schedule, and a small picture of Jesus Christ. Rain thrummed on the windows, which admitted gray morning light.

"They're not genuine, are they?" Eldon asked.

"Of course not," Nola said. "The Hummel people never made anything like this. I called Germany. And you're not taking any pictures."

"We couldn't use them anyway." Though I probably could sell one or two to the wire service, Eldon added to himself. Damn.

Art grunted, picked up a statuette and examined it with a connoisseur's fascinated distaste. The figurine was of a naked boy and girl. They had rosy, wholesome faces. Their activity was described in French among the pastel flowers that decorated the figurine's base: *Soixante-neuf.*

"They're pretty good fakes," Nola said. "The colors are off, and it's not the right kind of glaze, but they do look a lot like Hummels. Good quality—if you want to call this quality."

"They've got French writing on them," Eldon observed.

Art eyed him. "Improving your language skills?"

"There's no dope hidden inside or anything, is there?"

"They're solid."

"Where'd they come from?"

"Mail order. We found the catalogue in Archie's house."

"Lemme see?"

Art pulled the catalogue from a desk drawer. The glossy cover showed a tough-looking man and woman strapped into leather gear. Within were advertisements for an astonishing array of erotic items. A page headed "Hump-ems" was devoted to the figurines.

Eldon noted a Chicago post office box number at the bottom of the page. " 'Hump-ems'?" he said as he memorized it. "How do they get away with this?"

"You mean copyright problems?" Art said. "You think these people worry about that? Anyway, there are all kinds of Hummel knockoffs."

"A porcelain orgy." Eldon picked up a statuette of two lads intimately engaged. He read the legend on the base. "This is a phrase from Rimbaud or Verlaine, I forget which. They were lovers."

"Two guys?"

"Yeah. Nineteenth-century French poets. They wrote erotic poems to each other—"

Art took the catalogue away. "You ever read anything wholesome?"

"I'm looking for a book on how to play cards."

"Oh, yeah?"

"I've been to the Lucky Poke. The games there are crooked."

"Who told you that?"

"Saw it myself last night. A crooked dealer got the shit kicked out of him."

"Sounds as if the problem solved itself," Art said. "What were you doing there?"

"Archie Loris had a piece of the Lucky Poke action. I figure that his killing is connected to the gambling."

"Are we on the record—" Art began.

"—or off the record? Off the record, for now."

"Okay. And put down that damn statue before you break it." Eldon complied. "Thanks, Art."

"You'll hound me until I talk, so I'll talk," Art said. "But I don't want to see anything in the paper."

"Okay—for now."

"You're gonna have to be happy with 'for now' because there aren't any connections so far, Eldon."

"Archie had mob connections in Chicago."

"Yeah, and maybe they were after him for something. But we don't know what. Not money."

"Have you got anything at all?"

"I'm running a search on the National Crime Information Computer, trying to match up shotguns and M.O.s," Art said. "No luck so far. Nothing quite like this."

"Did you decide what kind of gun it was?"

"A 12-gauge. Your generic shotgun."

"You haven't recovered it, have you?"

"It's probably at the bottom of the bay. All we know is that it was fired at fairly close range, from the way the shot spread."

"What's 'fairly close'?"

"From the kitchen doorway."

"So a Chicago mobster marched into Archie's house with a shotgun covered with moss, paused at the kitchen door and blew him away while he was eating?"

"Looks like it." Art grinned, the lines in his face sweeping back from his mouth like curtains being drawn aside.

The smile's suddenness and lupine quality made Eldon uneasy; it always did. "Why didn't Archie run?"

"You saw how big he was."

"How'd a guy that large get around, anyway? How'd he get things done? Like buy groceries or clean the house?"

"When you own a string of girls, that stuff gets done."

"So who cooked the spaghetti?"

"Good question," Art said. "I've been shaking down whores, card-room people, and porn-hounds all over town. So far, nobody knows nothin'."

"Somebody's lying, then."

"So far everybody's story checks out."

"Then you've overlooked somebody," Eldon said, wondering whether Art had talked to Stephanie Hosfelder.

"Why d'you say that?" Art asked.

"Archie was killed by somebody he knew. He didn't try to run. He got wasted by surprise."

"Why do you think that?" Art looked amused. "You mean the mob sent a hit man he knew?"

"I think Archie was doing business," Eldon said, "and trying to make a point by eating while he did it." He thought for a moment. "The key is the moss. That's what's throwing you, right? NCIC can't match the moss with any M.O. in the files."

Art was briefly silent. "I had a dream last night. You were in it."

"Oh?" Eldon's skin prickled. Art's dreams about cases had a way of connecting with reality in unpleasantly surprising and sometimes dangerous ways. Art believed his dreams were messages from the Almighty. Eldon believed Art was a good detective who never stopped solving crimes, even when asleep.

"It was something about playing cards and flowers," Art said. "Archie was in the dream, too, though he didn't have a lot to say. And Melissa Lafky."

"Sounds like the day at the crime scene," Eldon said and added cautiously, "What about Melissa? And me?"

"I don't trust a woman who can do card tricks that well," Art said darkly. "She knows her job, though. In the dream, you were digging in the flowerbeds while she did card tricks. . . . That made me wonder if that shotgun isn't out there among the flowers."

"You said you thought it was in the bay."

"Probably is. Don't run out to Scoquel with a shovel. We went over the area around Archie's place with metal detectors. No shotgun."

"Frustrating," Eldon said.

"Not really," Nola said. "I've got all the scumbags in town doing legwork for me. Archie was into a lot of people. You ask enough questions, you shake enough people down, you shake things up and let 'em know you'll keep shakin' until somebody gives something up."

"How do you pick who to shake?"

"Often they pick themselves," Art said. "The patrol deputies keep me posted on who's in trouble for what, on who's receptive to cooperation because they're vulnerable. Then I drop by."

"Like in that Peter Lorre movie," Eldon said.

The reference to *M* clearly meant nothing to Nola. "One toad leans on the next because they don't want my heat," the detective said. "This is a small town; they know they have to live with me. It's not the best way to proceed but I want leads. I'll sort out the chaff." Art smiled again. "By the way, Eldon, why are you so sure it was *moss* wrapping the shotgun? I never told you that."

Eldon smiled back to mask his slip. "Reliable sources."

Eldon's stomach churned as he hiked back to the newspaper in the rain. That was a stupid slip about the moss, he thought. Art might catch on that I've been cozying up to Melissa. And his damn dreams never make a lick of sense—until it's too late.

He thought uneasily of the Lucky Poke. His eagerness to keep at the cards then seemed like a bad dream of his own, all too vivid. It was a crack in the resolve that had kept him going for six years in the rainy north woods. He felt as if he had committed a sin. He could see himself spending every night at the Lucky Poke, squandering his modest pay at the tables, putting up with the smoke and the overpriced beer and the likes of Chump-Change. Going native.

The *Sun* office was quiet when Eldon got there. Ad salesmen, secretaries, and composing-room personnel went about their morning duties. Fiske was pumping his hand exerciser as he pored over news copy, and Ambrose McFee was busy at his desk with page dummies.

"What brings you out in broad daylight?" Eldon asked McFee, for the sports editor usually worked the swing shift.

"Layin' out a Saturday sports feature," McFee said. "Don't drip on it."

"A friend of yours says hi." Eldon shook out his hat. "Simon Blood."

"Don't drip, I said. How do you know the limey?"

"We share a fishing hole."

"Isn't that like two cats sharing a sandbox?"

"Simon's okay. He helped me with my car."

"Simon's an interesting character," McFee said. "He's a sports drunk, like me. That's how we met. He's on the wagon now, too. Has been for a long time."

"He didn't seem to have a problem—" Eldon said, and stopped because it was a stupid thing to say.

"It never seems like a problem until it's too late." McFee seemed unoffended.

Maybe I should talk to Ambrose about last night, Eldon thought. Maybe later.

"Simon runs a nursery on the north end of town," McFee remarked as he returned to work on his page.

"A nursery?" Eldon said. "Got a phone number?"

"Somewhere. What's up?"

Eldon told McFee about the spattered flecks of mysterious vegetation at the scene of Archie's murder. " . . . and nobody knows what it is. I think it's important."

"Simon might know." McFee rummaged through a big address book stuffed with scraps of paper. "Here."

Eldon wrote down the number and called it from his desk.

"Sure, come on out," Blood told him affably. "We'll talk."

Eldon got directions and hurried to his car. He headed north along Bayside Drive, the Isetta fishtailing slightly on the wet asphalt.

He drove to a district of weatherbeaten warehouses, boathouses, and rental storage yards near the foot of the high bridge that spanned the Nekaemas Bay entrance. The skeletal quality of Port Jerome's waterfront was particularly apparent here.

Blood's nursery lay behind chain-link fencing at the end of a puddled, chuckholed street. The fence enclosed a forest of potted shrubs, flowers, saplings, and groundcover where rain sluiced off sheltering tarps and the corners of metal sheds. Eldon parked at the gate and walked to the office. He saw Blood through the window, feet on a desk, drinking tea and looking out into the downpour. Blood wore tooled cowboy boots. Today his Western shirt was purple and green. A big Union Jack hung behind him on the wall.

"Come in!" Blood said, getting up. "I didn't think I'd see you again this quickly. Your Isetta's still rolling, I see. Some tea?"

"Hell, yes."

"Earl Grey." Blood opened a tin and filled a tea ball. He dropped it into a mug, plucked a teakettle from a hotplate and poured steaming water into the mug. "All the comforts of home."

"Thanks for seeing me."

"I have lots of time." Blood handed over the mug. "Business is off because of the weather. Sugar or milk?"

Eldon put sugar in his mug and jiggled the tea ball on its chain.

Blood wrinkled his brow. "Have patience."

Eldon stopped jiggling the chain. He started to explain about the moss but Blood said, "Wait until your tea has brewed." When it had, they sipped tea together. I've got to bring Jimbo out here, Eldon thought. He and Simon can have a tea ceremony.

"Mum used to say that tea tastes best when rain is rattling on the windows," Blood said at last, with satisfaction. "Now, what's on your mind?"

Eldon told him about the moss. "Do you know what it is?"

Blood didn't even blink. "Certainly. The wire clinches it. I'll show you."

Blood pulled off his cowboy boots and slipped on rubber boots. He donned a hooded coat and led Eldon outside. Eldon brought along his mug of tea, enjoying the plume of steam that curled out into the rain. Blood headed down a gravel path toward the back of the lot. The path led under an arbor thick with climbing roses and past potted ferns, bleeding heart with rose-pink flowers, geraniums and hosta with big variegated leaves. There was a shed at the end of the path. "Around back," Blood said.

Behind the shed, a wide metal awning made a sheltered work area. There Eldon saw the menagerie.

Arrayed around were grotesque vegetable forms—a life-sized

swan, a leaping dolphin, a knee-high frog on a lily pad with a spider plant tendril growing from its gaping mouth, a Galapagos turtle, a kiwi bird. All were shaped from lush ivy or moss.

Blood said, "Topiary."

"Topiary?"

"The art of clipping shrubs into ornamental shapes." Blood stepped to a hedge shaped like a sea serpent rippling through the water. It was a series of sinuous ivy humps about six feet long, growing in pots. It had bulging eyes, horns, and a fanged maw, all made of vegetation, lovingly shaped.

Blood parted the growth with a finger. "Baltic ivy with eight-gauge aluminum wire for the frame. I'm rather proud of this. Normally, a hedge this size would be ground-rooted taxus or yew. But I've grown a movable one in pots, so one can move it around to catch the sun and surprise and delight guests."

Eldon had a crazy notion of what was coming. "How long did this take?"

"I'll show you." Blood lifted a four-legged wire and mesh framework from the work table. "This will be a bulldog. First comes the coarse wire skeleton—that's the eight-gauge stuff here. The finer chicken-wire overlay makes the shape."

Eldon got out notebook and pen. "Looks like a lot of work."

"It's extremely labor-intensive," Blood said. "Especially the chicken wire. Lots of snipping and tucking—you can damage your fingers, which is why I wear gloves now. It's clumsier, but I was getting too many scars."

Blood held out a hand. His fingertips were thickened with scar tissue, something like a guitarist's. "The frame is held together with waterproof tape or fine wire or twist-ties. Or hot glue. You can get burned."

"Is there a lot of call for this sort of thing?"

"Not much around here; it's only a sideline with me."

"So go ahead."

"Topiary ivy must be small-leaved, fast-growing, and hardy. You can use a good many other plants and mosses, too. The challenge lies in shaping your material. The green portion of almost every bush is only a thin layer like the rind of a watermelon. You decide to cut, say, a deep curve, and you wind up with an ugly hole and brown branches. It can take a year or two to green that hole, as new leaves finally emerge."

"So what does this have to do—"

"With the pimp's murder? Your tea's getting cold."

Blood waited until Eldon had slurped from his mug. "The last step is filling and planting," Blood said. "You stuff the frame with damp long-grain sphagnum and ivy cuttings. Fertilize and water. After a few months you have your beast."

"Wait a minute—what's 'sphagnum'?"

"A type of moss."

"Moss?" Eldon added the datum to what he knew and tried to render a total. He comprehended each of the facts but resisted bringing them together. His scalp tightened. "Exploding moss?"

"Bright chap." Blood beamed as if Baby Eldon had just taken his first steps. "The shotgun was fired through a piece of topiary."

"That's . . . *weird.*" Eldon hunched his shoulders and stared at the bullfrog, the sea serpent, the kiwi bird.

"It explains the spattered moss and bits of wire," Blood said. "It tells you a lot about the killer, too, if you think about it."

"You're doing the thinking for both of us at this point," Eldon said. "You tell me what it says about the killer."

"Don't you see, man? It takes months to grow a piece of topiary. It takes *skill.*"

"The killer was a topiary freak."

"A topiarist, yes," Blood said. "And a good one. I'll wager he tailored a piece of topiary for his nefarious purpose."

Good copy, Eldon thought, his mind kicking into gear at last. This tops the mummified foot in Schumacher's Landfill. This is better than the belly dancer who could eat broken glass. A guy growing a plant around a shotgun for months, just to kill a four-hundred-fifty-two-pound pimp. "Wait a minute. They didn't find any ivy—just moss."

"That's what clinches it!" Blood grew excited. "For topiary you need stuff that grows low and close so you can keep the shapes. That would be critical if you're trying to hide something like a shotgun. Moss is ideal."

"It's practical?"

"Making a topiary shape to accommodate a shotgun would be no problem, if you make the frame strong enough. Disney makes topiary fifty feet high with mechanized arms—Mickey Mouse waves at you."

"It would've had to have been portable."

"The murderer carries the topiary into the house," Blood said eagerly. "He lines it up with his target. He lets fly."

"Why would Loris let anyone do that?" Eldon asked. "It would be like inviting a flying saucer into your kitchen."

"Not if the victim were interested in topiary."

"He wasn't, that I know of," Eldon said.

But Blood was transported. "The killer's patient—you can't get long-grain moss in quantities bigger than about the size of a loaf of bread. And he knows which moss would best serve his purpose—"

"Which moss is that?"

"Baby's Tears would work well. *Soleirolia soleirolii.* It's actually not a moss, it's a groundcover. But we call it moss."

Eldon wrote it down, making Blood spell the Latin. "Has anybody bought something like that from you lately?"

"Just a few locals, gardeners well known to me."

"What about sales at other nurseries?"

"I'm the only one who handles topiary around here."

"Where were *you* the day of the murder?"

Blood laughed. "Drinking tea with Ambrose McFee. The perfect alibi."

"Sorry."

"Oh, you have to ask these things, I know. It's rather exciting."

"Sometimes I'd rather be fishing."

"We must go back to Sackett Lake together. Let me freshen your tea."

They went back to the office. Eldon took off his jungle hat and saw the sprig of moss he had hooked there. "What kind of moss is this?"

"Don't know," Blood said, peering. "Where'd you get it?"

"At Sackett Lake the day we met. Is it, uh, Baby's Tears?"

"No. *Soleirolia* is a Southern plant, doesn't flourish in the Pacific Northwest." The teapot whistled. Blood prepared fresh mugs of tea.

"Would this moss make good topiary?" Eldon asked.

"Who knows?" Blood answered. "It puts me in mind of an idea I'd like to try, though—topiary fishing flies for fishermen's yards. Giant replicas of their favorite flies. I wonder if there's a market?"

"How would you get the colors?" Eldon asked. "Mix different ivies and mosses?"

"That's just what you'd do," Blood said. "Though it's difficult. Different plants have different growing cycles. If you plug moss into an ivy growth, one will eventually take over the other. Or minimum water for one drowns the other. Or one shades the other. Mixing can be done, but it's twice the work."

"And the colors?"

"There are strains of moss that change color according to the kind of plant food and amount of light you give them. You not only make shapes but 'paint' them."

"I'll be damned."

"Certain bamboos change leaf or stem colors according to the lighting in the environment. Wandering Jew is normally gray and purple but becomes fiery red in sunlight. And so forth." Blood sighed. "There's no perfect combination of traits, so every mixed piece is a compromise. Only the rarest and most talented of us crossbreed plantings for special effects."

"A fishing fly sounds like a tough order."

Blood sighed again. "Chameleon moss is what we need. A species that combines every useful trait. Every topiarist dreams of it."

"Is that possible?"

"It's the Philosopher's Stone."

"Well, there's always fishing."

"Amen."

Eldon managed to get away after another cup of tea. He drove to a telephone booth and dialed Dr. Rosenak, the county medical examiner. Eldon and the M.E. were on good terms, and Rosenak was a man who enjoyed revealing things.

"Hi-ho, Eldon Larkin," Rosenak said. "I bet I know why you called."

"You do?"

"Never a murder around here that Eldon's not on the story."

Eldon wondered what eye-searing bow tie Rosenak was wearing today. "No rest for the wicked, Doc. Got a question for you."

"Shoot. By the way, when are we having lunch again?"

"Pretty soon, if you're still growing those great organic veggies."

"You know it. And I'm still using them to make Dagwoods."

Was a macrobiotic Dagwood possible? Eldon wondered. Well, never mind for now. "Have you got the results of the Loris autopsy handy?"

"Sure. Never had anything like it. He was so fat we had to use a small chainsaw to—but if I don't talk about *that,* it won't show up in the newspaper, will it?"

"True. But it's not the pimp I'm interested in today. It's your botanical knowledge."

"Oh?" Rosenak sounded surprised.

"You're a mushroom expert—"

"True enough."

"And a gardener. How are you on mosses and groundcovers?"

There was silence for a moment. Then Rosenak said slyly, "I know something about them."

Eldon knew it was time to ask the correct questions. "I thought you might. Were samples taken of the vegetation spattered around the murder scene?"

"Yes."

"Have you identified the vegetation?"

"Yes."

"What was it?"

"A commercial groundcover called Baby's Tears."

"*Soleirolia soleirolii,*" Eldon said.

"That's what I like about you, Eldon—you do your homework."

By Eldon Larkin
Sun *Staff Writer*

PORT JEROME—The shotgun that killed a football-hero-turned-pimp was concealed in a piece of topiary, a garden art form in which shrubs and mosses are shaped into decorative figures.

The bizarre twist in the slaying of Archie Loris of Scoquel was revealed Wednesday by Dr. Donald Rosenak, Nekaemas County medical examiner.

Rosenak performed the autopsy on Loris. He said tiny bits of Baby's Tears, a moss used in topiary, were found imbedded in Loris's chest, together with 12-gauge shotgun pellets and bits of chicken wire. Moss was spattered around Loris's kitchen, where his 452-pound corpse was found Monday.

The moss was singed and mingled with traces of gunpowder. That means it was propelled by the shotgun's blast, Rosenak said.

Gardeners use Baby's Tears to grow topiary figures and chicken wire to shape the figures.

Who killed Loris remains a mystery, although law-enforcement officials say his murder could have been a mob assassination.

Rosenak's findings suggest that the killer is an expert topiarist, according to Simon Blood, a Port Jerome nursery operator. . . .

"Is topiary microbiotic?" Fiske wanted to know.

Eldon looked up from his typewriter. The editor hung over his shoulder. "Just give this story good play tomorrow."

"It looks like good copy. A killer gardener—we'll get calls about 'bad taste' for sure."

"Maybe Bigfoot did it," Eldon said, feeling good.

"No way—You Are What You Eat," Fiske said. "How could a fully microbiotic diet such as Bigfoot's lead to violence?"

"Someone gets tired of sprouts and strangles the cook."

"Look into the microbiotic angle," Fiske said. "It's more productive than hanging around card rooms."

"The card rooms are part of the story, too." Eldon tried not to sound defensive.

"How much money did you lose the other night?" Fiske asked.

"What makes you so sure I lost?"

"You'd be counting out the winnings on Marsha's desk if you'd won," Fiske said.

"Uh, I lost thirty-eight dollars."

"Win it back."

Eldon resumed typing; Fiske moved off, as he had hoped. Eldon devoted two paragraphs to Simon Blood's explanation of topiary. Simon will appreciate the publicity, he thought, and chuckled as he visualized bushes shaped into giant fishing flies.

Eldon wrote rapidly. When he had finished, he typed "30" at the story's bottom and proofread it, using a soft black pencil to mark paragraphs and repair mistakes. Would the tightwad company that owned the *Sun* spring for word processors before he died of old age?

Who cares? he thought. Eldon fastened the newsprint pages together with a paper clip and dropped the story into the news–desk copy basket. If this lead amounts to anything, I'll soon have Melissa in my arms.

★ ★ ★

Eldon took Melissa in his arms and kissed her. She responded lovingly, squirming naked beneath him as they lay on the living-room rug. The telephone was ringing. The telephone was ringing—

Eldon's eyes popped open. The telephone was ringing in the living room. He was embracing his pillow. His electric clock said 3:12 A.M. The glowing red numerals hurt his eyes. He stumbled from bed. Goddamn it, he had to get an extension phone in the bedroom. Eldon slipped, bounced off the doorjamb, caromed into the living room and found the phone. "Yeah. What."

"Eldon? This is Marsha."

"I don't know any—oh, Marsha Cox. What the—"

"Listen, I'm at the hospital. The cops say for you to get down here."

"What for? You shoot somebody?"

"This is serious, Eldon. There's a woman in the emergency ward who's asking for you. She's in bad shape."

"Asking for *me?*" Eldon's stomach contracted. Melissa. "Oh, no! Was it a traffic accident—"

"No. They found her at the waterfront—raped and beaten to a pulp."

"I'll be right there!" Eldon slammed down the phone. His throat was dry and his breath came in gasps as he lunged after his clothes. She must've been snooping around on her own, he thought as he dressed. If only we hadn't made that damn bet.

He rushed out to his car. It was drizzling. "If you don't start I'll set you on fire right here," he told the car.

The threat worked. The Isetta turned over immediately. Eldon headed for the hospital. Only scattered street lights and meager scraps of neon illuminated the dark, wet streets.

Nekaemas Bay General Hospital blazed with light. The boxy, modern building stood at the back of a big lawn carved from the forest, as if someone had thrust a piece of urbanity into the wilds of the South Coast. An ambulance and a sheriff's car, their lights flashing, were parked at the emergency entrance. The dazzle blinded Eldon for a moment as he pulled up.

Then he picked out Marsha, waving from the doorway. She looked tired as she hurried down to the car and helped him pull open the door. "I was coming back from a real late school-board meeting and followed the ambulance."

"Thanks for calling."

"Don't worry," Marsha said kindly, "I'll write the copy."

She led him into the hospital and down a quiet white hall. The pungent antiseptic stink filled Eldon's nose. An ambulance crewman strolled past, and a couple of sheriff's deputies stood at the door to one of the treatment rooms. That was all. Where *is* everybody? Eldon wondered. The place should be crawling with law; an attack on a prosecutor was the equivalent of "Police officer down!"

"I don't have an I.D. yet—" Marsha began.

"Her family's in Eugene," Eldon said. "The D.A.'ll know how to get hold of them."

"What do you mean, the D.A.?"

"She's the deputy D.A. who came to our office. I took her to lunch, remember? Melissa Lafky."

"Oh, Eldon, I couldn't tell!"

Eldon's stomach churned. One of the deputies saw him. "Hi, Eldon. In here. Listen—it ain't pretty."

"Okay." Eldon took a deep breath. "Thanks." He stepped inside.

He couldn't recognize the woman on the bed. Her face was swaddled in gauze, distended like a grapefruit and raw with abrasions. Her blackened eyes bulged like dark golf balls. They were swollen almost shut. Her nose was broken. So were her front teeth. A plastic IV line ran into her splinted left arm.

The woman's eyes went to Eldon. Her head didn't turn; her eyes merely flickered sideways through her slitted eyelids. A noise that sounded like his name came from her throat. Her bony right hand pawed feebly.

Eldon thought he would faint. He fixed his attention on the hand as he walked stiffly toward the bed. Those can't be Melissa's fingers, he thought desperately. They're too long. Then he noticed the strands of long, lank dark hair that straggled through the bandages and lay tangled on the pillow. "Stephanie!"

"Who?" Marsha was just behind him.

"This isn't Melissa," Eldon said. "Melissa's hair is short. This is Stephanie Hosfelder." He almost added "thank God" but swallowed the prayer. Eldon bent close. "Stephanie, it's Eldon Larkin. I'm here now."

Stephanie tried to move her splinted arm and whispered something that sounded like "tape," but she couldn't bring her lips together. Her breath was foul. Eldon gently took Stephanie's right index finger. "Yeah, they've got your arm taped up. You'll be okay."

Stephanie kept trying to talk, repeating the one strange syllable and sometimes Eldon's name. Finally Eldon decided she was trying to say she'd been raped. "I know, I know, it's okay," he said. At last Stephanie subsided and Eldon stepped back from the bed.

One of the deputies came in and they talked quietly by the door.

"That's Stephanie—" Eldon said.

"—Hosfelder." The deputy nodded. "Yeah, we know her well. She's pretty bad off. Be a while before we can get anything out of her, if she even remembers. Uh, she a friend of yours?"

"A news source."

"What'd she say?"

"Just my name and something I couldn't make out. I think she was trying to say she was raped."

"We found her on the waterfront," the deputy said. "She'd been dumped in that storage yard by the pier—know where I mean?"

"Yeah. I talked to her there the other day. I guess that's why she asked for me."

"What'd you talk about then?"

"The Loris case. I was looking for leads. She told me about Archie Loris's gambling connections. Not much, nothing Art Nola doesn't already know."

"That's all? Did she mention any names?"

"Just Archie Loris. She used to be one of his girls. She was at the pier to service a ship."

"That ship's sailed," the deputy said.

"A guy brought her there but I didn't get a look at him."

"No doubt her new pimp," the deputy said. "He decided to show her who was boss."

"Jesus Christ. Did he beat her up for talking to me?"

"Naw. This happens all the time, Eldon. She probably didn't turn enough money aboard ship."

Eldon went out into the hall. Marsha was talking to a nurse and writing in her notebook.

"They don't know if she'll live," Marsha said, turning to Eldon with pen poised. "What did she say to you?"

"It didn't make any sense."

"Funny she asked for you."

"I talked to her just the other day. And I wrote about her wedding, about a year ago."

"Oh, yeah, that *Orient Star* business. I remember now. You're the one who got beaten up that time. Did her husband do this?"

"Her pimp. This is different from covering a school board meeting, huh?"

"Well, I can handle it, Eldon," Marsha replied sharply. "Routine assault on a streetwalker. Six or eight 'graphs, tops. Longer follow if she dies, because then we've got another murder. Right?"

"Yeah, that's right," Eldon said. "Sorry." How many times had he tossed off a synopsis like that himself?

Marsha put her pen and notebook away with a tired sigh. "It's awful. But I'd better get to the office and write it before I drop."

"Yes, you should. And thanks again for calling me. I was scared there for a while." The light-headed feeling returned as Eldon walked to the exit. I'm still scared, he thought.

But he realized as he drove home that he didn't so much feel scared as responsible. Stephanie must have been beaten because she had talked to him—why else would she have asked for him now?

But beaten by whom? By friends of Archie's? By Archie's killer?

By people scared by Nola's questions? Or just by her angry pimp? The questions ran through Eldon's mind as he got back in bed. He tossed and turned through what remained of the night, fretting, unable to sleep.

Finally he dozed off, to dream of cards and flowers. The dream gave him no rest. He crawled out of bed with the sun and chewed toast for breakfast. Even the Isetta seemed to run more slowly as he drove to work.

Eldon shambled red-eyed into the newsroom in time to see Frank drop a story into the copy basket—and to find that Stephanie's misfortune was, of course, grist for the mill.

"Dee-de-dee," Fiske said. "And what do we have from young Frank this morning? Anything tops the beaten strumpet?"

"Strong-arm robbery in a home," Frank said, sipping coffee.

"Anybody hurt?" Fiske asked. "Arrests?"

"Nah. The guy got roughed up a little. They're looking for the robber. It's small change."

"Our little Marsha brings us the lead story for today and goes home to bed," Fiske mused. "I found it in the basket when I came in this morning. She wrote a school board story, too. Eldon, you look like hell."

"I haven't had much sleep," Eldon said. "I went to the hospital."

"I know. Marsha left a note," Fiske said. "Hell of a thing. Well, this knocks your gardening story below the fold."

"It's not about gardening. It's about the Loris murder," Eldon said peevishly.

"It's too bad about that gal Stephanie," Fiske said. "I remember when she came in for extra copies of the issue that had your story about her wedding."

"Then don't be so callous."

"Good copy's where you find it," Fiske said. "That's the game we're in. Take the day off. Go fishing."

"I've got work to do."

"Take your camera along and shoot me some scenics," Fiske

said blithely. "I need wild art for the next slow day. 'Birds soar through a placid sky over Sackett Lake and there's no news today—' "

Eldon realized it would do him good to get his hands on his fishing rod. "Yeah. Okay." He went to his desk and got his camera.

Frank stepped over. "Say, Eldon, I think you ought to look into this robbery some more."

"I'm going fishing."

"Listen to what I'm trying to tell you. The incident log says Art Nola's on the case."

Eldon stopped. "Ohhh . . . Art wouldn't go out on an ordinary robbery—"

"When he's tied up on a murder investigation, that's right."

"—unless this robbery is somehow connected with the Loris killing!" Eldon suddenly felt as if he'd had a strong cup of coffee. "Who got robbed?"

"He lives near the boat basin," Frank said. "Name's Clete. Teaches part-time at the community college."

"I don't know him. What's he teach?"

"Music. He asked the cops to contact him where he moonlights, in case anything comes up in the robbery investigation. He didn't want them calling the college."

"Interesting. You say he teaches music?"

"Piano. You're sure you haven't met him? I think he moonlights at that restaurant you wrote about." Frank checked his notes. "Yeah—Oats in the Bowl."

"What's his name? His full name."

"Gordon Clete."

"Gordon—? Gotta get my notebook, Frank. The piano player knows more than he's telling."

14

Gordon Clete lived in a mobile home on a forested hillside, at the end of a muddy lane that wound up from the Nekaemas Bay boat basin. The sun shone through the Douglas fir, throwing dappled shadows on the trailer and making the water sparkle in the bay below. Eldon climbed from the Isetta and rubbed his bleary eyes. He could see fishing boats bobbing at anchor like battered toys. But getting the Isetta up the hill had been like driving a butter churn, which curbed his pleasure in the view.

A curtain flickered in the trailer. Someone was home.

Eldon mounted the porch. The door opened before he could knock. Sure enough—it was Gordon the piano player.

"Hi, Gordon," Eldon said.

"You. From the Lucky Poke—"

"Yeah. And Oats in the Bowl."

"What do you want?"

Eldon flashed his press card. "I'd like to talk to you."

"A reporter," Gordon said, appalled. "How'd you find me?"

"The robbery was on the sheriff's log."

"I didn't think of that. I shouldn't have called the sheriff. I'm in a very embarrassing position."

"Being robbed is nothing to be ashamed of." Eldon smiled reassuringly.

"If anything got in the paper—"

"It's not the robbery I'm interested in."

"Then what do you want? If anyone found out at work—"

"I'm working on a story. You can help me out." Here's where he closes the door in my face, Eldon thought.

Gordon stared, then seemed to reach a decision. "Come in." He stepped out of the way as Eldon entered, watching alertly as if ready to spring at him—or spring away. Then Gordon waved toward the living room. "Please sit down."

Eldon was pleasantly surprised by the furnishings. South Coast mobile-home decor ran to velour-covered furniture, paintings on black velvet, atrocious lamps, and *Reader's Digest* Condensed Books on end tables. This was different. Scandinavian furniture made the living room seem more spacious. A spinet piano with a metronome on top stood against one wall. Above the piano hung a framed sheet of Gregorian chant notation, parchment from some ancient illuminated book.

There was a stereo and a television set with a videocassette recorder beneath. A row of tapes next to the machine was askew where one had been removed. Bricks-and-boards shelving, filled with books in precise ranks, stood along one wall. A Native American rug of dark wool lay on the floor. Eldon noticed a neatly made queen-size bed in the next room.

"Forgive me," Gordon said. "I've had a bad night."

"Me, too." Eldon sat down.

"You never told me you were a reporter. I thought—"

"The Lucky Poke wasn't the place to mention it," Eldon said. "You're okay?"

"He didn't hurt me."

"Tell me what happened."

"You said you weren't interested in the robbery."

"No. But it might lead us somewhere else."

"In confidence? Off the record?"

"My word on it. I won't put you in the paper."

"Okay," Gordon said after a moment. "Coffee?"

"Hell, yes. I could use some." Even if it was instant, it would be an invitation to stay.

Eldon watched Gordon go into the kitchen, noting the little man's sturdy build and stride. I wouldn't want him to punch me in the face, Eldon thought. Funny he's so scared. But it must be scary to get robbed.

He browsed among Gordon's books as the sound of a coffee grinder came from the kitchen. Eldon had a theory that people could be plumbed by the books they owned. Whaddaya know, he thought, Gordon must speak French. Here's *Lovers* by Paul Verlaine in the original. And Genet's *Miracle de la Rose.*

There were books in English, too—among them James Leo Herlihy's *Midnight Cowboy,* Paul Goodman's *Making Do,* and poetry by Allen Ginsberg in the little black-and-white Pocket Poets editions that Eldon remembered from Berkeley. There were books on music and music history, as well. Eldon thumbed through *Lovers.*

Shortly, Gordon returned with coffee on a tray with sugar and cream and cups. "Do you read French?"

"Oui, monsieur, et je le parle aussi," Eldon replied. "Yes, monsieur, and I speak it as well."

"Et est-ce que vous vous intéressez de la littérature français?" Gordon asked, a smile crossing his face. "And you are interested in French literature?"

"Oui. J'était en Paris quand j'était étudiant. Maintenant je lis Rimbaud en français."

"I, too, spent time in Paris," Gordon replied in French. "You are reading Rimbaud in the original? Verlaine there is among my favorites. He and Rimbaud were close friends, as you no doubt know."

Gordon spoke eagerly. A barrier had fallen away. Eldon had seen it happen before—it was amazing what people would tell a newspaper reporter. It was even more amazing what they would tell him in a foreign language.

"I have read some of Verlaine," Eldon replied, closing the book. "And Rimbaud, too. But please tell me about the robbery. Let us continue speaking French. A foreign language provides the ultimate in privacy."

Gordon set down the tray, poured coffee, and took a chair.

Eldon smelled the coffee before he drank. "Whole bean," he said with pleasure. *"C'est bien."*

Gordon blew on his own coffee and sipped it. "I brought the

fellow over from the Lucky Poke to have a drink. He seemed nice enough."

"You did not know him?"

"Not really. I had seen him there a few times. We talked there, as did you and I."

"I see. Please continue."

"We came here after I had finished playing for the night. He . . . robbed me. He was a big guy."

"What did he take?"

"Money. My watch."

"Can you describe him?"

"A logger. Very strong. Muscles. Tattoos."

"On his arms? His hands?"

"His chest." Gordon paused, then decided to go through with it. "He . . . had his shirt off—"

He's a homosexual, Eldon thought, guessing the significance of some of the titles in Gordon's library. He picked up some rough trade and got robbed. I wonder how much of that goes on around here? Of course, thugs are a South Coast specialty—they come in all persuasions.

"This is not an enlightened community," Gordon said. "I do not have tenure at the college. I could lose my job."

"This is 1979, monsieur. Does the college care that you are, um—"

" 'Queer'?" Gordon demanded in English, his voice abrupt and sarcastic. " 'Gay' is preferred. It's been used in the subculture since the 1920s."

"Uh, yeah. Gay." Eldon switched back to English, too, trying not to sound apprehensive. Well, he's not going to jump on you, he told himself.

He forced his mind back to the interview. "Did the robber have a weapon?"

Gordon shook his head and rolled back a shirtsleeve to reveal an ugly bruise on his arm. "He was just strong."

"You look like you can take care of yourself—"

"I told you why I can't afford trouble."

"Then why call the cops?"

Gordon's lips clamped into a determined line. "He robbed me in my own place, goddamn it. I put up with a lot. But this is my home."

"What did the deputies say?"

"They were very professional."

"Who came out? I probably know 'em."

"A couple of uniforms. I didn't get their names."

"And wasn't there someone else?"

"Well, a detective showed up a little later—"

"Nola."

"Yeah. D'you know him?" Gordon asked.

"Sure. He's okay."

"He was very kind. Encouraging."

"About what?"

"About catching the guy, recovering my things."

"They call Nola 'Br'er Fox,' " Eldon said. "Don't sell him short, despite his sleepy look."

"I know what you mean." Gordon smiled a little.

"It means that sooner or later he'll figure out why you really were robbed," Eldon said.

"I told him I'm gay," Gordon said. "He didn't seem to—"

"I don't mean that," Eldon said. "I mean why really."

Gordon's stubborn expression returned. Eldon held up a hand. "I'm not here to hang you. I need information. I'm working on a story about Archie Loris."

"Why d'you think I know anything about that?"

"You work in the card rooms. You know the people there."

"Lotta cards, lotta people, Eldon."

"Lotta tunes, lotta laughs," Eldon retorted. "Those good-hearted guys and dolls, eh? Art Nola's making house calls on folks in that circle, and he included you."

"If I don't talk, what will you do?"

"Wait to hear that you've turned up murdered somewhere."

A tremor crossed Gordon's features. Eldon pressed on. "You might as well talk to me. Whatever you know, the more people you tell it to, the safer you're going to be." He let Gordon digest that. "Now—who shook you down, really?"

"As I told you—"

"Come on, Gordon—" Eldon looked quickly around the living room "—this place is neat as a pin. You say you got roughed up and robbed by a pickup, but not a doily's out of place."

"That's just how it happened."

"You were gonna fuck the guy—big rough logger, you say, a real mountain of manly muscle—he's got his shirt off, things must've been getting sweaty. But the bed's not even rumpled. What'd you do, change the sheets before you called the sheriff?"

For all Eldon knew, Gordon *had* made the bed. But the musician closed his eyes and said quietly, "Chump-Change."

The hairs prickled on the back of Eldon's neck. "You brought Chump-Change home to—?"

Gordon opened his eyes with a look of supreme disgust. "What do you think I am? He showed up here on his own. He was frantic—said Detective Nola was going around asking a lot of questions."

"Aha. Go on."

"When I saw Chump on the porch, I thought maybe he wanted me to help him get his job back at the Poke. Can you imagine that? After always leaning on me, threatening to denounce me as gay to the wrong people, get me beaten up some night, or cause trouble at the college."

"So why'd you talk to him?"

"He pushed his way in."

"You look sturdy. Why not push him out?"

"You know how he got that moniker? 'Chump change' is how—"

"—little money he'll kill you for. So he claims."

Gordon rubbed his bruised arm. "I wasn't about to try him."

"So what'd you give him? He wanted something from you, and

from the looks of that bruise, he got it." Gordon was silent. Eldon glanced around the room. "The videotape?"

Gordon started a little. "Okay, yeah. How'd you—?"

"There's a tape missing from the rack under the TV."

"That doesn't mean anything."

"Sure it does. It's absolutely the only thing out of place in here. What was on it?"

"Nothing that would interest you."

"Try me."

"I can't tell you."

"You told Nola."

"I didn't tell Nola," Gordon said. "I realized as soon as the deputies arrived that I shouldn't have called them, but until then I wasn't thinking clearly. I played dumb, told them I got strong-armed by a big logger—it was the first thing that popped into my head.

"Then Nola showed up. I realized that he hadn't come about the robbery. He started quizzing me about Archie Loris, who might've had reason to kill him and so forth. And then about the logger, when the deputies told him. I didn't let on about the tape."

"He believed you?"

"I don't know. He kept pressing me—that's why I had to admit I was gay, to make the story stand up."

"But Art didn't ask about the tape?"

"No. I don't think he knows about it."

"What was on the tape?" Eldon asked.

Gordon grimaced. "Archie."

"Archie doing what?"

"Playing with these—these weird little statues. You know those figurines, Hummels? Except these weren't like any Hummels I've ever seen. He was arranging them and rearranging them and giggling. It didn't make any sense."

"That's all?"

"Then he has sex with a whore. It's a home porno video. Man, it's gross, he's so fat. He's dressed up as a gas station attendant and—well, you don't want to see it."

"How'd you get the videotape?"

"The girl on the tape gave it to me. Stephanie. I know her from the Poke."

Holy smoke, Eldon thought. "Kind of lanky? Long hair?"

"You know her? She stole the tape when she left Archie's stable. Archie treated her pretty badly—you can see that on the tape."

"And she gave it to you—?"

"For safekeeping."

"She trusted you?" Eldon asked.

"Stephanie wrote some poems I put to music, one time at the Poke," Gordon said. "They weren't much; I just ham-and-egged some melodies. But she liked it—she didn't know any better. We got to be friends."

"That sounds unlikely."

"I didn't want sex from her."

"Ah."

"Look, I knew she was using me," Gordon said. "She didn't want to be caught with that tape. But sometimes you do favors, just to be decent—just to show someone like Stephanie that people *are* decent."

"Why didn't she destroy it?"

"I wondered that myself."

"So you watched the tape."

"She didn't say not to, Eldon. I had to know what was on it—it might've been incriminating." Gordon shook his head. "Poor Stephanie."

"How did Chump-Change find out you had this tape?"

"He said Stephanie told him."

I'll bet she did, Eldon thought, vividly remembering Stephanie's battered face and then their conversation on the waterfront. Chump-Change was Stephanie's pimp, he thought. That was what she meant when she told me to talk to the first person I saw at the Lucky Poke—Chump, of course, in the parking lot. And that's what she was trying to tell me about in the hospital—not "rape" but "tape." The videotape.

"And you gave Chump-Change the tape," Eldon told Gordon.

"I was afraid of what he'd do if I didn't," Gordon said. "That's why I lied to the cops. I can't get in any deeper." Gordon shuddered. "I don't know what's happened to Stephanie."

"She's in the hospital," Eldon said. "Chump beat the shit out of her to make her tell where the tape was."

"Good God!"

"You did the safest thing. But what's the tape *mean?*"

"I don't know. I don't know why Chump wanted it. What are you going to do?"

"Tell the cops. I won't be party to felony assault. Or murder."

"Murder? You mean Chump—"

"—maybe killed Archie for that tape," Eldon said. "But Stephanie had already split with it."

"She was so scared that Archie would fix her for running out on him," Gordon said. "She figured Archie wouldn't kill her because then he'd never get back the tape."

"That was good thinking, as long as Archie was alive," Eldon said. "She's just lucky Chump didn't kill her, too. Where's your telephone? I'm calling Nola."

"Just a minute," Gordon said. "You're going to do a story?"

"Yeah. But don't worry, I won't put you in it."

"I don't care about that anymore. I'm in this with you. I want to help you. I owe Stephanie."

"It's not your fault," Eldon said. "Chump-Change is dangerous."

"I could've defended myself better than Stephanie. I won't be pushed around anymore." Gordon gave a wan grin. "My secret's out, one way or another. I might as well stand my ground. And I want that tape back—for Stephanie's sake." He paused for a moment, blinking glistening eyes. "You know how that poor desperate kid used to try to cotton up to Archie? By bringing him crossword-puzzle books." Gordon cleared his throat. "Now, how can I help you?"

"Well, was there any topiary on the tape?"

"What's topiary?"

"Any shrubbery? I know it sounds odd—"

"What are you talking about? What can you do with shrubbery?"

"Never mind. Read today's paper." It would clinch everything if Loris had been into perversions with topiary, Eldon thought. That part doesn't make sense. Still—

"Why go to the sheriff?" Gordon asked. "You're an investigative reporter—we could solve the case ourselves."

"I don't solve cases," Eldon said. "I cover stories. I'm not a private eye. I'm a reporter."

"You're an investigative reporter," Gordon persisted.

"One who likes to stay healthy." But Eldon knew that any danger soon would pass. I win my bet with Melissa simply by turning in Chump-Change, he thought. I'll have cracked the case before Art, though not quite in the way Melissa expected.

Next I'll find out why that tape was so important, he thought. I bet it had something to do with the gambling. Eldon regarded Gordon. "You can help me."

"Good. How?"

"Keep your ear to the ground around the Poke. When do you play there again?"

"Not for a few days. I'm at Oats in the Bowl first, two nights from now."

"Well, when you get back to the Poke, let me know what you hear—about Archie and especially about that tape."

"Gotcha. I'll be discreet. I know how to do that."

"You can introduce me around, to people who know about the gambling underbelly."

"That's tougher, Eldon. They've got to trust you." Gordon shrugged. "You have to play cards."

Eldon swallowed. "Uh, no money. The *Sun* won't put up the cash."

"Money's not a problem." Gordon went into the kitchen and returned with a big tan crock incised with the word COOKIES. He removed the lid, took out a sheaf of cash and tossed it on the coffee table.

"The cookie jar is the last place anybody'd look, right?" Gordon asked. "There's a couple of thousand there. So money's not a problem, especially since it's not mine."

"Whose money is it?"

"Archie's. I was in debt to him like a lot of people. So why not put it to good use? He's never coming around to collect."

Melissa caught Eldon's wrist and gently kissed his index finger, then pushed his hand away. "No sale."

"What d'you mean? I've cracked the case!"

They sat in the Isetta at a viewpoint on U.S. 101, a discreet distance south of the county seat at Preacher's Hole. It was sunny, and the car's hatch was open to the warm breeze. They had a fine view of the Nekaemas Valley. Eldon had called Melissa at the courthouse after leaving Gordon and had told her they had to take a drive during lunch hour.

She had agreed, sounding intrigued. Now she tilted her head, looked down her nose and said, "An interesting theory—"

"Don't play lawyer! I've had a long night."

"—which will never stand up in court."

"I've got a witness. Circumstances—"

"Circumstantial is right," Melissa said. "A witness who tells the police one thing and a reporter another. And that topiary stuff you had in the paper today—"

"That's a great story!"

"It's one more loose end. How do we explain *that* to a jury?"

"I don't know. But you can at least charge Chump-Change with robbery—and assault."

"If Clete can keep his story straight . . . when and if that prostitute is able to tell us anything. There's no evidence yet for a murder indictment."

"You're weaseling out of our bet!"

"This would never even get to the grand jury," Melissa said. "Is this something you're going to rush into print?"

"Uh . . . no."

"And why not?"

"Because . . . I . . . need . . . to . . . verify . . . " Eldon got out. Admitting it was like having teeth pulled.

"So you don't have the scoop yet," Melissa said. "Our agreement was that you get the scoop on the Loris murder."

"I'm close."

"Maybe you are," Melissa said.

"I'm close to you right now." Eldon leaned toward her.

Melissa leaned away. "Eldon, you're sweet but you're too eager."

"I'm just glad you're safe! You should've seen Stephanie. At first I couldn't tell if it was her or you—"

Melissa was silent for a moment. "Have you told all this to Nola?"

"I've told you. You're a deputy D.A."

"Why not Nola?"

"Because I don't want misunderstandings about who cracked this case."

"Okay. No misunderstandings here. Now you tell Nola."

"Why don't you tell him?"

"If Art decides to make an arrest, I'll know your information's good. But if the D.A.'s office hands Art a warrant, he'll make the arrest whether he thinks there's grounds or not—and then he'll let us sort it out in court."

"This is too important to play games with," Eldon said.

"I'll make the report if you want," Melissa said. "But I don't want to draw attention to the fact that I'm seeing you. There could be problems."

"Like what? We're not breaking any laws—are we?"

"No. But there'd be difficulties if you have to testify."

"My word's not good? Put me under oath."

"Eldon, we're *friends.*"

"One of the other deputy D.A.'s can try the case."

"Why don't you turn the story over to another reporter?" Melissa countered. "This case is my responsibility. If the D.A. finds out about me and you, he'll bring in a prosecutor from the attorney general's office in Salem to take over, just to keep things very up-and-up. The state will bill us for that, and it's not cheap. He'll be very unhappy with me about the extra expense—especially because you're a reporter."

Eldon thought about it. He didn't want Melissa in trouble with her boss, and he didn't want to hurt the *Sun*'s relations with the district attorney. "An arrest by the sheriff is as good as an indictment—for our purposes?"

"That would be a scoop, all right. . . . " Melissa kissed Eldon. "Yes, you do kiss rather well."

"Teach me more about cards."

"Itching for revenge?"

"There's a gambling story at the Lucky Poke, whether Chump-Change is arrested or not."

Melissa looked worried. "You didn't take any of Clete's money, did you?"

"Of course not. That might look like a payoff."

"Exactly. Don't trust him."

"I might have to, eventually," Eldon said. "I may need him to bankroll me at the Lucky Poke."

"We'll talk about that later," Melissa said. "Now drive me back to the courthouse."

"Please! Another kiss before parting!"

Melissa touched Eldon's nose. "I have to get back. And you have to talk to Art Nola."

They drove back to Preacher's Hole and stopped outside the courthouse. Eldon admired Melissa's brisk stride as she went into the building, then looked around to see if anyone had noticed them together. It was only a matter of time before gossip made them an item. Eldon looked forward to that moment of triumph over the rednecks.

He called the sheriff's office in Port Jerome from a pay phone, but Art wasn't there. Probably off rousting the low-life, Eldon thought.

He could tell anyone at the sheriff's office what he had learned, but he wanted to savor Art's expression. I'll have beat him to a crime scene at last, Eldon thought.

Yet time was a-wasting. What if Chump-Change skipped town? If he was going to run, he'd have run by now, Eldon decided. Any murderer with sense would disappear quickly. Instead, Chump-Change was on a rampage: raping, beating, and looting, running like a frantic rat around his hoodlum's rut. It was just a matter of donning heavy gloves and grabbing the rat by the scruff.

I want to be there when the rat is grabbed, Eldon thought. For Stephanie.

He climbed into the Isetta. If I go back to the office, he thought, Fiske will find something irrelevant for me to do, probably some damn thing about macrobiotics. I ought to go get some sleep.

Eldon admired the flowers fringing the courthouse lawn and thought of the flowers in Scoquel and of Archie's house. It might be useful to have another look at the murder scene while waiting for Art to turn up.

He started for Scoquel. There seemed to be a new vibration in the Isetta. He slowed the car, then speeded up, trying without success to pinpoint the tremor. He sensed it only subliminally. It hadn't been there when he'd driven Melissa back to the courthouse. Or had it? Eldon squirmed as he thought about how much he'd paid for the car. I'll drive this thing until it falls apart, he vowed, and swooped down the Scoquel turnoff, where the iris fields gleamed in the sunshine.

Archie's house stood silent, the yard bordered by fluttering yellow tape reading POLICE LINE — DO NOT CROSS. Eldon parked, ducked under the tape, and went up the iris-bordered walk. The door was locked, but he could see into the living room through a window. The house was in disarray. Furniture had been shifted, drawers opened, couch pillows tossed on the floor. Sheriff's deputies had thoroughly searched the place.

Eldon followed the crane tracks into the backyard, where he was annoyed to find the rear wall of the house more or less back in place. The deputies had picked it up and leaned it against the house like a huge shingle. Eldon squeezed into the kitchen through the wedge-shaped gap, telling himself yet again that he had to lose weight.

The kitchen had been searched, too. Archie's lunch had been cleaned up. Eldon went into the living room, wondering whether any porno had been left behind. Good luck, he thought, finding the basket of magazines tipped over before the VCR. Nothing left but crossword puzzle books. And the deputies were probably having a great time running Archie's tapes.

There was a cabinet beneath the TV. Eldon took a doily from the mantel and used it to handle the latch on the cabinet door. On a shelf inside was a Betamax videotape machine. Loris did all right for himself, Eldon thought with envy. I could never afford a VCR.

The cabinet's lower portion held a tangle of spare parts—cables, zip cord for stereo speakers, extra connectors, a couple of sets of earphones, and so forth. Eldon glimpsed a dark rectangle far in the back of the cabinet.

Someone missed a videotape after all, he thought. Let's see if I can work this thing.

He jabbed the VCR's "on" switch and reached for the box. But the machine did not activate. And the box was empty. Eldon rose and turned a lamp switch. Nothing. The power was off. Eldon shut the cabinet door with a kick.

He strolled to the bedroom, toying with the doily as he peered around in the gloom. The cards lay on the waterbed where Melissa had dropped them. Eldon was tempted to stretch out and take a nap. I'd like to bounce her on one of these, he thought. But a waterbed was another thing he couldn't afford.

"Found anything you like?"

Eldon yelped and whirled to see Art Nola in the doorway.

"Art!" Eldon gasped for breath. "I was looking for you!"

Art pointed at the doily. "Did you help yourself to anything else?"

"I didn't touch anything." Eldon threw down the doily.

"You just didn't want to leave fingerprints," Art said. "I oughta frisk you, Eldon."

"Oh, frisk away," Eldon said snappishly. "I'm clean."

"Who told you I was here?"

"Nobody—"

"You said you were looking for me."

"I meant that I need to talk to you."

"What the hell are you doing here?"

"I wanted another look at the crime scene."

Art sighed. "Just like me. Figures."

"You scared me," Eldon said. "I didn't hear your car."

"I've been here for some time," Art said. "My car's in the woods. I saw you drive up. You never did know how to keep a low profile."

"Reporters don't need to, usually."

"Come outside where there's light," Art said.

They went back to the kitchen and slipped outside. Eldon realized as he blinked in the sun how stuffy the house had been. He was about to blurt out his story but decided to make Nola dig for it. He smiled blandly until the detective demanded, "What were you after in there?"

"I don't know, exactly. How about you?"

"The murder weapon."

"You said it was in the bay."

"I know, dammit. But I dreamed *something*. Maybe it's hidden in the weeds. Seaweed, field weeds, I don't know. Weeds. You keep hunting until something clicks."

"Me, too."

"So what did you want to see me about?"

This was the moment. "I know who murdered Archie Loris," Eldon said.

Art looked Eldon in the eye. "Talk."

Quickly, a little breathlessly, Eldon related his meeting with Gordon Clete and what Clete had told him about Chump-Change.

Art merely smiled. "That's not bad, Eldon."

" 'Not bad'?"

"We're already after Chump-Change. He's disappeared."

"Shit! I should've gotten to you sooner."

"When did you talk to Clete?" Nola asked.

"This morning."

"Chump disappeared last night. It must've been right after this robbery. Interesting."

"You don't seem that concerned." Eldon's heart sank. Perhaps his whole theory about the murder was wrong.

"Of course I'm concerned," Art said. "But fretting in this job takes years off your life. We put out an APB on Chump-Change— his real name's Gary Jouganatos—right after the Hosfelder beating. We knew he was her pimp."

Gary, Eldon thought. Mr. G. "How?"

Art's smile became lupine. "From lots of people. Chump-Change doesn't have many friends."

"You're charging him with the Loris murder?"

"We want him for questioning."

Damn, Eldon thought, so near and yet so far. "Are we on the record?"

"About Chump-Change, sure. He's had a record of petty crime and violence since he was a teenager. He was in MacLaren reform school up in Woodburn as a kid. Later he did county jail time in Bend."

"Okay. And how about the rest of it?"

"The rest of it's off the record," Art said. "I thought Clete was lying—a cop gets a nose for bullshit, and Clete's tastes aren't the sort of thing you blurt out around here. Too bad he didn't just come clean."

"He's afraid of Chump-Change," Eldon said, "and I don't blame him. I think Gordon's basically honest, even if he is a queer."

"You shouldn't call them that," Art said in a severe voice. "It's un-Christian."

Eldon was startled. "Okay, okay, 'gay.' Whatever you want."

"I meet all kinds in my job," Art said. " 'Hate the queers, hate the niggers, hate the Catholics up the block.' I sure get tired of hearing that stuff. Us normal sinners shouldn't be so high and mighty. We've got to set an example."

Eldon reddened. "I'm Catholic—"

"So you ought to know."

"And you ought to know about the tape that Chump-Change was after," Eldon said. He could almost see Art's ears perk up.

"What tape?" Art asked.

"Chump-Change stole a videotape from Gordon. It belonged to Archie Loris. Stephanie Hosfelder stole it from Archie and gave it to Gordon to keep for her."

"So that's why Chump went to Clete's place. And why you came here, now that I think about it. Find anything?"

"It's not here." Eldon told what he knew of the tape. "Gordon doesn't know why it's important."

"Blackmail," Art said.

"Blackmail who? Loris is dead. Stephanie's a prostitute."

"Maybe Clete didn't tell you everything that was on the tape," Art said. "Maybe there are other people on the tape. Maybe there's something that blackmails *him*."

"Gordon's admitted he's, uh, gay. Chump can't blackmail him now." Eldon decided not to mention Archie's money.

"The tape shows Loris fooling with those statues, you say?"

"Gordon says. Maybe it's a secret code? In the writing on the statues' bases?"

"That's an idea," Art said. "You read French—you tell me."

"Not that I noticed. It was just poetry."

"If you lined 'em up could they form a message?"

Eldon laughed. "Let's push 'em around your desk and see."

"The thing to do is find Chump-Change—and we will," Art said. "Guys like him never lay low for long. They're not smart enough. No self-discipline. And when you catch 'em, they sing."

Eldon nodded. But he could not imagine Chump-Change growing a topiary figure with a shotgun inside. We should be looking for someone else, he thought. Someone even more dangerous.

By Eldon Larkin
Sun *Staff Writer*

PORT JEROME—A man whom a Nekaemas County sheriff's detective described as a "small-time hoodlum" is sought for questioning in the gangland-style slaying of Archie Loris, the 452-pound former Port Jerome High School football star turned pimp.

Detective Art Nola said Gary "Chump-Change" Jouganatos also was wanted in connection with the savage beating of a prostitute and with a strong-arm robbery in a home near the Nekaemas Bay Boat Basin.

Nola would not say whether Jouganatos, 24, would be charged in the Loris killing or whether the murder and the other crimes were connected. He said that Jouganatos, who sometimes worked as a dealer in area card rooms, would be questioned about Loris's death and about the huge pimp's involvement in local social gaming.

Nola would not say whether authorities were looking into possible violations of state social-gaming laws.

Loris was shotgunned in his Scoquel home. Deputies said his killing had the earmarks of a mob assassination, fueling speculation that Loris was linked to illegal gambling. . . .

★ ★ ★

Eldon had rushed back from Scoquel to write. What a follow-up to the topiary story, he thought as he typed. They'll have to hang a flock of green rubber chickens to protest this.

He was groggy but typed steadily as he recounted that Gordon Clete was one of Chump-Change's co-workers and that Chump-Change had robbed him. Eldon decided to leave it at that. Gordon may have come out of the closet, but I don't think he wants to do it in the police columns of a newspaper, Eldon thought. Still, he's got guts.

Eldon smiled for a moment. Then his smile faded as he wrote about Stephanie Hosfelder, still in critical condition in the hospital. Eldon told himself that getting the news onto the street would help bring Chump-Change down.

At last he typed "30." "Where's Jimbo?"

Frank glanced up from his own work. "Press room, I think."

Fiske wasn't in the press room. But then, over the acrid smell of printer's ink, Eldon sniffed oysters cooking. He found Fiske tending a hibachi on the rear loading dock, grilling oysters in their shells, turning them with tongs. "Hey, those look good!"

Fiske swatted at Eldon with the tongs. "None for you."

"What d'you mean? I'm your official taster."

"You haven't been earning your pay."

"No? Here's another great story about the Loris case."

Fiske glanced at the first page. "Too bad it wasn't in time for today's paper. . . . Take 'pimp' out of the lead."

Eldon took out a pencil and replaced "pimp" with "gambling impresario." He eyed the hibachi as he wrote, his mouth watering, for he had skipped lunch. "Oysters aren't macrobiotic. I'd better eat those for you."

"I'll be the judge of that," Fiske said.

"They'll unbalance your yin and yang. What would Bigfoot say?"

"Bigfoot's not the question here. I'm not married to Bigfoot. I'm married to m' wife." Fiske licked his lips and rolled his eyes.

"I'm gonna cook up a special dinner for just me and her. Serve it by candlelight. I'm practicing so things'll go just right. My wife loves oysters."

"Why not take her to Oats in the Bowl?"

"I don't want to corrupt your tender mind with what comes after dinner, Eldon. You ought to think about trying something like this—you'd have better luck with women. Nothing like a good feed to put 'em in the right mood. You young guys lack imagination."

"Can I suggest a wine?"

"Something microbiotic." Fiske tonged up an oyster, produced a fork, and plucked the meat from the shell. He blew on it and took a big bite. "Mmmm, good! What kind of South Coast boy doesn't know how to cook seafood?"

"All of them. They deep-fry everything." Eldon remembered encountering a deep-fried salmon steak in a local restaurant and shuddered, suddenly depressed. Fiske had independently conceived the gourmet seduction dinner and was certain of success his first time serving one; the fact that the female dinner guest was his wife was beside the point. It reminded Eldon not only that he had missed lunch but that Melissa might yet slip through his fingers.

"That wine's got to have yang to it," Fiske said.

"I need more money," Eldon said. "I'm going back to the card room."

"No way. You know our deal."

"Read my story. You'll see why I've got to go back!"

"Dee-de-dee." Fiske tossed away the oyster shell and took Eldon's copy. He sat with his legs hanging over the loading dock and began to read. Fiske became intent, nodding and dropping pages onto the dock. He pulled out a pencil and corrected the copy against his knee, reading faster and faster as he marked the paragraphs.

Fiske reached the story's end and looked up. Eldon waited for Fiske to pronounce the words *"Good copy"* in a voice like an oily mortician's.

"It's okay." Fiske handed the story back.

" 'It's okay'? This is major stuff!"

"I liked your story about the barbered bushes better." Fiske turned back to the hibachi.

"This is a break in the case!" Eldon cried. "Chump-Change was the dealer who got tossed out of the Poke for double-dealing. The cops are practically trumpeting that there's illegal gambling going on. I want to blow the lid off—"

"Why should I pay when the sheriff and the D.A. will do it for us for free? And pretty soon, too, sounds like."

"Because it's *news,* Jimbo!"

Fiske picked up another oyster, forked out the meat and waved it to cool it. "This cookin' reminds me of years ago when I covered the blowtorch murder. I couldn't eat sausage afterward because of the smell."

Not this one again, Eldon thought. He began to shift from foot to foot. The blowtorch murder was one of Fiske's longest and most dismal journalism war stories.

"You remind me of a young sheriff's deputy at that murder," Fiske said, regarding Eldon's dance. "It was his first scene of mayhem, and he kept walking around in circles saying, 'His face is burned off, his face is burned off.' Which it was."

"Yeah?" Eldon stopped, wary. He hadn't heard this part before.

"He'd walk in circles awhile and then vomit awhile and walk in circles some more, talking about the burned-off face," Fiske said. "Finally the sheriff looked at him and said, 'Yep, she's burned off all right!' I doubt if that deputy's vomited since."

"What?"

"The smell doesn't bother me anymore," Fiske explained and chomped the oyster. "Point is, a crime's a crime. You're taking this personally, and I think I know why. It's that gal, isn't it?"

Eldon felt as if the terms of his bet with Melissa were tattooed across his brow. Trust Fiske to guess. He took a deep breath. "It's just that it was such good copy, Jimbo. We got to talking and—"

"I know this Stephanie was a source of yours, but you can't cover a story for revenge," Fiske said. "It spoils your objectivity. You know who that young deputy was?"

126

Eldon sighed with relief. "No, who?"

"Art Nola."

"No kidding?"

"He took it personally that someone had burned off a face. You might get *your* face burned off if you go nosing around the Lucky Poke just now. Or punched in, anyway."

"I'll chance it."

"I've got your safety to think about."

"And your budget."

Fiske ignored the gibe. "You need something to get your mind off this pimp and those cards. This topiary—is it microbiotic?"

"Of course not—"

"This might be a microbiotic murder, ever thought of that? Now that would be good copy." Fiske finished the oyster. "You've had a long day. Take the afternoon off. And think about that wine."

"I'll get some lunch," Eldon said pointedly and left.

He hiked down the street to Pop's Place, where he ordered a decidedly non-macrobiotic reuben sandwich with gooey yellow potato salad. He munched plastic-wrapped crackers, one packet after another, as he waited for his sandwich.

One videotape lies between me and winning the best wager I ever made, he thought. I've got to get hold of that tape. But how? Chump-Change might still have it, when and if the cops pick him up—which means it'll be impounded as evidence. Out of reach. Damn.

But would Chump-Change still have the tape? Maybe Chump took the tape to Archie's killer, Eldon thought.

There it was again: the idea that there was someone else still lurking on the fringes of the Loris case. That tape has blackmail value, Eldon thought. But for whom?

Holding people's paper must have been how Archie worked his will, since he was too fat to leave his house, Eldon thought. Follow the money and you'll find out who killed Archie and why. Money always means records. There's got to be a paper trail somewhere.

Maybe it was the card-room owners and not the mob, Eldon

thought as the reuben sandwich arrived. They hated Loris's guts because they owed him money.

He considered it as he chewed. There would have to be more trips to the Lucky Poke to insinuate himself with the gambling crowd, courtesy of Archie's money. That might be dangerous. And more card lessons with Melissa. That would be fun. After all, she'd promised. He ate faster, gazing out the restaurant window at the stationery store across the street. He got an idea.

After lunch, Eldon went to the stationery store. There he bought a package of rub-on Gothic letters and a blank white card and envelope. He walked to the library, where he sat at a table and used the edge of a quarter to rub letters onto the card, creating a facsimile of an engraved invitation:

The distinguished journalist

ELDON LARKIN

requests the pleasure of your erudite company

at his digs

for the purpose of continuing his instruction in

THE HOLY GAME OF POKER

Gourmet Seduction Dinner No. 3 will be served

R.S.V.P. — Black Tie Optional

Eldon studied his creation with pleasure. He had no idea what Gourmet Seduction Dinner No. 3 would be, but he'd think of something. He slipped the card into the envelope.

"Speak of the devil. Hiding from the boss, Eldon?"

It was Simon Blood, wearing a turquoise shirt with iridescent cactus flowers stitched across the yoke. "Hi, Simon. Are you hiding, too?"

"Just from the customers, since I'm my own boss." Blood sat

opposite Eldon and placed a manila folder stuffed with brochures on the table. "I'm doing research on your behalf."

"Yeah? I'll tell Fiske I've been out interviewing a source."

"Is that what I am?"

"Read today's paper. The medical examiner confirmed that the vegetation at the murder scene was *Soleirolia.*"

Blood beamed. "Told ya!"

"It's a great story," Eldon said. "I quoted you and put in the name and address of the nursery."

"Thanks for the plug." Blood tapped the folder. "I've been thinking about that topiary—couldn't stop thinking about it, really. Because of the skill involved."

"The skill?"

"Skill with topiary is how you find your man. Whoever wrapped that shotgun in moss knew just what he was doing."

"Yeah, so you said."

"There are people who do topiary in moss or even lichen. Real artists. Your man's one of them. He must be very good—portable topiary is almost always ivy, but this fellow works in moss."

"You mentioned that."

"I'm dying to know who he is myself. So I'm going to make some calls." Blood opened the folder and spread brochures across the table. "Someone among these knows your man."

Eldon examined the brochures. They were for topiary clubs scattered around the country. "I should've thought of this."

"I didn't think of it myself until you'd left," Blood said. "I didn't even know how to get in touch with some of these organizations. Luckily, I found this file here."

"I'll start calling—"

"Let me," Blood said. "You don't know what questions to ask. Topiary is a singular little world. Some of these groups are rather eccentric, suspicious of outsiders."

"That's ridiculous."

"Secret fishing holes are ridiculous, too."

"That's different!"

"Yes," Blood said, "anybody can buy a fishing license. But some of these specialized leagues have membership screenings that make the Rosicrucians look like the boosters for the high school band. Let me make contact; they'll talk to a professional. If I get wind of anything, I'll put you in touch."

"Suppose the killer didn't grow the topiary? Suppose he only commissioned it?"

"Then whoever made the piece can tell us who it was grown for. How many pieces of topiary have a shotgun inside?"

"How would you manage that, anyway?"

"I wonder," Blood said. "You'd have to keep the gun from rusting while the topiary grew. Perhaps if the shotgun were well greased and wrapped in plastic—"

"Would someone around here know how to do it?"

"No. But finding out who does know how will be easier than you think."

"I owe you one, Simon."

"Got any more fishing holes you want to show me?"

Eldon grinned. "That's asking a lot, but—you bet."

"I've got to get back to the shop," Blood said. "I'll call you in a day or two. Tell Ambrose hi. And save me some copies of that story."

Eldon blessed his fortune as he watched Blood check out the folder of brochures and leave the library. If Simon was right, dinner with Melissa would be a victory dinner.

Filet mignon, Eldon decided.

He glanced at the library clock. If he hurried over to the sheriff's office, he could send the invitation to Melissa through the county government interoffice mail. It would be at the courthouse in Preacher's Hole by the end of the day.

He left the library, walking briskly. It was sunny, but clouds were building on the horizon. A good omen, Eldon thought. Rain brought introspection and sharpened the wits. A good storm might even bring luck with cards. And he slept deeply when it rained.

At the sheriff's office, Eldon checked the dispatcher's log. There was nothing of interest this afternoon. He got an interoffice-mail envelope from the dispatcher, addressed it to Melissa at the D.A.'s office, and placed the dinner invitation inside. He put the envelope into the basket for outgoing mail and glanced at the dispatcher's status board: Art Nola was back from Scoquel.

Eldon went upstairs. Art sat pushing Archie Loris's obscene statuettes around his bare desk like big chess pieces.

"Enjoying yourself?" Eldon asked.

Art looked up. "Pull up a chair."

Eldon sat in the gray metal office chair next to the desk. "It must be a pleasure to handle fine china."

"I'm looking for coded messages."

"I was kidding about that."

"It doesn't hurt to check." Art pointed to the French poetry on the figurines' bases. "What do these say?"

"Lines from Verlaine," Eldon said. *"Jusqu'aux jolis tétins d'infante* . . . uh, let's see, 'To your little, childlike nipples, of—a, uh, barely pubescent girl.' And this one says *Fesses, dont la blancheur divinise encor la rondeur,* which is, 'Buttocks, whose whiteness makes their curves yet more divine.' "

"A code could be in English or French."

"Did Archie speak French?"

"He was a high school dropout. No French classes on his transcript."

"Then let's stick with English." Eldon looked at another statue. "This one's from Rimbaud: *Drôle de ménage!* 'Queer couple!' "

"Yeah, I see that," Art said dryly. "No message there—assuming you translated right."

"It's close enough."

"How about in French?"

"Not that I can see. Don't the state police have cryptographers? Or the FBI?"

"I can't waste their time with this." Art studied the figurines. "The deeds these cherubs are up to don't seem to form a pattern, either—"

"Maybe they pointed the way to a secret panel when they were lined up in Archie's living room," Eldon said. "Nothing on Chump-Change, huh?"

"If there were, I wouldn't be sitting here," Art said, and added, "Stephanie Hosfelder's still critical. She might not make it."

"Yeah." Eldon felt his weariness close in. "Let me know if anything breaks."

"Sure."

Eldon drove home, intent on dinner and sleep.

Ominously, the storm failed to develop. There were only spatters of rain as he drove up the ridge to his house. The clouds hung above Nekaemas Bay, seeming to glower like a sullen tomcat caught soiling a rug.

Eldon watched the sky through his front window and brooded about Stephanie as he ate a ham sandwich. He was bone-tired but not yet ready to sleep. He wanted dessert. He laced some vanilla ice cream with cognac and returned to the window.

The ice cream was good but the unsettled weather made for unsettled thoughts. I don't think Chump-Change killed Archie, Eldon mused. He's mean enough but not smart enough. But who did? Sure, a mob hit man—but who, exactly?

He went to bed still hoping for rain.

17

The clouds still hung heavy in the morning. Rain seemed imminent. Eldon called the hospital from his house. Stephanie Hosfelder remained in critical condition. He left without fixing breakfast.

He drove to work, parked the Isetta in the *Sun* lot, and walked three blocks through the quiet, damp streets to the sheriff's office to check the overnight log. Chump-Change had not turned up.

Eldon walked back to the office and found that he was the first news staffer to come in. Fiske usually was there ahead of them all, reading wire copy and planning the day's assignments. But this morning the wire service machine buzzed unattended. A couple of ad salesmen sat drinking coffee on their side of the office. Otherwise the place was empty.

Eldon went into the coffee room. There he discovered that the ad men had brought a large box of powdered-sugar doughnuts—his favorite. He gobbled one on the spot and took another back to his desk with a cup of coffee.

From his desk, Eldon saw people on the sidewalk, through the glass front doors. He craned his neck and peered as he chewed his doughnut. More pickets. No high school band this time, just a half-dozen adults walking back and forth with signs. Eldon couldn't read the signs. He watched the pickets buttonholing early passersby on their way to work, including *Sun* employees coming up the front steps. Secretaries, ad salesmen, and composing-room workers came in examining petition forms—doubtless copies of the petition that denounced him.

Come bright and early and drive it into the ground, Eldon thought sourly.

Marsha Cox came in with a petition in her hand and marched to Eldon's desk. "Wipe your moustache and look at this."

"Bah. That stupid petition—"

"Oh, it's a petition, all right."

Eldon made a show of stuffing the rest of the doughnut into his mouth as he read the sheet—and nearly choked. This was a new petition, calling for a vote on whether to establish a casino zone on the Oregon coast. "Holy cow," he got out as he gulped the mouthful down.

"A vote would bypass the Legislature," Marsha said.

"If they can get enough signatures to put it on the ballot," Eldon said. He looked around the office. His co-workers were *discussing* the petition, nodding to one another, actually taking it seriously! Some even pulled out ballpoint pens and signed their names to the forms!

"What's wrong with them?" Eldon demanded. "Do they want to live in a honky-tonk?"

"It's their right to sign petitions," Marsha said.

"Don't you realize what a casino zone would do to the fishing?"

"They're not going to put the card tables under water."

"There'd be too many people! We'd be overrun with tourists and crooks. Where's my notebook—?"

"They won't talk to you—they say you're biased."

"Wait'll they read my story in today's paper."

Marsha tittered. "That rubber chicken got to you, didn't it?"

"It wasn't macrobiotic," Eldon said with a sneer.

As if on cue, Fiske popped in the side door. His ugly teeth shone in a huge grin and he walked with a spring in his step. "Dee-de-dee! Did I hear the word 'microbiotic'?"

"You're late this morning, Jimbo," Eldon said.

"And quite cheerful," Marsha ventured.

"Dinner was great!" Fiske preened—like a college student who's scored on the first date, Eldon thought.

"I cooked dinner for m' wife last night," Fiske explained to Marsha. "Special event."

"That was sweet," Marsha said. "Men *can* cook, if they'll only follow the recipe."

"Oh, I had the recipe, all right!" Fiske skipped to his desk, grabbed a pile of press releases, and began sorting them. "Gonna be a good news day, I see—pickets out front again. They still mad at you, Eldon?"

"It's gone beyond that," Eldon said. "They want a vote on a casino zone."

"Better get some quotes," Fiske said.

"They won't talk to Eldon," Marsha said.

"Then *you* talk to 'em," Fiske said.

Marsha hurried for the door. Fiske lifted his Lucite-entombed pipe and regarded it. "Lemme see—Frank's gone down to the courthouse this morning. He can get the filing information about this new petition down there. Marsha can combine it with her stuff and we'll have a story."

"I can write it better!"

"We're running your story about that Chump-Change character today. You concentrate on that angle. We'll surround 'em with bylines. Meanwhile, make yourself useful—"

Fiske thrust the press releases at Eldon, who accepted them resignedly. They were daily grist for the news mill.

One of them caught Eldon's eye. The Nekaemas County clerk had gotten a grant from the state to pay for microfilming county records such as marriage licenses, military discharges, and liens.

Liens, Eldon thought. This could be a chance to follow that good old paper trail. And I don't mean Rimbaud or Verlaine.

He brushed powdered sugar from his desk top and opened his telephone book to the Yellow Pages. He copied out the names and addresses of the Lucky Poke and other taverns that offered social gaming. Then he called the clerk's office and asked the staff to check for liens against the establishments on the list. Eldon got a third powdered-sugar doughnut and more coffee while he waited.

Shortly the clerk's office called back. There were indeed construction liens against the Lucky Poke and most of the other card rooms. None of the lien holders were familiar to Eldon, nor was Archie Loris's name among them.

It's like betting in poker, Eldon thought, except in this game I know when to trust my hunches.

It was time to make some long-distance calls. He telephoned the state Corporation Division in Salem and asked for incorporation records on the contractors holding the liens. The state records listed the companies' owners. The name of Archie Loris did not appear among them. But Archie could have been a silent partner in any or all of the companies or simply worked under the table, with no formal connection to any of his debtors.

The next call paid off. Eldon telephoned the state Builders' Board and asked if there was a contractor's license in the name of Archibald Loris. There was, and it was the right man. The date of birth and Scoquel address were that of the dead pimp.

"Is there a D.B.A.?" Eldon asked.

"Yes. 'Doing business as' Banjo Boy Inc. Same address."

"Thank *you.*" What *was* Archie's thing about banjos?

Eldon called the Corporation Division once more and asked for incorporation data on Banjo Boy Inc. Back came the name of Archie Loris and several others with Nekaemas County addresses.

Banjo Boy was Archie's cover operation, Eldon thought. I bet I know who these other clowns are. He compared the addresses of the Banjo Boy officers with those of the card rooms on his list. None of them matched, but that would have been a bit too easy. There was one more call to make.

He telephoned the Oregon Liquor Control Commission in Milwaukie, near Portland, and asked for the names of liquor license holders for the taverns on his list. The names of four licensees matched those of directors of Banjo Boy Inc. Two lien holders in the clerk's records also had state liquor licenses, although in other counties.

Bogus construction liens against the card rooms, Eldon thought as he hung up. The liens get paid off with money from "nonprofit" social gaming. A nice way to launder the take. I wonder how much is involved? And how far the web stretches?

Let's see what Simon turns up, he thought. The bigger the story, the better. Picket me, will they? Spoil my fishing, will they?

Marsha marched back into the newsroom, her face flushed with annoyance. "They won't talk to me, either!"

"Bad taste?" Eldon asked innocently. "Bias?"

"They say they'll only talk to Ambrose!"

"Fine. Start your story, 'Pickets from a political movement started by a dead giant pimp paraded before the *Sun* offices today.' They'll talk after they read that." Eldon's phone rang. It was Frank, calling from the courthouse with the official particulars of the casino-zone petition.

"I can guess the sponsors' names," Eldon said and read off the names of the Banjo Boy Inc. officers.

"That's pretty good shooting."

"So they also happen to be officers of a construction company that holds liens against their businesses," Eldon said. "Company president—Archie Loris."

Frank whistled. "Nice work."

"It was simple."

"It's good copy."

"I'm waiting on one more source before I go into print with it," Eldon said. "We'll just do a story today about the petition. And I've got a story saying that the cops are looking for Chump-Change. The next step is connecting the petition drive to the Loris murder. The topiary could be the key."

"The topiary? How?"

"Never mind that for now. But I may need you to get back to your source in Chicago."

"I'm on it."

After Frank hung up, Eldon resisted the urge to call Simon Blood. He had to stay out of Simon's face, let him work. But Eldon mentally licked his chops. The bet with Melissa was nearly won.

He decided not to tell Fiske yet what he had discovered. Every reporter knew that a few facts could make an editor inconveniently agitated; on this particular morning, Fiske might take off like a rocket. He would keep his own counsel until he heard from Simon Blood.

But he could tell Melissa. He *had* to tell Melissa. Eldon phoned her at the D.A.'s office.

"Thank you for the charming invitation," Melissa said, her voice warm. "That was a surprise."

"I worked on it for hours."

"It's very creative. Unique."

"You're unique. I'm glad you like it."

"I'm flattered that you think I'm so erudite—"

"None more."

"—but I'm going to decline."

"But I need to play cards some more!"

"We'll play," Melissa said. "But you might learn more if we did it somewhere else."

"I'll be all business," Eldon said. "And I'm planning a great dinner."

"I think we should go out."

"Well—okay. Uh, we can get decent fried chicken at—"

"I was thinking of Oats in the Bowl," Melissa said.

"Huh?"

"I want to meet Gordon Clete. He may have to testify before the grand jury—especially if we go for gambling indictments later on. That's between you and me."

"Gordon'll figure it out for himself."

"Let him. I'll subpoena him eventually. But I like sizing up people in context."

"Is that why you came to the newsroom the other day?"

"Very perceptive, Eldon." Melissa added softly, "I liked what I found."

"It's a date. What can I say?"

"Find out when Clete plays at the Oats again."

"Tonight, as a matter of fact."

"Good—let's go. Bring your appetite." Melissa put a throaty intonation on the final word.

"I have something that'll whet your appetite, too."

"What's that?" Melissa's voice was almost a whisper.

Eldon dropped his voice. "A list of people who have liens against their own card rooms. Business partners of Archie Loris. Looks like a money-laundering scheme."

A pause. "You may have a winning hand—if you can prove that. Eight tonight, Oats." Melissa hung up.

Through the glass front doors, Eldon saw a storm front roll up from the south. No doubt it was already raining on Preacher's Hole. Eldon chuckled as raindrops smacked the glass and the pickets scampered for cover.

He looked over to see Marsha at her desk, just hanging up her own telephone. Amazingly, she smiled at him. Eldon was certain she was about to say something particularly cutting. "Well?" he asked.

"I have decided to let Louis back into my life."

"I thought *he* dumped *you.*"

"Louis just called. He has seen the error of his ways."

Score one for Marsha as well as for Fiske, Eldon thought. God. "Well, it does get lonely here on the coast," he said.

"Fortunately, we have our work, don't we?" Marsha said, still smiling.

Eldon returned the smile. "And how."

Rain fell steadily all day. Fiske bannered Eldon's story about the search for Chump-Change across the top of the day's front page. Beneath was a picketing photo and Marsha's story. To Eldon's glee, Marsha used the insulting lead that he had suggested, although Fiske, albeit with a grin, toned it down.

Frank called from Preacher's Hole after lunch. The county seat's antiquated storm drains had backed up, and Main Street was a river. Eldon took the information from Frank for a next-day weather story.

He stayed at his desk throughout the afternoon, making weather calls and hoping in vain to hear from Simon. If he has any sense, he's home in front of his fire, Eldon thought finally and put the matter from his mind. He called the hospital to check on Stephanie. Her condition was unchanged.

Eldon cobbled together a weather story as the day drew to a close. He planned to kick back at home for a few hours before meeting Melissa. But then the inevitable reports of storm-related traffic accidents started coming in over the police scanner.

Sixty-five inches of rainfall a year here, and people still drive like maniacs when it rains, Eldon thought with an unhappy glance at the clock. He managed to keep abreast of things by phone until an empty Shell Oil truck sheared off a telephone pole on Bayside Drive, killing power along the waterfront for forty-five minutes, and Fiske sent him out to take a picture. It was a long day.

It was after 7:30 P.M. and growing dark when Eldon escaped the newsroom and headed for Oats in the Bowl. He was tired and uneasy. The Isetta seemed unstable, no matter how carefully he drove. The rain played tricks with perspective and distance in the twilight, making the deepening shadows among the trees seem cold and frightening. Even macrobiotic food would taste good tonight.

Oats in the Bowl was a beacon in the storm. The restaurant's lights glowed warmly through its stained glass. Fat raindrops gleamed in the radiance as Eldon pulled up and parked. Melissa waited on the porch in a dark green trenchcoat, navy-blue beret, and boots. She looked like a sentinel in the growing darkness. As he hurried onto the porch, Eldon heard piano music over the sound of the rain.

"Clete's inside tickling the ivories," Melissa said as she permitted Eldon to peck her on the cheek. "Does he know we're coming?"

"No."

"Good. He won't have time to change his story."

"He wants to help. Why would he lie?"

"He lied to Nola, didn't he?"

"Some. People get funny when they see a badge."

They entered the restaurant. The fragrance of sandalwood mingled with the odor of food. Gordon sat playing the piano. Chopin, Eldon thought. A few customers idled over meals. The pony-tailed waiter came over and said the restaurant was about to close. Eldon started to protest. Gordon saw them and called, "They're friends of mine. At least give 'em some tea."

The waiter shrugged and brought cups and a pot of peppermint tea, then hung a "closed" sign in the doorway, went into the kitchen, and started cleaning up.

" 'About to close,' " Eldon grumbled. "I'm hungry!"

Melissa poured tea, opened the pot's lid, looked inside, and extracted a deck of cards. "Shall we play? Keep your mind off your stomach."

"Strip poker?"

Melissa laughed. "Let's keep our clothes on. Five-card draw. You need practice." She shuffled the cards, her smile oddly innocent as she cut the deck.

"There's nothing to bet with," Eldon said.

"What about these toothpicks?"

There was a glass bowl of toothpicks on the table.

"Okay." Eldon took a handful and Melissa did the same. Eldon saw another bowl of toothpicks on the next table and brought that over, too.

"That was a good story in the paper today." Melissa began dealing.

"You saw it? Thanks. I try to be provocative."

"It provoked me to talk with Art Nola, to speed up the legwork."

I've cooked my own goose by confiding in her, Eldon thought. But what can I do? It's all going in the paper anyway. His fingers were sweaty as he picked up his cards.

Customers filtered out as they played. Eldon held his own, somewhat to his surprise. Was he getting better or was Melissa going easy on him?

The pony-tailed waiter finished in the kitchen and came out.

"I'll lock up and put the key in the drop slot," Gordon told him. The waiter rang out the cash register and stashed its contents in a small safe beneath the counter, then hung up his apron and left. Gordon closed the piano lid and came to their table. He looked cautiously from Eldon to Melissa and back again.

"I saw your story in the paper," Gordon said. "I didn't expect it to appear . . . so quickly."

"We're a daily newspaper," Eldon said.

"Yeah—well, you treated me okay. Good thing you didn't look me up at the Poke, though. That would've been awkward." Gordon turned to Melissa. "I remember you, but I never got your name. Eldon, who is your pretty colleague?"

Melissa pulled her badge case from her purse and let it fall open. "Melissa Lafky, district attorney's office."

"Oh." Gordon sat down slowly. "Not a colleague."

"I want to ask some questions," Melissa said.

"I've already talked to Detective Nola—"

"I know. Play poker?" Without waiting for an answer, Melissa dealt Gordon in. He looked startled, then smoothly picked up his cards.

Not another card shark, Eldon worried as rain rattled on the windows.

"I've talked to the cops and I've talked to the newspaper, so I might as well talk with you," Gordon said. "Nola's hanging around the bars and card rooms, leaning hard on people for information. Lots of them are nervous."

"Art's kind of hard-nosed, yeah," Melissa said. "They should give him what he wants."

"Nola wants Chump-Change, and no one knows where he is. Eldon's story in the paper today didn't calm them down. The owners are frantic. There are so many skeletons buried around the Poke that it's like a cemetery."

"The skeleton I'm interested in is that videotape," Melissa said.

"You told her about that, Eldon?"

"You can trust Melissa."

"Do I have a choice?" Gordon glanced at his cards and bet five toothpicks. Then he repeated what he had told Eldon about the theft of the videotape.

Eldon, who had two aces, saw Gordon's bet. Melissa matched the bet, too. Gordon drew one card. Eldon drew three cards. Trash. His luck had turned—or had Melissa abruptly made him a prop? One bad hand doesn't make a turn of luck, he told himself sternly.

One card for Melissa. "So you don't know why Chump-Change wanted the tape?"

"No." Gordon bet ten toothpicks. "He forced his way in and grabbed it."

Eldon folded. Gordon threw him a sharp grin. "That's right, Eldon; you stay on the sidelines where the big kids can't hurt you."

"And the tape showed Archie and Stephanie Hosfelder having sex?" Melissa asked. "I call." She showed jacks and threes.

Gordon had nines and fives; he frowned, for Melissa had won. "Yeah. The tape starts with Archie pushing these perverted statues around—"

"Do the statues mean anything to you?" Melissa passed the deck to Gordon, who shuffled and began to deal.

"No," Gordon said. "I think they were just one way that Archie
. . . worked himself up. We'll play five-card stud now, if Eldon
knows how—"

"I know how," Eldon said.

Gordon dealt one card down and one up to each of them. Eldon
had a king up. "King's bet," Gordon told him. "That means it's
your move, Elvis."

"What's this 'Elvis' stuff?"

"A little card-room banter," Melissa said. "Keeps the pressure
on."

Nobody said a word at the Lucky Poke, Eldon thought. Nervously, he bet three toothpicks. Melissa and Gordon saw his bet.
Gordon dealt another round, face-up. Melissa, showing an ace, bet
four toothpicks. Gordon and Eldon bet the same.

"Eldon says you owed Archie Loris money," Melissa said.

"You and Eldon do share a lot of confidences."

"He also told me you're gay."

"That's no secret anymore." Gordon dealt the next round.
Eldon got another king.

"I needed money because a friend was coming from Portland to
live with me," Gordon said. "I don't make enough to support
two."

He dealt another round. Another king up for Eldon.

"Wasn't your friend going to get a job?" Melissa asked as the
betting proceeded.

"It's tough to find work here—you know that."

"What's your friend do?"

"He's a painter. No skills."

"A house painter?"

"An art painter. As I said—no skills." Gordon smiled faintly.

"How about working as a dealer?" Eldon asked.

"No," Gordon said. "I'm in that scene deep enough. Look what
it's gotten me. But he's not coming—it didn't work out."

"I'd bluff you now," Melissa said to Gordon, "but I don't know
about Elvis here."

It's only toothpicks, Eldon thought, and shoved out a pile of them. "Stop calling me 'Elvis.' "

Melissa showed two pair.

"Shit," Eldon said.

"We were together in Portland," Gordon said, conceding defeat by tossing down his cards. "He was going to move down here and paint. Get away from his problems."

"What kind of problems?" Melissa asked.

"He drank—drinks. That's why I didn't want him working in the card rooms. I thought a change of scene would help; the teaching job opened up here, so Port Jerome is where I went. But he never followed. I realized later that we were in the process of breaking up when I moved here. Though having arrived, I find that I kind of like it."

"Too bad you don't like to go fishing," Eldon said.

Gordon threw him a sour look and became silent.

"My deal," Melissa said, taking the deck. "Five-card draw with a wild card. Name your lucky number, Eldon."

"Six, of course," Eldon said with a smile, thinking of Melissa's card trick on the day they had met. He got a pair of nines in his hand. Hey, pretty good, he thought.

Gordon took two cards. Eldon and Melissa each took three cards. Eldon kept a serious face only with an effort. He had drawn a third nine!

Oh, baby, he thought and rested his hand on his "money."

Gordon glanced at him and bet ten toothpicks.

"Raise twenty," Eldon declared.

"Whatta man!" Melissa said, and to Eldon's delight folded.

"Okay," Gordon said, "see that and raise you twenty-five."

Eldon threw in the rest of his toothpicks. "Whatcha got?"

"Three jacks." One at a time, Gordon showed a jack of clubs . . . a jack of diamonds . . . and the six of spades.

Eldon showed Melissa his three nines and asked, "Did I play so badly?"

"No, that was all right."

"It was dynamite," Gordon said, collecting the toothpick pot. "Keep it coming; you've got talent, baby."

His victory seemed to make him talkative again. "Moving from Portland cleaned me out. Archie had money, so I borrowed from him."

"Why not go to a bank?" Eldon asked.

"No collateral."

"How'd you afford your VCR, then?"

"That was a gift from my lover," Gordon said. "He sold a painting just as I left for Port Jerome. It turned out to be a good-bye present. Anyway, Archie was in the loan business, so . . . "

"You keep rough company for a music teacher," Melissa said.

"Places like the Lucky Poke are where you play music around here," Gordon replied. "It's fascinating, stimulating—not like the college or Oats in the Bowl." He leaned forward. "I play better music there. The loggers, the smoke, the cards, the smells. The tension. The dirty deals. I eat it up."

"Tell us more about that loan," Melissa said.

"That was Stephanie's idea. She knew I needed dough and suggested Archie. Bad idea, huh? Just as well that Archie wound up dead. I couldn't have made the payments, because of vigorish."

"That might be reason for you to kill him," Melissa said.

"Plenty of people had that reason, so here's a better one," Gordon retorted. "You want to talk about blackmail? Archie found out I was gay—it was never any secret, but I never made a big thing of it either, and I got by. He threatened to put out the word at the Poke, make an issue of it. He told Chump-Change, just to give me a taste of what could happen."

"What was their relationship?" Melissa asked.

"Chump and Archie? Chump did the odd dirty errand for Archie. But Chump and Archie didn't get along. It's kind of funny, now that I think about it—Chump-Change wanted to emulate Archie. But Archie couldn't stand that. It only increased his contempt."

Eldon recalled Chump's words from the Lucky Poke: *I'm draw-ing per diem!* But from whom? Not Archie.

And not from the card-room owners, either, Eldon thought with chagrin. They're not involved in the killing—finding that paper trail was just too easy.

"You can't fight everyone," Gordon said. "I'd have been watching my back every second. So I said to Loris, 'What do you want?' And that pervert said, 'I want you on tape.' For one of his porno shows. Can you imagine that?"

"Good grief." Eldon thought of Archie's dead Roman-emperor face.

"Stephanie bought me clear," Gordon said.

"How?" Melissa asked.

"She agreed to be on his damn tape," Gordon said, "instead of me."

"Why?" Melissa asked.

Gordon said simply, "She's my friend."

Eldon looked at the scattered cards with a burst of empathy for Gordon. Poor bastard, he thought, looking for love in unfriendly places—just like me.

"Stephanie never thought she counted," Gordon said. " 'I'm just a whore anyway,' she said. I tried to tell her she was wrong. Archie took her up on it just to hit at me—said he'd decided to give me a little more time on the money, after all. Stephanie's worth a hundred of that fat degenerate. I wish I *had* killed him."

"But you didn't," Melissa remarked. "You were teaching a music class at the college at the time of the murder."

"Well—I admit I'm glad you did your homework, Ms. D.A."

"Nola checked it out for me."

"I still wish I'd done it."

"What'd Archie make the tape for?" Eldon asked. "His collec-tion?"

"Stephanie told me Archie was going to sell it to a 'big bidder,' but she didn't know who."

"The mob," Eldon said. "It's obvious they killed Loris for the tape. I thought it must have been the card-room owners but they have too sweet a setup."

"I think Chump-Change did it," Gordon said. "He took over some of Archie's girls and wanted the rest."

"No, Chump's mean enough but too stupid," Eldon said. "This isn't his style. The first thing Melissa said at the crime scene was 'This is a mob hit.' "

"The killer *was* someone Loris knew," Melissa said. "He did know Chump-Change, from what you say, Gordon."

"But who told Chump about the tape?" Eldon said. "He beat Stephanie half to death to find out where it was. I think someone *sent* him after that tape. I'm looking into that now."

Melissa pounced. "What have you found?"

"You and Br'er Fox will have to keep reading the paper," Eldon said with a grin. "Meanwhile, Gordon and I have a project in mind."

"Which is—?" Melissa asked.

"He'll bankroll me in the card rooms with the money Archie loaned him. Whatever dirt I dig up about social gaming goes in the paper—and I'll tell you, of course."

"You'd name names? Reveal your sources?"

"I'll name criminals. Why should I protect them?" Eldon mentally crossed his fingers. There's always the Oregon Shield Law, he thought. She can't force me to reveal sources, even in court.

"But that won't solve the Loris killing," Melissa said.

"I'm betting it will," Eldon said.

"The ultimate dirty deal," Gordon said.

"What happens to that money is between the two of you." Melissa's expression was bland—a real poker face, Eldon thought. "But I'd hope any citizen would come to me if he had information bearing on a criminal investigation."

You do know how to bluff, Eldon thought. Only you don't know about Simon Blood, my ace in the hole. I'll track down Archie's killer. And he'll lead us to Chump-Change and the tape in the bargain.

But Eldon looked again at the cards scattered on the table and suddenly was daunted. What if Simon doesn't come up with anything, he wondered, and I lose the whole two thousand with no results? I've got a hell of a lot riding on Simon Blood.

Melissa smiled. Could she read the doubt on his face? "Good thing you can tap a lot of cash," she said. "You may need it."

"One thing, Eldon," Gordon said, "I can't guarantee that anyone will talk to you."

"When they're scared is when they sometimes talk the most," Eldon said. "They *should* be scared of Nola."

"They're more scared than that," Gordon said as a gust of wind and rain hit the windows like a fist. "I'm just a piano player with big ears—but I think they're afraid for their lives."

Afterward, out on the porch, with rain falling steadily and light from the windows glittering on puddles in the parking lot, Melissa said to Eldon: "You can probably trust him. But keep an eye on him."

"Do I have a choice?"

"Give him receipts for that money. It makes you look more honest."

"I *am* honest!"

"I mean, if you have to testify." Melissa glanced back into the restaurant, watching Gordon preparing to shut off the lights. "He plays poker pretty well—not as well as me, of course."

"You mean you *let* him win in there?"

"Well, now, I couldn't use sex, could I?" Melissa asked with a sidelong grin.

"A bet's a bet," Eldon said tartly, a little hurt.

"Just teasing, Eldon. I think I'd be better off welshing on the mob than welshing on you when it comes time to collect."

"You got that right. And I am going to collect."

Melissa turned toward him as Gordon turned out the lights. "You're pretty sure of yourself. Why?"

"Keep reading the paper."

"What're you going to print?"

"My review of this restaurant, for one thing." Eldon stepped in; Melissa kissed him. It was a long, lingering kiss that seemed to blend smoothly with the rain. "Eldon—please be careful." Then she was down the steps, dashing to her car in the rain.

Eldon watched her drive away. Then he plunged into the downpour, getting pretty wet before he got inside the Isetta. He shut the hatch and sat for a moment listening to the rain thrum on the car's shell, then gave a short, sharp whistle. What a woman!

He started the car and headed into Port Jerome. He was still hungry. It wasn't too late to find a sandwich somewhere. He could go home and fix something to eat, of course, but he needed to wind down; otherwise, he would lie awake all night thinking of Melissa and seething with frustrated lust.

Eldon strained his ears as he followed the winding road into town, trying to sense the new vibration in the Isetta. The noise of the rain made it impossible. He topped the rise and headed downtown. Lights on the buildings below threw off a watery gleam, like beacons on sunken ships.

The *Sun* office was lit up. Ambrose must be there, working on the next day's sports page. Maybe he wants to go out for a burger, Eldon thought. I should talk to him anyway . . . about this card thing.

If he didn't do it now, he probably never would. Eldon pulled into the parking lot and let himself in the side door.

McFee was typing at his desk in the empty newsroom, sitting cross-legged in his cranked-up swivel chair. The chair kept rotating to the right, as usual. McFee's purple baseball cap was pushed back on his head.

"I'm writing that casino column," McFee explained when he saw Eldon.

"You're 'agin' it, I hope?"

"You bet I'm against it," Ambrose said. "Back in the days when I was drinkin' and chasin' other people's women, I got drunk and stomped on in most of their lousy bars. I *know* what this is all about."

"What's it all about?" Eldon asked.

"Well, if you think Archie Loris turned out bad—"

"Loris started bad, from what I can tell."

"—consider how many more high school athletes will wind up that way if there are casinos around here," McFee said.

"Jocks are stiffs, anyhow," Eldon said.

"They're a precious national resource," McFee said. "Loris weighed in at a cool two-twenty in high school. He was a South Coast football god of his day. He died weighing four-fifty-two, an overloaded blimp fit only for the non-American sport of sumo— maybe."

Eldon doubted that Archie had gained two hundred pounds in local card rooms, but he said, "The seven deadly sins, right."

McFee glowered up at him. "Look how the Japanese have taken over the car industry. I don't want to have to cover sumo. I may have to vote Republican in '80."

"Don't do that."

"I'll do what's necessary." McFee's fingers flew across the keys of his typewriter. He was a flawless typist since he had stopped drinking. "I haven't lectured my readers on clean livin' since the last Pioneer Days Festival."

"When Paavo the Finn tried to kill you."

"That's what got me on the wagon. Nothing like a close brush with death." McFee blinked his huge blue eyes. "So what's eating you?"

"Uh, what?"

"You want to get something off your chest."

"How do you know?"

"Because you're hovering," McFee said. "Usually, you're glued to that phone the second you walk in here, even this late. And because I've seen that kind of look before—at church."

"It's not a drinking problem," Eldon blurted out.

McFee nodded. "So talk."

"Cards," Eldon said quietly, thankful they were alone.

"Cards?"

"I'm worried I might be a compulsive gambler."

"Yeah?" McFee peered at him with interest.

"Don't look at me that way. I'm not a bug."

"It's just that I never met one before."

"I want to talk. I want a burger."

McFee jumped down from his chair. "Let's do that. The column'll keep awhile."

There were no hamburger establishments handy, but the Timber Topper nearby served broasted chicken.

Eldon launched into his story as they walked there through the rain. It sounded crazier the longer he talked: dead giant pimps, women lawyers doing card tricks, gay piano players, and card-room intrigue. The downpour had slackened. Lights reflected off the wet street and store window displays, throwing ominous glints upon chainsaws, truck tires, rock crystal jewelry, and myrtlewood salad bowls.

Eldon told McFee about his bet with Melissa.

"—and so there I was, in this three-way poker game, interrogating Clete and trying to outguess Melissa *and* Art Nola, and Art wasn't even there. Gordon and I cooked up this scheme where he'll bankroll me in the card rooms while I do an investigative story. Melissa knows about that deal but not officially. By the end of the night I wasn't sure if I was coming or going."

"Or if Melissa was impressed," McFee observed, jumping over a puddle.

"I think she cheats at cards," Eldon said.

"But in a good cause." McFee threw Eldon a wink. "Love."

"Chasing women always got you in trouble."

"Drinking's what got me in trouble," McFee said firmly. "And the girls had to be tall. They still do. Point is, I'd been carrying on like that since puberty—maybe since before puberty. How long have you been worrying about all this?"

"Well . . . just since I made that bet."

"Doesn't sound *too* serious, Eldon."

They reached the Timber Topper. An ax was imbedded in the tavern's door. McFee seized the haft and pulled, and they went inside.

The place smelled of old cigarettes and flat beer. It was nearly empty of its redneck clientele—maybe because it was a week night or maybe because the Timber Topper didn't offer social gaming, Eldon thought. The jukebox was mercifully silent.

"Hey, Bucky," McFee called, "couple o' He-Man Chicken Baskets, if ya would." They sat in one of the dark booths beneath a neon sign advertising Blitz beer. "You've never had this problem before?" McFee asked.

"No. Cards used to bore me."

"How d'you feel when you play?"

"How do you mean?"

"Do you sweat, get nervous, start gulping alcohol, stuff like that?" McFee gave an evil grin. "Do you get kind of an *erotic* thrill out of it?"

"No! Of course not."

"But now you can't stop when you play?"

"Uh, maybe I just *think* about not stopping. I mean, suppose I really couldn't?"

"Then I suppose you'd be a compulsive gambler. But it doesn't sound like you are. That kind of problem doesn't usually spring full-blown from the brow of Zeus, y'know—I'm here to tell ya."

"Ambrose, I hate losing."

"You wouldn't be much of a reporter if you didn't," McFee said. "D'you want to talk to the priest? Monsignor Stonum helped me a lot."

"I don't want to go back to church."

"Oh, well! Here's the chicken. Thanks, Bucky."

The bartender set down bright plastic baskets lined with waxed paper and filled with chicken so overcooked that the skin was hard as greasy slate. French fries were heaped alongside, garnished with little white foil ketchup packets.

McFee tore open his packets and squirted ketchup over his fries, then picked up a drumstick and chomped it.

"It's like I'm about to jump into a pool of sharks," Eldon went on.

"Well, you've got a lot riding on this story," McFee said.

"I *want* to jump in."

"Your problem isn't cards, it's this woman, Melissa."

"She's worth it." Eldon didn't know how much better McFee's observation made him feel. "I've got to go through with this, and I don't want to make a fool of myself."

"Well, if you figure out how not to, let me know, because you'll be the first," McFee said.

Eldon brightened a little. "If Simon Blood comes through, my problems are solved. Thanks for his phone number, by the way."

"What about Simon?"

"He's trying to trace Loris's killer." Eldon explained about the topiary organizations. "I might be able to unravel Archie's mob ties."

"That would make the casino petition look like a sideshow."

"Look, when is your column going to run?"

"Day after tomorrow."

"Rewrite it," Eldon said. "I found out today that the card-room owners and Archie had a dummy company to launder the take." He laid out the details of the lien scheme to McFee. "I was going to wait on using it, but Melissa knows about it now, too. Put it in your column."

"That's a nice little scoop." McFee giggled like a delighted little vampire preparing to sup. "I can already hear 'em squeal when I call 'em up for comment."

"It'll keep the story alive while I wait on Simon. And if you're the one calling for comment, they won't pay attention to me while I hang around the card rooms."

"Don't mention it. . . . You know, Eldon, if you were a compulsive gambler, I don't think you'd be trying to torpedo a proposal to bring more gambling to this town."

"I don't know if it's a rational thing like that."

"Oh, I used to attend the opening of every new bar," McFee said. "Mostly to get the free beer, of course. Listen, is there much chance it was simply the local card-room operators who had Archie killed?"

"I doubt it. They've got a fat setup."

"Unless fat Archie was squeezing 'em too hard. Kill Loris, absorb his operation and profits, and accept the thanks of a grateful community."

"If it was local, Art Nola would've made a pinch by now," Eldon said. "And this petition campaign wouldn't make sense; Archie was in on the casino-zone idea from the first."

"And safer." McFee took a crunchy bite of chicken and followed it with fries. "Wonder who exactly did kill Archie?"

Eldon shook his head and followed suit. *And safer,* he repeated to himself with a little chill. There it was: big money on the table and a wild card somewhere in the deck. Had he learned enough poker to find it?

19

The next morning was sunny. Eldon felt better, more confident. He'd slept like a log, thanks to his talk with McFee and a stomachful of chicken and fries.

I can go fishing if this weather holds, Eldon thought as he started the Isetta to go to work. Maybe Simon can join me.

He tightened the eight ball on the gear shift, threw the car into gear, and hurtled downhill. The Isetta rocked and bounced as he sped for the flats. Eldon hit the brakes at the bottom of the hill and stopped with a satisfying squeal of rubber and a scary shimmy. Wait—was that a rattle?

He gunned the engine and abruptly turned left. Maybe he could shake something loose. He rocketed across the Wapello Slough Bridge and up Bayside Drive.

A police siren blasted. Eldon saw flashing red and blue lights in the rearview mirror. He'd blundered into a speed trap. He hastily prepared excuses as he looked for a place to pull over. The patrol car pulled abreast as Eldon slowed. The deputy inside beckoned him to follow.

I'm not going to get a ticket, Eldon realized. There must be a big accident up the road. A high-speed escort to the scene is first-class service.

He hung on the patrol car's bumper all through town, trying vainly to spot the flares and emergency lights ahead that would mark the accident. At the north end of town, they slowed and headed into the warehouse district.

The deputy turned down a side street that Eldon didn't know. He made another turn and then another, bouncing through water-filled chuckholes. Then they were driving along a chain-link fence enclosing a disorderly potted garden and metal sheds—Simon Blood's nursery. The deputy had taken a short cut.

The patrol car halted at the nursery gate, its siren winding down to a growl. Art Nola waited there as another deputy stretched yellow crime-scene tape across the entrance.

Eldon's stomach churned as he parked and opened the Isetta's door. Now he was aware of every bit of greasy chicken he had eaten the night before.

"Blood's dead, Eldon," Nola said.

Eldon clutched the fence. "What happened?"

"Murdered. Shot through the head. You don't want to see."

Eldon struggled to focus. "Why'd that deputy bring me here?"

"I sent him to your house after you. I have questions."

"Questions?"

"I found the body," Nola said. "I read your story about the topiary and came over to talk to Blood. I figured—"

"—that if you could trace the topiary, you could trace the killer," Eldon said. "So did I. That's what Blood was doing for me."

"What did he find out? And don't say 'confidential source' or I'll run you in."

"He didn't find anything. Or hadn't yet. He was going to call me if he did."

"The office has been ransacked," Nola said. "It's supposed to look like robbery, but I don't think so. We don't know if anything's missing yet."

"There's a file folder from the public library. It's full of stuff about topiary associations."

"Would you know it if you saw it?"

"I guess so—"

"It's chaos in there," Nola said. "You could spot it faster because you've seen it—if you want to go in. I won't make you."

"I'll go in. I've got to cover the story."

"Call in someone else from the *Sun*."

Eldon tried to work saliva into his dry throat. "I'm not just playing reporter, y'know."

"All right, then. We've covered him up." Art ducked under the tape and headed for the nursery office.

Eldon followed. But the sense of distance that insulated him at murder scenes did not take hold. His feet crunched on something; he looked down to see that he was walking on pieces of a shattered teapot. Tears stung his eyes.

Nola came back and grasped Eldon's arm. "You don't have to do this."

"Just let me get my breath."

"You're hyperventilating, trying too hard."

"It's not as if his face is burned off."

Nola looked at him oddly. "Let me help you. Try not to touch anything."

He guided Eldon into the office.

The disarray didn't register for a moment. Then Eldon saw things all too clearly. The desk was overturned, its drawers scattered and broken. Papers, pencils, gardening magazines, and broken packets of seeds covered the floor. The telephone was smashed.

The hotplate on which Blood prepared tea lay in a corner, still plugged in. The red-hot element had scorched some paint. The Union Jack had been ripped from the wall.

A pair of feet in tooled cowboy boots stuck out from behind the desk. Both boots pointed to the right. Eldon forced in a deep breath and stepped around the desk. A sprawled form lay covered by the Union Jack. There was blood on the flag—but not so very much, Eldon thought with surprise. An arm in a bright plaid shirtsleeve was flung out to one side.

Eldon stared at the waxy hand. "Do you want me to identify him?"

"Not necessary," Nola said. "Why don't you look for that folder?"

"That flag. He was an American citizen."

"It's all we had to cover him with."

Eldon pulled his eyes from the shrouded form and looked carefully around the room, trying to spot the folder. "I don't see the file. He might have taken it home. . . . "

"His wife says not," Nola said.

"He had a *wife?*" Blood had never mentioned a wife. "Kids?"

"No kids."

"No kids," Eldon repeated, pulling out his notebook. "What did they shoot him with?"

"A handgun," Nola said. "I'd say a .38. We'll have to wait for the autopsy to be sure, of course."

"They shot him in the head, you said. How many times?"

"Just once."

"Where?"

"You don't need to—"

"Where?"

"Between the eyes, Eldon."

"Fiske will want a photo," Eldon said. "Well, the hell with him today."

"Why don't you come outside?" Nola asked. "Thanks for looking around."

Sackett Lake is all mine, Eldon thought bleakly. "We were going to go fishing."

He looked again at Blood's waxy hand. He remembered the hand alive and holding a string of fish, remembered it handing him a cup of hot tea, remembered it stroking topiary. Suddenly, the chicken and fries started coming up. He got outside just in time.

He threw himself against the building and vomited. The world contracted, then finally unclenched. He stared at the ground and gasped for breath. You barely knew him, Eldon thought, stunned by his own violent reaction. But Blood . . . was a fisherman.

Eldon almost laughed at the absurdity. Yet that was what was at the bottom of it. You liked him better than you knew, he told himself as a rope of sour drool ran from his mouth. He heard a car pull up and the door open and slam. Eldon looked up to see Melissa staring at him.

He croaked in humiliation. Melissa dashed inside. Eldon pressed his cheek against the cool, damp wall. Slowly the cramps ebbed, replaced by fury and shame. The same M.O. as Archie, he thought. Shot close up.

Melissa returned. "Eldon. You're sick—"

Eldon straightened and wiped his mouth. "He got killed because of me—and you."

"What the hell do you mean?"

"He didn't even know about our bet."

"Hush." Melissa glanced back; Nola had come to loiter in the doorway.

Art's ears are all too keen, Eldon thought, as his cherished sense of clarity rescued him at last. "Come with me." He headed for the topiary shed.

"What is it?" Melissa demanded, following.

Eldon rounded the shed. Blood's topiary menagerie stood as he remembered it. No, something was different. . . .

"Did the dead man make these?" Melissa asked.

"Shh." That was it—the sea serpent's long rippling body had been pushed slightly askew.

Obscene topiary, Eldon thought suddenly, with an electric sensation. That's how the killer got close to Archie. Archie loved dirty images. Statues. Porno tapes. He didn't stir from his house, so people had to bring him things. Girls. Porno. Topiary.

Someone had brought Archie an immensely filthy Hummel, formed from shrubbery with the shotgun inside somehow. And there had to be a trail.

He felt Melissa's gaze as he studied the topiary; it felt as if a surgeon was about to graze the hairs on the back of his neck with a scalpel. This is what she's like in court, he thought. This is the real game for her, not poker. For me, too. Well, I'll give her something to chew on.

He examined the hedge. What the hell was he looking for? He ran his hands along the serpent's mossy body and then he found it—a patch of moss and wire about an inch on a side was missing from an inconspicuous spot.

"A sample's been taken." Eldon grabbed the topiary frog. "This one, too—see the inside of the frog's right leg? And the dolphin's tail has a notch clipped out of it—"

Melissa grabbed Eldon's shoulder. "Don't touch any more. You've made your point."

"Can you lift fingerprints off topiary?" Eldon asked.

"I'd like to try," answered another, familiar voice.

Eldon looked up to see Art Nola. "All you need to find is—"

"A topiary expert who likes firearms," Nola said.

"The FBI'll help you now," Eldon said.

"You can help, too," Nola replied. "Can you remember anything about those brochures? Names of organizations, anything? It'll save us legwork if you can."

"I can't remember names," Eldon said. "They were all over the country—California and New York. The Midwest, too. Archie had Chicago connections—"

"That big nursery in Medford might have that information," Melissa said. "Jackson and Perkins."

"Good thinking," Nola said. "Eldon—don't put anything about

the topiary in the paper. The killer'll read it and know we're onto him."

"No deal. I'm not keeping this out of the paper. I owe it to Simon."

"You'll let the louse that killed him get away."

Eldon didn't respond. Nola regarded him intently. He'd love to make me back down, Eldon thought.

"I'll call Jimbo Fiske," Nola said.

"Be my guest!" Eldon wondered what Fiske would say.

"I'll call him now." Nola left the shed.

"Want to call off the bet?" Melissa asked after Nola's footsteps had crunched away. "You can't beat the FBI."

"The bet's still on," Eldon said. "I wonder how much longer before Art figures out about you and me?"

"He doesn't care," Melissa said. "He cares about this case, though. I was wrong about that."

"I told you about Br'er Fox," Eldon said.

"So you did. What are you going to do?"

Eldon tried to keep his voice level. "My gambling stories will be a memorial to Simon. I'm calling Gordon Clete right away."

"Better hold off—"

"I'm not laying off this story!"

"I don't mean that," Melissa said. "Think it through. Someone kills Archie Loris. Then the attack on Stephanie. Now Simon Blood's dead. They all got close to this case. Gordon had better lie low for a while."

"Maybe you're right."

"Loris and Blood are similar M.O.s. The Hosfelder beating is completely different. But they're all connected."

"They're connected by the topiary," Eldon said. "And the killer's still in town."

"He stuck around to kill Blood, anyway," Melissa said.

"I'll warn Gordon. But I won't back off on the coverage."

"I'm worried about you. Writing more stories might be danger-ous."

Eldon wanted to give a devil-may-care grin but managed only a grimace. "All part of my romantic occupation, ma'am. Nobody kills cops or reporters. It causes too much trouble."

They both looked uneasily at the topiary menagerie.

Eldon tried to start writing his story in his head as he drove back to the *Sun*. But it was no use; he would have to do it on paper. He had written stories before about murder victims that he had met while they were alive—but never about one whom he had known well enough to like. He caressed the eight ball with a wet palm.

He was still unsteady when he entered the newsroom. Fiske was pacing the floor, working his hand exerciser and slapping his thigh with his copy of *Sasquatch and UFO*.

"We're putting it all in," Fiske announced.

"Art Nola called you," Eldon said.

"Art called me and the sheriff called me. I bet the FBI calls, too."

"What did you tell them?"

"That we're in the news business."

"Thanks, Jimbo."

"It's good copy. Did you get any pictures?"

"No." Eldon wet his lips. The taste of vomit was still in his mouth. "Simon was a dedicated fisherman. A damn good guy."

Fiske stopped. "You knew this guy?"

"Yeah. . . . I never saw a friend dead before."

"Must've been rough." Fiske resumed pacing. "Never mind the pictures. I sent Frank over there. He'll handle the story."

"I want to write it."

"And I want you objective," Fiske said. "You can't cover this. Type up your notes and put 'em on Frank's desk. I have something else in mind for you."

Eldon took a deep breath. He wasn't sure he could get through writing the story anyway. "Okay. You're right. But I get to write Simon's obit when the time comes."

"The obit's yours."

"Thanks, Jimbo." Eldon went to his desk and rolled a newsprint

sheet into his typewriter. Fiske started circling the desk. Slap-slap-
slap went the magazine.

Eldon tuned Fiske out and wrote several paragraphs on separate
sheets of newsprint; Frank could paste them into the sequence of
his story as he saw fit. His stomach twisted as he described the
murder scene, but he managed it. Frank'll need this, Eldon
thought. Art won't let any more press inside the nursery, now that
we don't play footsie.

Eldon typed:

> Samples had been cut from topiary figures at Blood's
> nursery. Nola refused to comment on the possible sig-
> nificance or whether Blood's murder was connected to
> the pimp's. . . .

Fiske intercepted the sheet as Eldon pulled it from the typewriter. "What *is* the significance?"

"They're connected—but I couldn't get that on the record.
Blood was trying to find out for me who made the topiary. It
might've led us straight to the killer."

"You never said. What did he find?"

"Er, nothing—" Eldon hesitated.

"Well?"

"I *did* get the connection on the record, kind of. Melissa told
me—"

"Then put it in. I'll have Frank play it up high."

The phone rang on the news desk. Fiske rushed off. Eldon
cranked another sheet into his typewriter, sorry now that he'd
opened his mouth. He and Melissa had merely been talking. He
hadn't actually *told* her he was writing a story. He wasn't obliged
to warn her, of course.

Defiance welled up in him. She knew why I was there, he
thought. We both were at the scene of a murder in our official
capacities. What does she expect?

Eldon wrote:

A Nekaemas County deputy district attorney linked Blood's murder to that of Archie Loris and to the near-fatal beating of a prostitute in Port Jerome.

Melissa Lafky said at the scene that topiary was the likely connection in the killings. Spattered topiary was found at the Loris murder. Blood was a topiary expert, and samples had been taken from topiary figures growing at Blood's nursery. . . .

I won't mention the topiary file that Simon got from the library, Eldon decided. I'll give 'em that much—for now.

Melissa would be mad as hell. Eldon grinned. Upping the ante.

"You done yet?" Fiske came over to collect the copy. "I'm running your restaurant review today. Finally got some space inside."

"Good." Eldon got the Medford telephone directory and looked up the number of the Jackson and Perkins nursery. He called the nursery and in a short discussion learned a disappointing truth: Jackson and Perkins specialized in roses. Topiary wasn't their thing at all.

That's that, Eldon thought as he hung up the phone.

"You don't look so happy, Eldon," Fiske said. "I'm not happy, either."

"Thanks, Jimbo. That's nice of you to say."

Fiske walked over holding the Lucite cube in which he had sealed his pipe. "I shouldn't've done this, Eldon. My wife liked this pipe."

"I thought you two were on a health kick."

"She says I don't smell right without smoking my pipe."

"Get another pipe. She'll get used to it."

"It's not the pipe. Microbiotic eatin' has changed my metabolism. I smell different."

"I don't smell anything."

"If I start another pipe, God knows what I'd smell like—like a sasquatch, maybe." Fiske held up *Sasquatch and UFO*. "Bigfoot's microbiotically correct smell keeps off predators."

"Nothing's eaten you yet," Eldon pointed out.

"That might be only a matter of time," Fiske said. "That's why I want you to look into—red tide."

"What?" For a moment, Eldon could think only of communist invaders.

"Red tide is killer parasites, borne on the ocean waves—affects oysters and clams." Fiske tossed *Sasquatch and UFO* on the desk. "The background's in here."

"I know about red tide. I thought this was the New Age issue."

"The Maya calendar is the cornerstone of the New Age," Fiske replied. "It connects everything: chaos cycles, dinosaur extinctions, plate tectonics, microbiotics. What it all adds up to is red tide at any time. Get out to the boat basin and talk to the oyster farmers."

"If we had a red tide, there'd be a statewide health alert."

"You gotta help me, Eldon. This could make or break me."

"What're you talking about?" Eldon watched beads of sweat break out on Fiske's forehead. "Are you okay?"

"My wife and I are at a delicate point," Fiske said.

"You've been married for years. You're rediscovering love."

"That's what I mean. The oysters."

"The oysters?" Eldon's disturbed stomach rumbled in warning.

"They're a powerful aphrodisiac. If a red tide destroys the oysters now, I'm as good as finished."

Eldon wanted to flee the newsroom, into the sunlight and fresh air. And maybe to vomit again. "Yeah. Okay. Sure."

"Good man. I—" The telephone rang on the news desk and Fiske sprinted to answer it. *"Sun.* Jimbo." He clapped his hand over the receiver and whispered delightedly, "It's my *wife!"*

Fiske began chattering to his beloved like a schoolboy.

Eldon called the Pacific Fishery Management Council in Portland and the National Oceanic and Atmospheric Administration in Seattle. Both said there was no sign of red tide.

I've got to go see Gordon, he thought. I've got to tell him that the plan's off. I can't risk his life the way I did Simon's.

He dialed Gordon's number but got no answer. He's probably at the college, teaching, Eldon thought. He said not to contact him there, but this is an emergency.

Eldon picked up his notebook and camera and waved good-bye to Fiske, mouthing the words "oyster ranch." Fiske shooed him out, still wrapped up on the phone with his wife.

Eldon started the Isetta and aimed it for the community college. But first he would go to the hospital and look in on Stephanie.

The hospital's corridors had the same dreary look in broad daylight that they'd had in the middle of the night. Maybe it was the lighting and maybe it was the smell of the antiseptic.

"I'd like to get the condition of a patient," Eldon told the businesslike woman at the reception desk.

"Name?"

"Stephanie Hosfelder." Eldon spelled it.

"You're a relative?"

"Eldon Larkin from the *Sun*."

The operator made a call, spoke briefly with someone. "She's out of intensive care—"

"Excellent!"

"—and listed in serious condition."

"Can I see her?"

"No visitors."

"What room is she in?"

"We can't give out that information."

"But I can check back on her condition?"

"Yes, certainly."

"Well, thanks."

"You're welcome."

Eldon strolled away, intending to head to the main offices, where he would demand to see the hospital administrator. But a perverse sense of reportorial aggression sent him instead to the gift shop. There he bought an inexpensive arrangement of dried flowers and a get-well card. He peeked out of the shop to make sure that the receptionist's attention was elsewhere, then headed down the hall into the hospital.

He wandered from nursing station to nursing station, asking in an amiable and confused way for Stephanie Hosfelder's room and proffering the dried flowers. A nurse made a call to get the room number and directed him to the third floor via the elevator.

He stepped out of the elevator and practically into the arms of a deputy sheriff. The deputy was leaning on the nursing-station counter, chatting up a slender nurse with a long nose and dyed blonde hair worn in an early-1960s flip. The deputy was the same one who had met Eldon in the emergency ward the night Stephanie had been brought in.

"Hey, Eldon," the deputy said. "That for me?"

"For Stephanie. I hear she's better."

"No visitors," the nurse said.

"She's under police guard," the deputy said. "I can't let you in there. Sorry."

"Can't I just give her these?" Eldon asked.

The nurse checked her watch. "I'll take them in to her. It's time for her shot."

Eldon handed over the flowers and card. "How's she doing?"

"Better." The nurse went down the hall.

Eldon and the deputy watched the nurse's trim backside until Eldon asked him, "What's 'better'? Is she conscious?"

"On and off," the deputy said. "She's pretty weak."

"I've got to talk to her."

"And put it in the paper? The sheriff 'ud have my badge."

"She was asking for me the night she came in."

"She ain't asked for you since."

"Aw, I wouldn't—"

"Off the record?" the deputy asked.

"Yeah! That's good enough—"

"I mean me, not her," the deputy said. "Off the record, Eldon, it's not going to do you any good to talk to her. She doesn't remember anything."

"What? Amnesia?"

"Naw, she knows who she is. She just doesn't remember anything past the afternoon of the day she got creamed. Bad concussion, knocked out the short-term memory."

"Like an auto accident," Eldon said.

"That's affirmative. We don't even know if she can identify her assailant."

"Has she said anything about a videotape?"

"You mean the tape Art Nola's looking for? Now, how'd you find out about that?"

"I talked about it with Art," Eldon evaded. "Has Art questioned her yet?"

The deputy shook his head. "She's in no shape to talk to anybody. We're going to sit with her until she is—and make sure nothing happens to her in the meantime. Know what I mean?"

"I think so." Eldon said. That means the killer's still around. This is mob stuff, all right. And I bet I know where Chump-Change is: with the shotgun at the bottom of Nekaemas Bay or filling a shallow hole out in the woods.

The nurse returned. "Her vital signs are better."

"Thanks for taking in the flowers," Eldon said.

"I'm sure she appreciates them," the nurse said.

"I might come around again," Eldon said.

"We'll be here," the deputy said affably. He and the nurse exchanged smiles.

Eldon went back into the elevator and enviously waved goodbye as the doors closed. He had never had the knack of chatting up women. He was sure that the nurse wouldn't have given him the time of day, socially speaking. I'm not macho enough, he thought as the elevator descended. Maybe I should buy some jeans that are too tight for me and sling them under my belly, to get in the swing of things.

He had not yet stooped to that; his clothes were shabby but at least they fit. And he'd acted resourcefully just now. That made him feel like eating something at last. He went to the hospital cafeteria and bought shredded wheat and milk. He sat at a Formica-topped table, chewing and taking stock.

A police guard on Stephanie—the search for the killer was still hot! But there seemed to be no way to get hold of the mysterious videotape; and without Stephanie's help—which might never be forthcoming—he might never understand its significance.

I've lost the bet, Eldon thought.

Strangely, the realization gave him a lift. A burden had vanished. It was like the time he'd realized that he wouldn't take Bernice back if she had turned up on his doorstep.

It's just me and my notebook and my fishing rod, Eldon decided. Back to basics.

He was free to cover the story as he found it. Explore the card rooms. That would be good copy. The murders would make a nice sleazy background on which to pin the card-room owners. He'd make the stories real shame-of-our-city stuff, teach the rednecks some standards at last. He owed Simon that much.

Eldon realized bleakly that Dr. Rosenak soon would be cutting up Simon's body. He tried not to visualize the slashing autopsy cuts, the extraction and dissection of Simon's brain and organs. But Rosenak might recover the bullet that had killed Simon. And that could be enough to trace the killer.

The chance remained that Eldon might turn up something leading to the killer through Gordon's contacts. Not that they were promising—odds were he'd get only rumors, suppositions, blue-sky fantasy, and outright lies. Still, he might come up with something solid on the murders, which would still mean a win with Melissa.

Eldon felt better as he ate the shredded wheat. He just might still be in there swinging.

20

The Nekaemas Community College campus was pleasant, with low, sprawling stucco buildings and well-groomed lawns. Eldon had spent little time here; schools were Marsha's beat. I may have to amend my habits, he thought, admiring some of the women students as he hurried along. I should come out here and find some feature stories.

It was lunchtime. Students lolled on the lawn eating, talking, and playing guitars. It reminded Eldon of idyllic days in Berkeley. A *Sun* delivery truck pulled up to the student union. The driver loaded the day's edition into the dispenser box there and drove off.

Eldon bought a paper. The story of Blood's murder was splashed across the top of the front page. Eldon forced himself to read with a critical eye. Frank had done a good job of melding his own reporting and Eldon's into a comprehensive story. Eldon saw that Frank hadn't picked up much additional information at the murder scene—but he had tackled the unenviable job of interviewing Blood's widow.

I couldn't have done that, Eldon thought and stopped reading. It was the first time he'd thought such a thing about a news story. Was he losing his edge?

He had to find Gordon. He got directions to the music building and headed up a winding path, the paper tucked under his arm. He walked briskly, puffing a little, and found Gordon lounging on a bench under a tree in front of the building, talking earnestly with a young man with a rucksack and drinking from a tall waxed-paper cup.

The student looked at Eldon curiously as he bustled up.

Eldon realized that he was breathless and a little flushed.

Gordon broke into a pleased grin and raised the cup in a toast. "Eldon—this is a surprise. Sit down, *mon ami*. Jim, you must excuse us."

The student looked amused as he collected his rucksack and moved off.

"Toi et moi sommes déjà notoire," Gordon said. "You and I are notorious already."

"Cut the crap," Eldon said in English.

"Want some iced tea?" Gordon indicated a camp thermos beside the bench and more cups.

"Yes. I'm thirsty." Eldon handed over the newspaper as Gordon drew the tea. "That man was my source. My friend," Eldon said. He snatched the cup, took a slug of iced tea, rinsed his mouth, and spat the tea on the grass.

Gordon's smile died as he read the murder story. "Being your friend can be hazardous."

"Simon got too close to the Loris case."

Gordon nodded. "Same as Stephanie. It's obvious."

"We've got to drop the card-room project," Eldon said. "I can't ask you to take the chance."

"Not on your life," Gordon said. "I owe Stephanie." Then Gordon winked and added, "I can't come on too holy. This is going to be fun. I told you I like dirty deals."

"Don't make light of it."

"I'm not. Have some more tea." Gordon took Eldon's cup and carefully poured. "I've kept my ears open in the card rooms."

"I thought people were too scared to talk."

"They were for a while. But people read the newspapers, even in the gutter."

"I should post that over the door of the *Sun*."

"They read about the case, and they're angry and scared over what happened to Stephanie. Why keep your mouth shut when they're going to get you anyway?"

"What'd they say? Will anyone talk for print?"

"Not yet. . . . But they say the killer's still around."

"That's out-of-date information," Eldon said wearily. "It's obvious, because he killed Simon Blood to cover up his trail. But now he's gone—he has to be, because there's nobody else connected with the case that he needs to kill."

"They say he wants something—badly."

"The videotape, of course," Eldon said.

"If the tape's important, then your friend at the nursery was in the wrong place at the wrong time." Gordon studied the *Sun* again. "Killing someone for topiary is damned weird. Now I see why you asked me about it—"

Eldon nearly choked on his tea. "Good God."

"You okay?" Gordon asked.

" 'Killing someone for topiary . . . ' " Goosebumps rose on Eldon's skin despite the warm day. *"That's* why the killer's still hanging around—not because of the tape. To get more topiary. That's why he took the topiary samples at Simon's."

"He killed your man because of a *plant?"*

"He took cuttings at Simon's nursery," Eldon said. "He knew about the nursery because I quoted Simon in a story about the Loris killing, about the topiary they found in Archie's kitchen."

"Simon's topiary—was it special? Was it rare?"

"No, it just takes a knack to grow and shape." Eldon stared at the pleasant surroundings, the sun-dappled trees, the green lawns, and the strolling students. His skin crawled. He thought again of his theory that Loris's killer had used a topiary statue to get into range.

"I vote we follow the tape," Gordon said. "And don't tell me about risks, Eldon. It was a risk for me to move down here."

Eldon thought it over. At last he said, "All right. When do you play over at the Poke next?"

"In three nights."

"I'll show up then."

"No, pick me up at my place. We'll drive over together. You'll be my very good friend, looking for a good game."

Eldon squirmed. "Well, why do we have to—"

"If they're looking for one thing, they won't see the other," Gordon said. "I just got the idea from that student. We'll let the money do the talking. Archie's money."

"We're going to play this very cool."

"Don't worry. We won't even hold hands."

Eldon drank some more tea to cover his embarrassment. "Oh, I nearly forgot—we ran the review of Oats in the Bowl today. Mentioned your music but not your name."

"Just as well. Seems it doesn't pay to be too prominent."

"No. . . . Listen, *don't* ask any more questions. Don't call attention to yourself in any way."

Gordon put a finger to his lips. "Quiet as a mouse."

"I've got to head out," Eldon said. "Got a story to do about oysters."

"Tu as vraiment un travail intéressant," Gordon said. "You do have an interesting job." He added with wicked enjoyment, *"Les huîtres sont aphrodisiaques, tu sais.* Oysters are an aphrodisiac, you know."

"Yeah, I know," Eldon answered in English. *"Bon jour."*

He headed down the path. He glanced back to see Gordon greeting two more students, a young man and a young woman, and offering them iced tea.

As soon as Eldon had left the campus he was back on the undiluted Oregon South Coast. The college's modern buildings gave way at once to weatherbeaten stores and dwellings along the familiar winding road to the boat basin and the oyster ranch. Their ramshackle condition seemed to symbolize Simon's death. Once you're in Nekaemas County, he thought, there's no way out.

But he perked up when he approached the roadside flea market. The nameless place was housed in a sprawling, tarpaper-faced building. It had been there for years, a jam-packed junk store owned by a grumpy Scotsman whose white beard seemed to bristle with a resentment of its own. Eldon disliked the Scotsman, but the place was great for used books. He would treat himself to one today. An addition to his library could cheer him as readily as a good meal.

A portable marqueelike sign in the junk shop parking lot announced various "bargains." There was a new message on the sign today: VIDEO RENTALS HERE! Big-city technology had reached the South Coast, and it was only 1979. Definitely worth stopping, Eldon thought.

The Scotsman came to the shack's door. He was dressed as usual—a dirty gray sweatshirt and a moth-eaten green plaid kilt. He watched suspiciously as Eldon parked, working his lower jaw back and forth as if grinding sand between his teeth. The Scotsman always did this, as if he thought Eldon planned to steal junk or torch the shack. Eldon had never learned the man's name. The Scotsman's conversational skills largely consisted of pointing in response to inquiries and snarling, "Over there!" He also counted out change, in a tone suggesting that he would rather have his fingernails pulled out.

Eldon nodded to the Scotsman and strolled into the shop, wondering as always what the rough-hewn inhabitants of the South Coast had to say when they saw the Scotsman's kilt. Whatever it was, Eldon suspected that they didn't say it very loud.

There were a half-dozen battered gray plastic suitcases stacked at the counter. Those must be the videocassette recorders, Eldon thought. He got hold of some used machines.

Eldon winced when he saw the steep rental prices. Betamax videocassettes in frayed cardboard sleeves were on display behind the counter's dirty glass—women-in-prison movies, old Westerns, Hammer horror movies, and *The Wild One,* starring Marlon Brando. He resolved to rent a VCR when he could afford it.

He wandered among plank tables piled high with ragged clothes and dented kitchen utensils, to the sagging shelves that held the second-hand books. He had carried off from here Churchill's *The Second World War* in hardback, all six volumes, for twelve dollars. He had once found the big paperback edition of Kenneth Clark's *The Nude: A Study in Ideal Form* in good condition, for a quarter.

Eldon enjoyed the Scotsman's resentment when he unearthed such treasures.

He rooted through the science fiction, enjoying the covers on the dog-eared 1950s- and 1960s-vintage paperbacks and worked his way into the mystery novels. A murder mystery was unappealing in the wake of Simon's death, but Eldon got interested in *The Tularemia Gambit* by a writer named Perry who lived in Port Townsend, Washington. It seemed to be a mystery about disease.

The book was in good shape; Eldon had decided to invest fifty cents in this Northwest writer when a banjo string twanged. He glanced up but saw only the Scotsman, watching to make sure that he wasn't trying to palm the book.

The unseen musical browser plucked out a rickety "Camptown Races"—the tune was just recognizable, for one of the banjo's strings seemed to be missing.

Eldon peeked around the shelf. In the opposite corner of the room, under dusty fan belts hanging from a beam, a squarely built man stood examining a banjo. He wore a porkpie hat and a drab overcoat, like a character in one of the old detective novels on the shelf at Eldon's shoulder.

Eldon stared, for the man held the banjo almost as if it were a rifle, and he looked like something the Scotsman might try to sell: a manikin with pale, dry-looking skin, thin hair, thick-fingered hands with bluish dirty nails, clothes shabby and with a dull, worn sheen—everything about him used, used, and used again, used too much.

The man had a face like moldy Gouda cheese, a cheese that peered with resentful intensity through eyes like flat greenish chips of stone with no luster to them. He stooped and picked something up and shuffled toward the front of the store, holding the old banjo by the neck.

Now, he's a prize, Eldon thought as he watched the man go to the counter. He saw as the man emerged from behind the counter that he also lugged a VCR in its plastic case.

"Did you take that from behind the counter?" the Scotsman

demanded with his usual malevolence. "You can't come behind the counter."

"You went outside," the man replied in a slow, dry voice. "I'm renting it." He held up the banjo. "This is how much?"

"Ten dollars," the Scotsman said.

"How much?" Same slow, dry tone.

"Ten dollars."

"How much?" Same tone—but now the man exuded a palpable air of malice.

The Scotsman shifted uncomfortably, his mean little eyes fixed on those across the counter. "Eight dollars," he said at last. "I need a driver's license for the rental."

"Shit you do." The man shoved his hand into his overcoat pocket. For an irrational moment, Eldon thought he was going to yank out a pistol. What the man did yank out was a wad of greenbacks in a money clip. He tugged out bills in the amount of the VCR rental, wadded each one up, and dropped it on the counter. Then he said, "This is for the banjo." He crumpled three more one-dollar bills, put the money clip away, and picked up the banjo and the VCR case.

The Scotsman said nothing and didn't move. But Eldon saw a tremor in his hands as they gripped the counter.

Met your match for mean, Eldon thought, and stepped up to pay for his book.

The other man stared at Eldon. His lusterless eyes flicked upward and locked. Eldon realized after a moment that the man was staring at his hat, apparently fascinated by the fishing flies there. Then the man turned and went out the door.

I hope I never meet *him* at Sackett Lake, Eldon thought.

The Scotsman snatched up the wadded bills. Then he grabbed *The Tularemia Gambit* and glowered at the fifty-cent price tag. "Seventy-five cents."

Eldon paid and left. He got outside to find that the man with the banjo and the VCR had vanished. He hadn't heard a car pull away.

No one was walking down the road. Becoming invisible is a good trick to know, he thought. I wonder if Melissa can do it.

Eldon didn't call Melissa that day or the next. The bet was history and he was embarrassed. He had talked big and taken a fall.

That night Melissa called him, at home.

Eldon was sitting in his easy chair eating ice cream and reading Verlaine, trying not to think about Simon, when the phone rang. "Yeah?"

"It was a .38 Special," said a woman's voice.

Eldon, still switching over from French, didn't recognize the voice for a moment. *"Qui est-ce*—uh, who is this?"

"Melissa."

"Oh! I didn't realize it was you."

"A million miles away," Melissa said fondly. "Nose in a book."

"Uh, yeah—what was that you said?"

"Blood was killed by a .38 Special," Melissa said. "Rosenak just recovered the bullet."

"Where are you?"

"At the medical examiner's office. The bullet's intact. There's a good, clear set of rifling grooves."

"They can trace the gun, then? Through NCIC?"

"They'll try. It could take weeks. No guarantees."

"Thanks. I wouldn't have known." A white lie—Eldon knew that Rosenak would have tipped him off.

"I haven't heard from you for a couple of days," Melissa said. "Is anything wrong?"

"Yeah—no, I mean. I'm going to the Lucky Poke tomorrow night." Eldon added lightly, "I'll watch out for anyone packing a .38."

"You do that." Melissa paused, then said, "I watched the autopsy. My first."

Eldon shuddered. "You okay?"

"Yeah, I guess. It's part of the job."

"I'll bet you could use a drink, though. Come on over."

"I'll take a rain check," Melissa said in a breathy voice and hung up.

She's playing this for all it's worth, Eldon thought. Really stringing me along.

Clearly Melissa wasn't ready to write off their bet.

She wants to lose, Eldon thought with a pleasant shiver. Or does she? She was "losing" the night we played strip poker. She was "losing" at Oats in the Bowl. This could be another ploy to lead me down the garden path. . . . And I'm enjoying it.

Well, a tip's a tip, Eldon decided and called Frank. The phone rang several times before Frank answered, his voice somewhat breathless.

"Frank—it's Eldon."

"Perfect timing, man. Lemme call you back."

"No, listen—they got the bullet that killed Simon Blood."

"Yeah?" Now Frank was interested.

"It's a .38 Special—"

"Oh, great. That caliber's as common as dirt."

"There's a clear set of rifling grooves on the slug. They're checking them through NCIC. Can you tap some sources?"

"It's tough to get NCIC leaks," Frank said. "The network can trace unauthorized queries back to the source."

"You've got to try. We've got two murders with a similar M.O. and we know the type of gun for one of 'em. Surely someone can—"

"It's a big country with a lot of criminals in it, Eldon." Frank sounded distracted; he was breathing harder. "I'll make some calls."

"Tonight?"

"Tomorrow!" Frank hung up.

Eldon stared out the front window and across the bay, to the north shore where the trees threw long shadows in the evening light. That gun exists *somewhere,* he thought. And so does this topiarist. If I can put them together, I might have a winning hand.

═══21═══

Frank called back in the morning, while Eldon was eating cereal for breakfast. "Chicago's two hours ahead," Frank explained. "Got an early start, thanks to the time difference."

Eldon heard pots banging in the background. Someone was fixing breakfast at Frank's place.

"Tracing that pistol panned out," Frank said.

"So soon? Hey, all right!"

"I learned that Art sent a query to Chicago. The Chicago people tapped other sources on his behalf. Since these were authorized queries, my pal on the Chicago paper got a look at 'em at his end, through his sources."

"Yeah? And?"

"The riflings match a revolver used in a hit on a crooked contractor named Lizzio in DeKalb, Illinois, in 1968. The gun's a Smith and Wesson Model 10. It was made in 1925, according to the serial number."

"That's a classic piece."

"And how. It's a New York Police Department service revolver that went missing in 1944."

"How'd it get out of NYPD's hands?"

"The cop who owned it died in '44," Frank said. "The gun apparently went to his son in the Navy, who then was killed in the Philippines. After that, who knows?"

"And the gun finally turns up here," Eldon said.

"The 1968 case was never solved," Frank said. "But the M.O. resembled the Loris and Blood killings. The Lizzio hit also resembled some other unsolved hits in the Midwest, including a couple of Chicago bookies. Different weapons were used in those, but the upshot was the Chicago cops got four suspects."

"Any of 'em know about topiary?"

"Not that I heard," Frank said. "Two are doing life in Joliet, making furniture. One's on the street but had an alibi. The fourth one's been dead for years. They didn't question him, needless to say."

"Was he dead before or after that '68 hit?"

"After. Poisoned."

"Poisoned?"

"He had gambling debts. And guess what?"

"What?"

"He knew Archie Loris. Worked with him, you might say."

"Worked with him how?"

"Well, remember the prostitute who led to Archie's downfall in Chicago? The one he beat on with the banjo?"

"Yeah—"

"She was in this guy's stable. The poisoned guy's."

"Why didn't you say, dammit?" Eldon cried.

"Just laying the cards down one at a time," Frank said cheerfully, "to make the relationships clear."

"But you've got details? Names, dates, places, so forth?"

"You bet."

"Put 'em on my desk because—"

"—this is *good copy!*" they yelled together.

"It's perfect," Eldon said. "Simon's killed by this pistol after asking questions about Archie's murder, which is tied to the mob. We'll run this story. I'll start in on the card-room investigation and use it as the follow-up to whatever Nola runs down. It just might all connect."

"Ah, my breakfast is ready," Frank answered. "Grapefruit, eggs over easy, bacon, toast with marmalade, coffee. What're you having?"

"Cold cereal, you bastard."

"That's not macrobiotic," Frank said with a chuckle. "See you at the office."

"Just be sure you're there on time. . . . Who's cooking over there?" Eldon wondered suddenly if it was Melissa.

"My librarian friend," Frank answered. "She was very discouraged about the loss of the topiary resource file. She sought consolation."

"That doesn't matter now."

By Eldon Larkin
Sun *Staff Writer*

CHICAGO—A pistol used to kill a Port Jerome nursery operator has been linked to a mob-related murder in Illinois 11 years ago.

Police in Chicago said ballistics records showed that the revolver that killed Simon Blood at his nursery was the same weapon used to kill Thomas M. "Palermo Tommy" Lizzio, a contractor and underworld figure, in DeKalb, Ill., in 1968. Lizzio was an underworld associate of Archie Loris, the 452-pound Port Jerome high school football-player-turned-pimp who was murdered in his Scoquel home. Police say the killing of Loris also was mob-related. . . .

"Dee-de-dee!" said Fiske. "Just like Eliot Ness."

Eldon decided it was time to strike. "I need more money to gamble."

"No way. You've got money left."

"But we've got to hit this hard, Jimbo!"

"What d'you plan to do? Hand out bribes?"

"I plan to play cards."

"Make do with what ya have. And I haven't forgotten about the red tide."

"Or plate tectonics. Or Bigfoot."

"Both those subjects led to some *good copy,* y' know."

"I just wish I hadn't lost so much skin the times they did," Eldon said.

Frank came over to Eldon's desk, pushing his glasses up his nose. "How's it going?"

"I've got to find those topiary brochures," Eldon said. "They don't have extra copies or anything?"

"What they had was in the file, I guess."

Marsha strolled over. "Try *The Encyclopedia of Associations.*"

"You're kidding," Eldon said. "I never heard of it."

"It's got every association that you ever heard of."

"Including topiary?"

"Including gardening, anyway. I was a librarian once."

"I'd have taken you for one if I didn't know you were a journalist," Eldon said sincerely.

"I was a library aide, really. I shelved books and catalogued things while I went to school."

Eldon blinked. "Thank you, Marsha. That's worth a try."

"You are the sort of person who can sometimes use guidance, Eldon."

"Frank, call your girlfriend," Eldon said.

Frank grabbed the phone. A few moments later he looked up with a grin. "They've got it, all right."

"I'll go over after deadline," Eldon said.

"I'll go now," Marsha said.

Eldon arrived at the library to find Marsha thumbing through a big blue book.

"Here it is," she said.

"Look up gardening associations in Illinois. Illinois is where Archie started. Got to start somewhere."

The encyclopedia mainly listed trade and professional organizations. Among them were professional gardeners' associations, including some for Illinois.

Eldon wrote down the phone numbers and hiked back to the

newsroom. He began making calls with the usual grab-bag of results. Some numbers had been disconnected. Others did not answer. But Eldon got through in many cases, usually to people in garden stores, and began the tedious process of explaining again and again who he was and what he wanted.

The gardeners could provide little information. Most knew nothing about topiary at all. Others knew about it but weren't in touch with any topiary societies. Eldon exhausted the possibilities in Illinois. His heart sank. He'd hoped for a quick and dirty hit, something in the Chicago area. But his luck wasn't running.

When he ran out of numbers in the Midwest, he'd start on another region of the country. This'll be good for a few days, Eldon thought. There are only forty-nine states to go.

He kept the phone glued to his ear so that Fiske wouldn't bug him about "red tide" as he worked his way east.

He wanted to make as many calls as possible before businesses back there closed for the day. Indiana was the state just east of Illinois. Nothing on Marsha's list for Indiana. Forty-eight states to go. Ohio. He started with a number in Cleveland.

The number rang through to a garden store, where a man with a thick Middle Eastern accent decided that Eldon must be a bill collector. It took several minutes to get that misconception straightened out—or so Eldon thought. He began asking about topiary, carefully enunciating each syllable of the word; the man abruptly said, "Call extension service!" and hung up.

Eldon stared at the receiver. Good God, the guy was right. Fifty state departments of agriculture were at his beck and call.

Eldon glanced at the clock. There was still time. He called Columbus, Ohio, information and got the number of the state agriculture department. He called them and asked for the public affairs office.

The flack there was a jovial man with a twangy accent who told Eldon, "There's a crusty son of a bitch in Dayton who's a topiary freak from way back. Name of Carl Stowe. Used to be a newspaper reporter himself, as a matter of fact. He still writes a garden column for the local paper, smokes awful cigars, has a pet pig. He's into a million scams, including topiary. Here's his number."

"Thanks," Eldon said after he'd copied it down.

"He'll paste your ears back, but that's just for show. But he loves topiary—he'll talk."

One of the legion of faceless helpful sources, Eldon thought as he hung up and prepared to dial Stowe's number. But let's see if this pays off before I get too grateful. He braced himself for the worst and dialed.

"Stowe." It was a snarl.

"Stowe the topiary man?"

"Yeah. Why?" Stowe sounded like a troll at the bottom of a well.

"I want to talk about topiary."

"Coulda guessed that." But the voice softened slightly. "Whaddaya wanta know?"

"About topiary organizations in the Dayton area."

"I *am* topiary in the Dayton area."

"Is that so?"

"Yeah. And it's getting late, I gotta get home and prune my shrubs."

"I need to know about topiary groups. I'm looking for someone who might've done a particular piece of work, probably on order for a customer."

"What kinda work?"

"A pornographic figure—"

"Is this a damn joke?!"

"No, this is Eldon Larkin. I'm a reporter for the *South Coast Sun* in Oregon. The statue probably was at least a couple of feet tall and had room enough inside to conceal a 12-gauge shotgun."

A silence. "That would be some piece of work."

"That's why I'm trying to find out who grew it."

"I used to work on a newspaper," Stowe said at last, quietly.

"How come you got out?" Keep him talking. "Money?"

"Couldn't stand the polyesters." Stowe's voice began to pick up steam. "The blow-dried hair on the managers. A new managerial class that tramples the bones of Murrow, Pulitzer, Ernie Pyle, Billy Russell . . . " Stowe paused, as if waiting for a response.

"The Crimean War correspondent," Eldon said. "He covered the Civil War, too."

"You know Russell?"

"I've read some of his stuff."

"The War From the Landing at Gallipoli to the Death of Lord Raglan," Stowe said reverently. "Eighteen fifty-five."

"Brilliant," said Eldon, who hadn't read the book.

"I threw in Russell to see if you really were a reporter," Stowe said. "Anybody can blow off Murrow or Pyle. Or Hemingway. Bah."

"Why would I lie?"

"I don't mean *lie!*" Stowe cried. "I mean put on airs! Daintily twiddle your manicured fingers on the typewriter keys. Sip your espresso and nibble your raisin toast! All kindsa journalism dilettantes these days—we need more cigar smokers—"

"I'm covering a murder," Eldon put in hastily.

"A murder? Why didn't you say?" Now Stowe sounded like a hungry man confronted with a feast. "Is it . . . *good copy?"*

One of Fiske's generation, Eldon decided. Well, he knew how to deal with that. "You bet. A four-hundred-fifty-two-pound pimp connected with gambling and the Chicago mob. He got it in the chest with a 12-gauge hidden in topiary."

"Oh, that's good stuff! What I wouldn't give to cover a good murder again!"

"This one's pretty good, all right."

"I remember the time I walked into this bedroom and there was the victim's head on the end table, looking at me with these big blue eyes—"

"I ought to have my editor tell you about the blowtorch murder," Eldon said. "Anyway, this pimp was heavy into porno—"

"Ha ha! Four-hundred-fifty-two-pound-pimp 'heavy'! Ha ha!"

"—and I figure that's how the hit man got close to him: offered him a porno topiary figure."

"Hey, that's great! This pimp sounds like a real assistant-managing-editor type!"

"Topiary was spattered all over the scene," Eldon said. "And a friend of mine who was a topiarist got killed yesterday for asking too many questions about it."

Stowe uttered an animal growl. "Was he a good friend?"

"Yeah. A good friend."

"You're so lucky! How many reporters get to write good copy for personal revenge?"

Eldon heard a heavy object slam upon a desk and then what sounded like paper being spilled. "Yeah—here it is, kid," Stowe said. "There's a topiary club near Chicago that might have what you need to know. A very exclusive group."

"Will they talk to me?"

"*These* topiarists normally are very stubborn because they have a very special rep," Stowe replied. "They're porno topiarists."

"No shit, Carl?"

"An elite outfit, you might say," Stowe said. "Very specialized. Think a lot of themselves. But they're going to talk to you, *because they owe me!* They've consulted me several times."

"You must know a lot about topiary."

"I know *everything* about topiary. Without me, they'd be nothing, just a bunch of brush-cutters. I taught them the secret of growing first-rate topiary bazooms—"

"How would you grow a figure with a shotgun inside?"

"Put the shotgun inside a plastic tube," Stowe said. "The gun would have to be greased and wrapped, because topiary takes a long time to grow. On second thought, just grow the topiary around the tube and slide the shotgun in at the last minute."

"Be a good way to get rid of the gun afterward, too," Eldon said.

"Sure," Stowe said, "just slide it out and pitch it. Here's their phone number and their post office box. You wanta talk to Edna."

"Edna what?"

"Just Edna. No last names."

Stowe read off the numbers. A light came on in Eldon's brain. The post office box number was the same as that on the fetish catalogue that Art Nola had shown him at the sheriff's office, the day they'd examined Archie's bogus obscene Hummels. That catalogue had come from Archie Loris's house.

Eldon had memorized the number but hadn't written it down afterward. He stared at the digits he'd just scrawled on note paper. Yes, this *was* the same number. . . .

"You still there?" Stowe asked. "This is enough to make me wanta go back into the newspaper business. Your paper got any openings?"

"I don't think so," Eldon said. "But you could send a resumé."

"Just talkin'," Stowe said. "Send me clips of your stories, will you?"

"I'll send clips," Eldon said.

After he had taken Stowe's address, Eldon called the Chicago number.

A chipper-sounding woman answered at once. It proved to be Edna and Eldon guessed she was middle-aged. Edna started gargling like a teenaged talent-show singer with mike fright once she found out he was a newspaper reporter—but she didn't hang up. Lying about being a reporter was something Eldon never did. Anyway, lying usually wasn't necessary—it was amazing what people would tell a reporter.

But he did not mention the murder.

"How did you get this number?" Edna finally got out.

"Carl Stowe."

Edna gave a lovelorn sigh and at once recovered her self-possession. *"Carl! I'd do anything for him!"*

"He said you can tell me about a particular piece of topiary that someone out here commissioned. I think it's a human figure."

"Human figures are our specialty," Edna said. "But I certainly can't tell you who it might've been grown for—we're very discreet."

"This is off the record, of course. I'd never say that you said."

"You must know Carl pretty well," Edna ventured.

"Oh, Carl's a great guy," Eldon said, "in spite of those cigars. He reminds me of the editor I work for."

Edna squealed. "You *must* know Carl if you know about his cigar—those cigars of his, I mean."

Eldon decided that for all her talk about discretion, Edna had a potent appetite for notoriety—and hadn't had a thought above the belt in years.

"This particular figure would've been three feet tall or so," Eldon said, "and it would've incorporated a length of plastic pipe somehow. I wish I could be more specific—"

"That's the 'Banjo Boy,'" Edna said at once.

"So the pipe formed part of a banjo?" Eldon asked.

"Heavens, no—the banjo was grown," Edna said. "That was part of the *art*. The pipe was to hold a garden hose. The Banjo Boy was to be a fountain, as I understand it."

"A fountain? How so?"

"The client would wheel it around the garden and run the hose up the pipe." Edna cackled as she warmed to the subject. "It would be a thrill just to *run the hose up the pipe!*"

"But it was a realistic figure?"

"It was modeled after a German Hummel, and very artfully done. The Banjo Boy was playing a banjo, of course, and he had on the cutest little topiary vest and hat and *not another stitch!*" Edna started giggling uncontrollably. "The hose went in at the rear, *up the statue's keester!*" Edna screamed with laughter, finally mastered herself and finished as she gasped for air: "The pipe was—was covered with growth, stuck out of a . . . but surely I don't have to draw you a picture?"

Eldon managed to laugh. "No, of course not! Hey, that's great—that's really clever. Listen, I need to know—"

"I can't tell you the name of the client." Edna was back in control now.

"The client is Archie Loris, who lives out here in Oregon," Eldon said.

"Oh. You've talked to him, then?"

"Uh, yeah, I've seen Archie. But I want to talk to the artist."

"He wouldn't tell you?"

"No—"

"Well, then, I can't—"

Was Edna wavering? Something teasing was creeping into her tone. Eldon tried to sound a little anxious.

"Look, I'm . . . very interested in the artistry. Personally interested," he said. Put that way, it was true enough. "Carl said you'd—you'd help me."

"Oh, my, do we have someone on the hook here?" Edna's voice turned luscious and breathy. "This isn't *really* for a newspaper after all, is it?"

"I'll get in touch with him if only you'll tell me his name."

"We don't see much of him. I'm really not sure how to get hold of him. A rather private man. He travels a lot on business. . . . But I can't leave a friend of Carl's *on the hook*. So here's the name—"

"Oh, thank you," Eldon said, pencil ready.

"Mr. Leon Grazel." Edna spelled the last name.

Another memory floated up. Something Stephanie had said when they had talked on the wharf. A name. An initial, actually. Mr. G.

22

Eldon ended the conversation with Edna only with difficulty. He didn't like to hang up on helpful sources—he often needed them again. But neither was Edna one to let go of a potential client or topiary association member. She described the benefits of topiary association membership in increasingly lascivious detail. Eldon was able to disconnect tactfully only after agreeing to be on the mailing list for the same quarterly pornography catalogue that had gone to Archie.

Was Edna the leather-clad woman on the catalogue cover? Eldon decided not to ask; either way, he would be disappointed. He gave her the *Sun*'s mailing address. The catalogue would make a nice newsroom conversation piece, a counterpoint to *Sasquatch and UFO* and something new for Marsha to goggle at.

Should he tell Melissa what he had discovered? Or tell Art Nola? Or should he keep it to himself while he sniffed around the gambling scene?

I can still win the bet, Eldon thought, a vision of wrestling sensually with Melissa between the sheets burning in his mind. All I need is information leading to an arrest. This looks like it.

If I can pull this off, I'll never bother to gamble again, Eldon thought. And I'll get the girl in the bargain. Tonight's the night to move. Now or never; I might not get up the nerve to do it again.

Eldon headed out the side door to his car. It was quitting time, anyway. He could tell by the way Fiske's finger twitched on the Lucite cube that it was time to disappear before he found himself calling irritated officials and shipping agents at their homes during dinner with stupid questions about what blight might be about to descend on Northwest marine life.

Fiske can cover the red tide himself, Eldon thought as he slammed the Isetta's door. He can write an editorial against it, like Xerxes flogging the sea.

He started the car and bounded out of the parking lot. In the corner of his eye, he saw Fiske spring through the *Sun*'s side door, waving and yelling. "Don't see a thing," Eldon told the rearview mirror and laid rubber down the street.

He heard a clunk as he slammed through the gears. He gripped the wheel fiercely, scarcely daring to slow down as he turned onto Bayside Drive. The Isetta teetered as it took the corner; for a moment Eldon thought he was going over. But the car stabilized and completed the turn.

Eldon listened to the chugging engine. Something seemed different. An unusual vibration? The Isetta was a subtle beast, not like his weirdly customized but ill-fated van or his ancient Citroën, which had complained of its ailments as loudly as a spoiled three-year-old.

Eldon queasily waggled the steering wheel. He remembered his first date with Bernice. He'd been so nervous that he'd thrown up. He'd had to stop the Citroën and get out by the side of the road and vomit. His wife-to-be had been tactful, but Eldon wondered if that moment hadn't sown in her the seed of doubt that had grown into the mighty tree from which she'd finally left him swinging in the wind.

I wonder if Gordon ever threw up on an important date with a guy? Eldon wondered. I'll have to ask him sometime.

He crossed the bridge to Regret, where log rafts drifted in the slough. The logs were white with seagulls preening their feathers or sleeping. Others bobbed in the water among the logs. More gulls glided in to join the flock. Must be a storm at sea, Eldon thought. I could use a little rain tonight, for luck.

He felt like a bomber pilot preparing to take off for an air raid as he taxied down the pitted road along the slough and lined up the car at the intersection for the charge uphill to his house. He reviewed the reverse-H shift pattern to be certain he would shift smoothly as he accelerated. He was preparing for takeoff. . . .

No—he was preparing to make a cast, and the top of the hill was where he wanted to put his fly.

That was better.

He committed himself.

The car sprang forward and hurtled right up the hill. Eldon imagined a big, infinitely long fishing line running out behind him. The Isetta popped to the top of the hill like a fly alighting on the water. Eldon rolled into his driveway and headed into the house.

He grabbed the phone and called Frank. "Those calls paid off."

"What did you find out?"

"A name—Leon Grazel. Stephanie talked about a 'Mr. G.' He grew the topiary figure that was used to kill Archie—a big Hummel with a banjo and a hard-on with the shotgun inside."

Frank hooted. "That tops Fiske's blowtorch murder!"

"I'm going to the Poke tonight, start playing cards and asking questions. You got anything going?"

"No," Frank said. "Want me to come with you?"

"No," Eldon said. "I just want someone to know where I am."

"Okay. If you don't come to work in the morning, I'll drive over there and look in the dumpster for the body."

"If it comes to that," Eldon retorted, "Melissa's all yours."

"Thanks, Eldon, but that may be a bigger bite than I care to chew."

The exchange was a suitable bit of bravado on which to end their conversation. He called the D.A.'s office. By good luck, Melissa was still there.

"Eldon!"

"I wanted to say thanks. The tip about the gun paid off."

"How?" Melissa asked eagerly.

"Fella named Leon Grazel, at the end of a tangled path. He killed Loris and probably Simon."

"Spell the name. I'll give it to the sheriff."

Eldon did. "I think I win our bet."

"If they arrest him," Melissa said with an airy laugh.

"When the warrant's issued," Eldon said. "Catching him is your problem. And so's coming to dinner again."

"Oh, boy, you're a good cook. What're we gonna have?"

A salad, bread, wine, and some cheese, Eldon thought, running over recipes in his mind. A Waldorf salad—and for dessert, grapes. Eldon imagined Melissa naked, feeding him grapes. "I'll let you know," he said. "For now, wish me luck."

"Why?"

"Tonight's Lucky Poke night. There's still a gambling story. I owe Simon."

"With two murder raps, this Grazel will never get out of jail," Melissa said. "I'll make sure of that. That ought to square you with Simon Blood."

"There's Stephanie, too," Eldon said.

"You know, Eldon, that's what I like about you," Melissa said, "your sense of obligation."

"Catholic upbringing."

"You'll have some sins to confess after we have dinner," Melissa said with a chuckle. "You're going to the Poke alone?"

"Well, Gordon will be there. And I told Frank about it, at our office."

"Just so you've got backup," Melissa said.

"This actually has been one of my safer assignments."

"You'll have to tell me about some of the others—over dinner."

"You bet I will."

"Remember to stick on twelve when you're playing blackjack, and in poker never try to fill an inside straight."

"Yes, ma'am."

When Eldon left his house to pick up Gordon, he saw that clouds were rolling in high over the bay. A little rain is what I need to make the luck run my way, he thought.

He found Gordon waiting on his porch, tapping the edge of a fat envelope against his leg. He wore a dark shirt, gray slacks, and a tan car coat with big pockets.

"Ok-*ay*." Gordon almost danced with anticipation as Eldon got out of the car. "The game's afoot."

"This is not a game," Eldon said.

"Sure, it's a game," Gordon said. "A card game. A detective movie and I'm supplying the sound track. Honky-tonk piano."

"Just don't call attention to yourself," Eldon said with irritation.

"You *need* a sound track," Gordon said. "Without me, who'll talk to you?"

"Listen, did Stephanie ever mention a 'Mr. G'? Or the name Leon Grazel?"

"No. Who's he?"

"Grazel probably killed Loris and Simon Blood."

Gordon whistled. "Are we going after him?"

"Hell, no. The police can do that. We're proceeding as planned. Understood?"

Eldon got ready for an argument but Gordon merely gave a brisk nod and handed over the envelope.

"Okay," Gordon said. "Here's the money. Let's go or I'll be late—and let me drive, will you? I'm keyed up."

"Okay." Eldon tossed him the keys.

Gordon pulled open the Isetta's door and climbed inside as Eldon stood weighing the envelope. "Well, come on, Eldon. I'm not going to grab your knee."

Eldon climbed in next to him and hauled the door shut. "Think I can get 'em to cheat me tonight?"

"You don't have to," Gordon said. "All you have to do is win and lose money."

"I've already done that."

"Economies of scale," Gordon said. "Makes a better story, the more money that's involved. And it's all on Archie. Hey, I like this eight ball—"

It annoyed Eldon to hear a piano player talking like a reporter, but he knew Gordon was right. He covered his irritation by explaining the secrets of the Isetta's gear-shift pattern. Then, to his chagrin, Gordon started the car and headed smoothly down the trail toward the boat basin, shifting without difficulty.

"I want to have this story in print before they finally pick up Chump-Change," Eldon said.

"He's disappeared for good," Gordon said.

"Art Nola doesn't think so," Eldon said.

Gordon glowered at him. "Let me ask *you* a question—how could you think I'd pick up scum like Chump-Change? I don't walk around with my head in my pants any more than you do."

"Is that still bothering you? I said I was sorry. It was just something that occurred to me. It's my job to think things like that, and I didn't know you then."

"You got that right. You have no idea what it's like to be gay in a place like Port Jerome."

"Why stay here, if it's so bad?"

"I told you all about that. I didn't realize until later that we were in the process of breaking up when I moved here."

Eldon smiled.

"Something funny?" Gordon asked.

"My ex-wife pulled something similar," Eldon said. "And Melissa's right—you keep rough company for a music teacher."

Gordon relaxed and grinned. But it was a friendly grin. "Fairies should like things a little more delicate, hey?"

"Everyone likes things 'a little more delicate,'" Eldon said, "unless they're criminals."

The Lucky Poke's yellow sign seemed to gleam with special malignity as Gordon drove into the club's parking lot and parked the Isetta. But it began to rain as they crossed the parking lot, and Eldon's heart lifted a little as they went inside.

Hell had not changed—the smoky atmosphere and red wallpaper, the stale, paralyzed ambiance under the brassy lighting. They never even replace the smoke, Eldon thought, feeling his throat seize up.

There were not many customers; it was a week night.

"Looks pretty quiet," Eldon said. "There's two empty seats at the poker table."

"I don't see anyone I'm tight with," Gordon said. "You'll have to hang out for a while."

"That's me," Eldon said, "part of the scenery. I'll get us some beers, on Archie."

Gordon gave Eldon a smile and a clap on the shoulder, then went to the piano and began warming up. Eldon paid for two draft beers—the bartender was the same tired woman who had been there on his first visit—and took one to Gordon. Then Eldon went to the poker table and sat down.

No one acknowledged him except the dealer. "Twenty-dollar minimum, five-dollar ante." She was small and slab-faced, with an incredibly shiny pile of hair and thick glasses. She held one shoulder higher than the other, head thrust pugnaciously forward.

God, look at that wig, Eldon thought as he pushed over the money and received a pile of chips in return. Why doesn't she just wear a coonskin cap? He felt pity for the woman's deformity until she shrugged and switched shoulders, dropping the one and raising the other as she shuffled the cards, her head rolling like an orange on a plate. Her mouth pumped something like a fish's when she spoke. "Ante up."

The players received their cards. Eldon got two fives. Well, that was okay. He'd see what developed.

What developed was not encouraging. Eldon's first hand was so weak that he folded. On the second round, he wagered some money on a pair of fives. But a fat fisherman whose face was spotted with moles topped him with three tens.

Eldon was certain that everyone could see that he was the greenest player at the table. Well, it's Archie's money, he thought. I'll bet he never expected to invest in a newspaper.

Gordon started playing a country tune as the second hand was dealt. Something about winning and losing. I've got to do better, Eldon thought. I've got to win a few hands or everyone will say that I wrote the exposé just because I lost. He felt his anxiety rising, knew that the game already was starting to get the better of him.

The cards went down once again. Eldon wagered seventy-five dollars on a pair of sevens and won because all but one other player folded and the remaining player, an old man in a hand-knitted beret and half-spectacles, tried to bluff him unsuccessfully.

Eldon felt better as he raked in the chips. Not a big win but a confidence-builder. I've got to hang in here, document things, he thought. Give the story some color.

But the next three hands were disasters. In short order, he lost nearly two hundred dollars, most of it to the fisherman, who was coming on strong. I've got plenty of money, but I can't start throwing it around, Eldon thought. It'll attract attention. People will suspect a setup.

Perhaps he'd go a hundred more and then drop out, return another night. Or he could dip into his pocket and—

Someone took the other empty chair. A woman. Eldon glanced at her and clenched his jaw to keep it from dropping open. Melissa—in disguise as the perfect South Coast barfly. She wore heavy eyeliner and shoulder-duster earrings and had done something to her hair, fluffed it up somehow. She was dressed in a tight denim skirt and a faded plaid Western shirt with the top two buttons revealingly unsnapped. She had long red false fingernails, and her wrists were decorated with cheap, heavy jewelry.

Yet it was Melissa. She gave a brassy smile. "How ya doin' there, hon?"

"Oh. Ah. Just fine." Eldon realized he was staring. He looked away, reddening. Melissa had played it just right, made his unthinking recognition look like a once-over in a bar. She sounds like she never finished high school, he thought with awe.

Somewhat to Eldon's shock, Melissa took out a cigarette and a lighter and lit up. He nearly gagged. She smiled again and then appeared to lose interest in him as the dealer called for the ante and dealt the cards.

"How're you tonight, darlin'?" the fisherman asked Melissa.

"You just better keep your mind on your cards," Melissa told him with a flirtatious smile.

It was clear at once that Melissa and the fisherman were now the dominant players at the table. They traded victories while Eldon and the others sniped around the fringes, dashing in now and again to claim a small pot. Eldon played more boldly, anxious to win back Melissa's attention. He had some success. But when he over-bet on a weak hand, she took his money without a word.

She wasn't flirting now, either with him or with the fisherman, whose enthusiasm for Melissa now was clearly dampened. The fisherman's pile of chips was getting smaller. Eldon played more boldly but a little more wisely, and found that he was winning again.

At last, Melissa announced, "I'm out." She stood up and took her chips.

"Night, babe," the fisherman said. Melissa threw him a brief, uninterested smile and sauntered away from the table.

Eldon rubbed his forehead. Should he spend more of Archie's money or get the hell out? He wasn't fascinated anymore, just tense and sweaty. His eyes burned from the cigarette smoke. He became aware that Gordon had stopped playing. He glanced over at the piano. Gordon's coat and tip glass were still there but Gordon wasn't. Probably taking a break, Eldon thought.

Melissa was at the bar, drinking a beer. Eldon watched her until the dealer broke in: "You gonna watch those legs or ante?"

"The legs," Eldon said heavily and got up from the table.

He walked stiffly to the bar, trying to work the kinks out of his own legs. "Buy you a beer?" he asked Melissa.

She looked at him. She was smoking another cigarette. "With what?"

"My mad money."

"Okay, honey. Just don't get any ideas."

"I'm sure you're not that kind of girl." Eldon signaled for two beers. "You're a pretty good poker player, though."

"Well, you knew that," Melissa said.

"What are you doing here?"

"Watching out for you. I don't trust Clete."

"And what is the point of the getup?"

"Do you like it?"

"Does the D.A. know you're doing this?"

"Not exactly."

Eldon glanced around. "You came alone?"

"Why not? It's perfectly safe."

"Not in that skirt."

"I wore my black garter belt, too. . . . Believe me, Eldon, I can take care of myself."

"Well, you sure took care of that fisherman."

Melissa nodded and blew a perfect smoke ring. "Sure did. Men hate to have a woman beat them at cards. By the way, that game is straight—now that I've left it."

"Huh?"

"Keep your voice down." Melissa smiled alluringly as she spoke. "How d'you think you managed to win as much as you did?"

"Oh. I see. Thanks. . . . Couldn't the dealer tell you were cheating?"

"I wasn't cheating. I just played so you would win. Didn't do it enough for anyone to get suspicious." Melissa kept smiling, eyes wide and locked on Eldon's. He found himself leaning toward her as the bartender set two beers before them.

Melissa giggled, shaking her head playfully as if Eldon had ventured an intimacy. Her dangling earrings glittered as they swung under the brassy light. "I'd sure like to know where the money here is going."

"You mean the house rake?"

"Yeah. The owners don't keep it all. If we can figure out that, we'll know who killed Loris and why."

"Grazel killed him. And Simon."

"And why?" Melissa asked. "Money is why. It always is. Find out who's on the receiving end and it will tie up a lot of loose ends."

Eldon looked over at the piano. Gordon had not yet returned. "I wonder where he is?"

"He'll be back. He wouldn't leave his tips. Relax and enjoy your beer."

But Eldon found Gordon's absence ominous. The minutes ticked by. Finally he said, "I think I'll go look for him."

"Calm down."

"I'll just check the men's room—"

"He didn't go into the restroom. He went outside. He's probably having a smoke. *I'll* go look for him."

"He doesn't smoke—" Eldon began.

"The air in here is too close," Melissa said. "And do you really want to go poking around outside, when people now know you have all that money? I don't trust him. He's been gone too damn long."

"But what about you—?"

"If he's up to something and sees you, he'll cool it. But he doesn't know who I am." Melissa swung off the bar stool and sauntered toward the door.

Eldon nervously sipped his beer as he watched her go. Where was Gordon? Where were the people Gordon was supposed to introduce him to? Had he been had? He was about to go to the blackjack tables when Gordon came back in from the rear of the building and sat down at his piano.

Of course, there's a rear door, Eldon thought. He went over, trying to be casual. "Where've you been?"

"Just took a break," Gordon said. "Walked around the building. The cigarette smoke gets to me."

"So where's the contacts?"

"That's what I was doing out back—looking for some of the girls. Their clientele slips in and out the back door. No one's out there—it's raining. Except that woman who was at the card table. I don't know her. Might be a freelance—"

Eldon had to grin. "That's Melissa."

"What? No shit? She looks completely different."

"It's a talent of hers," Eldon said.

Gordon shook his head. "She could turn a few tricks, looking like that—"

"Never mind that. I want contacts."

"There's nobody around I'm tight with," Gordon said. "Your best bet is to keep playing cards."

Eldon knew he had to be patient. He went back to the poker game and played two more hands, winning a little. But he couldn't get into the rhythm of play; he kept glancing toward the front and back doors, waiting for Melissa to return.

The dealer rolled her teeter-totter shoulders. "Did she take off with your wallet?"

"Family pictures in it," Eldon said and left the table.

He went out front. Cool, rainy air hit his face like the slap of a wet towel. Rain gusted in the light of the Lucky Poke sign and spattered the hoods of cars and pickups parked in front of the club. Eldon felt a real pang of worry. Where was Melissa?

A couple of loggers lounged in a nearby pickup, smoking and chugging Coors from cans. Eldon wondered why they were drinking in the truck when they could do it inside. Then the pungent reek of marijuana reached him on a gust of rain. Eldon walked to the truck, waving and grinning before he tapped on the foggy passenger window.

The logger rolled down the window. Three fingers of his right hand had been sawed off at the first joints, and he held the burning reefer unself-consciously between the stumps. He had a chin beard and a terrible case of acne. "Hi, there," he said with a cheerful, vacant smile.

"I'm looking for a girl—"

"I sure wish we had one in here, pard!"

"We don't look like girls, do we?" the driver asked and cut loose with a belt of stoned laughter. He was an Indian with long black braids under a baseball cap. His nose looked as if it had been flattened by a shovel. "Can't help ya!"

"My girlfriend came out of the club and didn't come back," Eldon said, shivering in the rain. "It was just a little while ago. You been here long?"

The loggers blinked and looked at each other. Finally, the passenger admitted, "I'm not sure how long we've been here. D'you know, Dewey?"

"Sure wish I did!" The driver roared with laughter again, grabbed the steering wheel, and made humping motions. "Malcolm, gimme that joint."

"You want a toke?" Malcolm asked Eldon.

"Thanks, I'm just doing beer tonight," Eldon said.

Malcolm passed the joint to Dewey. "Your girlfriend gave ya the slip, huh? What's she look like?"

"Good looking—" Eldon said.

"They all are," Malcolm said, shaking his head slowly at some memory.

"She's about five-five, brown hair, a plaid shirt, and a real tight skirt—"

"Whee-*ooo!*" Malcolm said. "We remember her, don't we?"

Dewey gave a war whoop. "We remember that skirt! Was *that* your girlfriend?"

"Yeah—" Eldon said.

"That was no girlfriend—that hadda be a *hooker!*" Malcolm waggled a sawed-off index finger. "Did she make off with your money, pard?"

"No, I just want to—"

"I'm sure you do," Malcolm said. "She was definitely a hooker. Sorry, but it's true; say what you will."

"My friend's right," added Dewey, a little dangerously.

"We know we're right," Malcolm said. "D'you know why?"

"I just want to know which way she went," Eldon said.

"Well, pard, she went off with her pimp, is the way she went. He was real firm about taking her along. Guess he had some action scheduled for her."

"Her pimp?" Eldon grabbed the pickup's door handle in horror. "Who?"

Dewey gave a snort. "That little green-faced rodent, deals cards here sometimes. Except I thought he got run off—I was kind of surprised to see him. What's-his-name—?"

"Goes by Chump-Change," Malcolm supplied.

"How could he line up a woman looks like that?" Dewey asked. "Didn't I hear he was in some trouble with the law—?"

"Which way did they go?"

"You must really want that skirt," Dewey said.

"Well, wouldn't you?" Malcolm asked and pointed a finger stump into the darkness. "They went that way. In an old car, had fins on it. Listen, pard, you're askin' for trouble, you mess with that pimp—"

Malcolm was pointing toward the cutoff to Preacher's Hole and points south.

Eldon scrambled across the gravel and sprang up the Lucky Poke's steps, nearly slipping on the wet concrete. Preacher's Hole? Eldon wondered and then thought, Scoquel! They're going to Archie's house.

He rushed inside to Gordon. "Chump-Change has kidnapped Melissa."

Gordon kept playing. "What? How?"

"He forced her into his car," Eldon said. "Couple of guys saw it in the parking lot. Where's a phone? I'm calling the cops—"

"Phone, hell—let's go after them." Gordon brought the tune he was playing to a smooth conclusion, picked up his tips, and headed for the front door, shrugging on his jacket as he went.

Eldon started for the door but Gordon threw his arm around his shoulders and gave him a brief, comradely squeeze—just long enough to stop him, just enough for people to notice, not long enough for anyone to conclude anything. "Back in a bit," he told the bartender.

They stepped out into the rain, and Gordon headed for the car.

"We're calling the cops!" Eldon said and then remembered that Gordon still had the car keys. "Give me the keys."

"No. And don't try to take them." Gordon faced him in the rain with a determined expression. "Come on—or I'll go without you."

Eldon looked wildly around for aid but saw only the goggling faces of Malcolm and Dewey through the fogged windshield of their pickup.

It won't do Melissa any good if he knocks my block off and leaves, Eldon thought. If I go with him, I can phone for help somewhere.

"Okay," he said. "But I drive. You'll just have to trust me, like I've had to trust you. I know where they're going—Archie's place. I know the way and you don't."

"All right." Gordon climbed into the car. He handed over the keys only after Eldon got inside and pulled the hatch shut.

Eldon got the car started. Good job, he told himself. I'll head downtown to the sheriff's office and . . .

But a metallic glint caught his eye. He looked down to see Gordon draw a Bowie knife from one of his coat's big pockets and rest it on his thigh.

"Where the hell did you get that?" Eldon demanded.

"Piano player's got to have some protection," Gordon said.

"What're you gonna do?"

"Stick it in Chump, if I get half a chance. I should've had this when he came to my house."

Gordon didn't raise the knife or threaten Eldon with it. But the message was plain. Eldon pulled out of the parking lot and headed down the road.

They drove in silence, light from the occasional highway lamppost flashing on the knife's blade. Eldon imagined that the slap of the windshield wiper and the hiss of the tires on the wet road amplified every noise the car made. He became certain that there was a new rattle in the car's rear. He listened to it, fiddling with the eight ball on the gear shift.

Finally he asked, "When we get there, what're we going to do?"

"Get her back."

"Killing Chump-Change is not the way to do it."

"Too bad it won't come to that," Gordon said. "Chump's fine at intimidation and at beating up women, but that's all——"

"He's mean as hell."

"We outnumber him."

"You were scared of him before," Eldon said.

"That was when I thought I had something to hide," Gordon said.

"Suppose he's got a gun?"

"Did those guys you talked to say he had a gun?"

"No——"

"We sneak up on him, take stock. Get help if we have to."

"What's he looking for in the house?"

"We don't know that he's headed there," Gordon said.

"Where else would he be going?" Eldon asked.

"South," Gordon said. "To California. But there's something he wants in Archie's house first. Probably money."

"But what's he need Melissa for?"

"A hostage. He sees this hooker at the Poke and grabs her. He needs someone to drive for him, someone to do for him. That's how guys like Chump-Change think."

They were coming into Preacher's Hole. The town's streets had been rolled up long since, and the dark buildings looked like tombs. Rain beat steadily on the Isetta's roof.

"There's a sheriff's station in the courthouse," Eldon said firmly, "and we're going there for help."

"The hell we are—"

"What're you gonna do, Gordon? Stick me?" Eldon felt the airy clarity that he achieved at murder scenes and accidents. He seemed to see the Bowie knife in keen detail, even though it was dark.

Gordon studied him for a long moment. "You're right," he said at last. "Let's get to the sheriff."

"Good man. We'll be right on the patrol car's tail."

Eldon headed for the courthouse, steering down dark streets that seemed like funnels. But he was appalled to find that the courthouse was dark, too. They pulled up to the door of the sheriff's station to find the little office dark.

"Where's the deputy?" Gordon demanded.

"On patrol somewhere," Eldon said. "He could be anywhere in this part of the county."

"Head for Archie's," Gordon said.

"No, we phone the sheriff in Port Jerome—"

"And lose another half hour waiting for a car to show up? We don't have any choice now, Eldon. Step on it."

The Isetta vibrated like an out-of-synch eggbeater as Eldon put the pedal to the floor. The shaking gave a weird perspective to the darkness, made the passing trees seem huge and the road as if it spilled off into nowhere.

At last they reached the Scoquel turnoff. Eldon twisted the wheel vengefully. Gordon yelped like a kid on a roller-coaster ride as they plunged down the turn.

Eldon fought the wheel as the Isetta rocked precariously and fishtailed. "Slow down!" Gordon pleaded.

"The house is ahead—" Eldon pumped the brakes.

"Turn out the headlights! He'll see us!"

Eldon stabbed at the dashboard, missed the button, grappled with the wheel as the Isetta started another downhill plunge. Suddenly there was a grinding, snapping noise from the car's rear. It was as if someone had thrust a broomstick through a bicycle's spokes. Eldon seemed to hear Simon Blood explaining calmly as the Isetta rolled upside down and skidded along the road on its top: *The drive couplers rattle when the bolts start loosening up. If they break, you stop.*

They slid into a tree. The lurch slapped Eldon's head against the side window. His ears rang. The motor flooded and died. The headlights threw their beams uselessly into the forest as Eldon and Gordon untangled themselves.

"God-damn!" Gordon said.

Eldon fought for breath. "You okay?"

"Yeah. Let's get out of here—" Gordon fumbled with the door handle. "It's jammed!"

"I know how to get us upright," Eldon said. "We need to roll the car away from the tree. Stand on the ceiling and brace your hands against the floor. That's it—"

"I've lost my knife," Gordon said, getting into position.

"Good," Eldon said. "We need to rock in unison. I'll start to count. On three, we roll to the right. The car should flip right over."

"Shut off the headlights!"

Eldon tried to punch the headlight button, found he was clutching the eight ball. He shoved it in his pocket and hammered at the headlight button. It was broken. The lights stayed on. "The hell with it," he said. "Let's get rocking."

They braced their hands and started rocking side by side. On Eldon's count they threw themselves to the right. The car moved only slightly.

"We're wedged somehow," Eldon said. "Again."

They started rocking once more. "All right," Eldon said. "Ready—one—two—"

A flashlight beam stabbed through the side window. Gordon yelped. Eldon closed his eyes and turned away from the blinding glare.

There came a nasty chuckle and then an all-too-familiar voice: "Well, look at 'em dancin' in there like a pair of crazy Rockettes. Nice of you boys to hang out a light."

Eldon's stomach turned over. He squinted out the window as the speaker upended his flashlight to shine the beam up his chin, the way Eldon remembered doing at Boy Scout camp.

It was Chump-Change, chewing gum. The flashlight trick provided no improvement.

Chump tapped the window with something big and dark and heavy. Eldon saw the muzzle of a .38-caliber revolver in the flashlight's gleam. Chump-Change gave his trademark shark's smile. "Fish in a barrel," he said.

Gordon backed into Eldon and Eldon tried to flatten himself against the far wall of the car as Chump-Change took aim.

But then another voice spoke: "No. Pull 'em outa there."

The voice was slow, dry, and malicious—and also somehow familiar. Eldon threw himself against the window. Two people were illuminated in the Isetta's skewed headlights. One was Melissa, standing disheveled with her hands clasped atop her head. The other was a man in an overcoat and porkpie hat, rain dripping from its brim. He held a black semiautomatic pistol.

Chump-Change turned to argue, and the beam from his flashlight briefly highlighted the other man's face. It was a face like an evil, blotchy cheese with little eyes that glittered in the beam's sweep.

It was the face of the man he had seen in the Scotsman's junk store.

=23=

"Aw, c'mon, Mr. G!" Chump-Change said in a whine horribly like a schoolboy's. "I wanta do 'em! This is my chance."

"No it isn't," the other man said. "There's witnesses."

Mr. G, Eldon thought, feeling his stomach clench and his throat suddenly go dry. Leon Grazel.

Chump-Change waved his pistol at Melissa, who stood shivering in the rain. "I'll do her, too. You bet I will."

"But there's yet another witness," Grazel said.

"Who?" Chump demanded, bewildered.

"Me, stupid," Grazel replied. "The thing you have to learn in this business, Juggy, is never to trust anybody. Now get those two outa there and bring 'em into the house. I want to talk to them. We're getting wet."

"C'mon, don't call me 'Juggy.' I'm Chump-Change."

"I'll call you what I want. You're working for me."

Chump-Change began a frantic little short-stepping dance, as if uncertain what to do. Grazel watched silently. At last, Chump-Change thrust the revolver into his belt, picked up a big rock in both hands, and hurled it clumsily into the Isetta's windshield.

The windshield shattered, showering Eldon and Gordon with chunks of glass. The rock almost smashed Eldon's foot.

"Good job," Grazel said. "You two in the car—climb out slow. You're covered."

Eldon crawled out into the mud on his hands and knees, taking care not to cut himself on the broken glass. Gordon followed. They climbed to their feet and put their hands in the air.

"My car," Eldon said. "It wasn't even paid for."

"Pregnant roller skate," said Chump-Change, who had pulled out his revolver once more. "Hey, check out that Bowie knife, there on the ground. Bad dudes here."

"You know either of them?" Grazel asked.

"I know 'em both," Chump-Change replied scornfully. "Couple of fairies hang out at the Lucky Poke. This one's a piano player. The one with the silly hat's his new boyfriend."

"What brings you two out here?" Grazel asked. "And don't say you were on a drive in the country."

Gordon tossed his head toward Melissa. "He took off with one of our girls. We want her back. You okay, Melissa?"

"I'm okay," Melissa said, teeth chattering slightly.

Chump-Change guffawed. "So *that's* what all this was about! After Archie was dead, you decided to start your own string, with her and Stephanie! I bet you peddle your boyfriend's ass, too. Gordo, I didn't think ya had it in ya—"

"Shut up, Juggy," Grazel said. "Bring them inside."

Chump-Change stepped behind Eldon and poked him with the revolver. "March, assholes."

"Don't do that," said Grazel sadly. "It shows him right where the gun is. He could turn around and take it away from you."

"Him?" Chump-Change said, but he stepped back.

"He's just learning the trade," Mr. Grazel explained to Eldon. "Now, back to the house—you first, hon."

Melissa picked her way unsteadily over the wet ground. Eldon realized that she was barefoot. Good way to keep someone from making a break, he thought.

"Can I put my hands down?" Melissa asked. "My shoulders hurt."

"Just keep 'em up there, hon," Mr. Grazel said. "You can get more comfortable inside."

Mr. Grazel's voice was as dry and even and deadly as when Eldon had first heard him speak in the Scotsman's store. He lumbered along like some armored turtle; but Eldon thought he was merely conserving energy for the moment of action.

Archie's house was dark except for a single golden light in one window, like a star. An electric lantern. The power was still off. Melissa's teeth chattered as she stumbled along in her bare feet. Grazel walked silently but Chump-Change was breathing in Eldon's ear as if he'd just run the hundred-yard dash.

Gordon spoke cheerfully to Eldon in French. *"Eh, est-ce que tu penses qu'on a une chance de les avoir? Ils sont deux, nous sommes trois,"* he said. "Hey, do you think there's a chance of jumping them? Two of them, three of us."

"Ne sois pas stupide. Ils ont des revolvers. Parle anglais!" Eldon replied as Grazel threw them a sharp glance. "Don't be stupid. They've got guns. Speak English!"

"Shuddap that fairy talk," Chump-Change said and jabbed Eldon again with the revolver.

Eldon forced himself to laugh. "Okay, okay. He was just telling a joke."

"I'll bet!"

They ducked under the swinging evidence tape and went up the walk. Mr. Grazel called a halt. "Juggy, go open the door. Cover them as I bring 'em inside."

"Okay, okay." Chump-Change did as he was told.

"Hon, you go over and stand with your friends," Grazel told Melissa. She stumbled over and tearfully embraced Eldon. Eldon hugged her, half beside himself with terror. Grazel watched them, holding his pistol almost casually at about waist height. "Okay, hon, that's enough. Step away from him—now."

Eldon thought he heard Melissa whisper, *"Play along,"* as she stepped aside, but Gordon coughed and, with the noise of the rain, he couldn't be sure. What's she going to do? he wondered desperately, pull the six of spades from Grazel's ear?

Chump-Change waved from the door with the revolver. "Okay, bring 'em in."

Grazel tilted his head toward the house. "Single file."

They filed inside. The electric lantern stood on the table that had held Archie's figurines, now pulled to the center of the room. The lantern threw big shadows on the walls and made the room seem cavernous. It gleamed on the metal of the banjo Grazel had bought at the Scotsman's; it leaned in one corner.

There was new disarray. All the furniture had been pushed around, and the contents of the VCR cabinet had been dumped on the floor. Grazel and Chump-Change plainly had been searching.

Grazel looked Eldon over. "You were in the junk store," he said. "I had a feeling about you. Empty your pockets on the table. You can start with that weight or whatever it is in your right-hand pocket."

Eldon slowly drew out the eight ball and put it on the table. He'd had a vague idea of hurling it in lethal fashion. He balanced the ball carefully on the hole in the bottom where it had screwed onto the Isetta's gear shift, afraid that if he dropped it, Chump-Change would be startled and fire. Eldon put his wallet on the table.

"Anything else?" Grazel asked.

"I have to reach into my coat again."

"Do it slowly."

Eldon pulled out the packet of money and placed that on the table, too.

Chump-Change whistled. "Sure enough, they were doin' some business. I thought they were up to something when I spotted 'em tonight at the club."

"Isn't it lucky I made you go there?" Grazel said. He said, "Thank you," to Eldon, then looked at Gordon. "Now you do the same—what's your name?"

"Gordon."

"Ah. Gordon Clete."

Gordon emptied his own pockets, including another wad of Archie's cash. "Look, we don't know who you are or what this is all about—"

"Oh, I doubt that," Grazel said.

"—so why don't you keep the cash and let us walk home?"

"I want to keep the girl, too," Chump-Change said.

"We were just about to go through the contents of her purse when you showed up," Grazel said, a slight edge to his voice as he glanced at Chump-Change. "But we'll get to that in a minute. You two fellows sit down on the couch and take off your shoes. Hon, you can take that chair there."

They all sat down. A sharp gust of rain struck the windows as Eldon fumbled with his shoelaces. It reminded him of playing cards with Gordon and Melissa at Oats in the Bowl. He fervently wished himself there.

"Une vraie tempête ce soir," Gordon declared with a reckless grin as he pulled off his shoes. *"On pourrait courir rapidement et se rendre loin, si on nous en donne la chance.* A real storm tonight. We could run fast and far, if we get the chance."

"He's remarking on the weather," Eldon explained and gave Gordon's ankle a nudge.

"Fairy talk," Chump-Change said.

"A cultured man," Grazel remarked. "Rather too cultured for a would-be pimp. Juggy here is more that sort. But Archie Loris was a pimp, and he was an art collector." Grazel seemed amused. "Well, to business," he said. "I know who you are, Gordon, and I want the tape."

"What tape?" Gordon asked.

"The tape that Stephanie gave you for safekeeping."

"Juggy took it." Gordon threw Chump-Change a savage smile. "Or didn't he tell you?"

"That's *Chump-Change* to you!"

"It was the wrong tape," Grazel said. "It was some abomination entitled *The Fat Man Pumps Good Gas,* starring Archie. I despise bad pornography."

"That was the tape Stephanie gave me," Gordon said. "That was the tape your pal took. I don't know what tape you want."

"Perhaps luckily for you—if it's true," Grazel said.

"I wouldn't double-cross you, Mr. G," Chump-Change said nervously.

"No, even you wouldn't be that stupid," Grazel said.

Chump-Change stepped to the table and fingered Eldon's envelope. "There's a lot of cash here. Maybe they sold the tape."

"Open the wallets," Grazel ordered.

Chump-Change opened Gordon's wallet and flourished another wad of money. By the light of the lantern, the wad threw a huge shadow on the wall, like a prehistoric bird or a giant bat.

"Whee-ooo!" Chump-Change started to pocket it.

"Put that down," Grazel said. "Check the other wallet."

Eldon sat silently, waiting for the inevitable. Chump-Change found his press card almost immediately.

Grazel silently studied the card, looking at Eldon and back to the card, as if making sure that the I.D. photograph matched. "Eldon Larkin. I've been reading your stories. You've finally tracked me down."

Eldon forced a grin. "How about an interview?"

Grazel stared at him. "The lady's purse, Juggy."

Eldon watched as Chump-Change scooped up Melissa's purse and dumped the contents on the table. Please God, he prayed, don't let her be carrying her—

"That's a badge!" Chump-Change said. "Oh, shit!"

Grazel trained the semiautomatic squarely on Melissa's middle. "Get your hands back up! Now!"

Melissa obeyed. Mr. Grazel opened the black leather case. The badge glittered in the lamplight. " 'Nekaemas County District Attorney's Office—Deputy District Attorney.' You sure can pick 'em, Juggy—a reporter and a cop."

Eldon felt Gordon shift his weight on the couch. No, he thought, don't try it. You'll get us killed. . . .

"I thought she was a hooker," Chump-Change said. "Then those two showed up with a wad of dough and Larkin and her started talking—"

"Juggy, you're a stupid fucking imbecile," Grazel said. "Your brain is a rock-solid bolus of shit that you take out of your head and lick when you want to think."

Chump-Change trembled. His eyes filled with tears, like a child who desperately wanted to please a stern parent.

"To think this was my last job," Grazel said with a sigh. "I should've known something like this would happen. I should never have come back here. That's another thing about the business, Juggy—your luck always runs out."

"There's a squad of sheriff's deputies on its way, thanks to him," Melissa said. "Give up now."

Grazel shook his head. "If this was a setup or even a vice sting, there'd have been cops all over, the moment Juggy forced you into his car. Larkin and Clete wouldn't even be in the equation. No, you three are operating on your own. Why?"

Melissa shrugged. "Okay. It's true. There was money to be made."

Grazel gave a little snort.

Eldon tried to think of an additional lie, but his throat might have been laced shut. He merely squeaked for air.

Chump-Change sneered at him. "You're in way over your head—you and your stupid hat." Chump-Change raised the revolver.

But Grazel said, "Just a minute. Let's see that hat!"

Eldon sat petrified. When he didn't move, Chump-Change cocked the revolver. Gordon cursed, snatched Eldon's hat and jumped up to throw it on the table.

Chump's .38 went off with a huge bang. The noise seemed to puncture Eldon's brain. The flash was blinding. Gordon pitched forward, hit his head on the table, and fell to the floor. The impact made the lantern rock and knocked the eight ball off the table. Eldon sat deafened, blinking at spots before his eyes. He heard the eight ball bounce on the floor far away, through the ringing in his ears.

Gordon lay curled on his side, unmoving. Eldon slid off the couch and turned him over. Gordon rolled slackly, eyes half-open and fixed, blood from the ugly gash in his forehead where he had hit the table running down one cheek. There was a bullet hole in the center of his chest. There seemed to be less bleeding there than from the cut and Eldon thought crazily as he clutched Gordon's shoulders that the bullet wound couldn't be as bad.

Chump-Change flipped his revolver up like a gunslinger and blew smoke from the muzzle. "Scratch one faggot."

Grazel made a strange, honking sound. *"Je suis aussi un homme cultivé!"* he told Eldon. "I, too, am a cultivated man!"

Eldon, sickened, realized that the honking was laughter. Then his nausea was swept away by the clear, distant feeling. I've just been along for the ride until now, he thought with an angry clarity. But if I want to get out of this alive, I'm going to have to take these bastards. And I will.

"It's a good thing—believe me, Juggy, a *damn* good thing—you shot him and not Larkin," Grazel said at last.

"That one now, this one later—what's the difference?" Chump-Change demanded.

Grazel regarded him. His gaze grew hotter, his stony eyes more lustrous in his pale, lumpy face. "The hat."

Chump-Change pushed it across the table.

Grazel examined the hat in the lantern light and then asked Eldon sharply, "Where'd you get this?"

"At—at a surplus store in Berkeley—"

"No! This! I saw it when you were in the store, but I wasn't sure." Mr. Grazel plucked something from the hat and held it out. His hand was in shadow. Then Grazel brought his hand nearer the lantern and Eldon saw it—the sprig of moss from Sackett Lake.

"Fishing." It was all he could think to say.

"Fishing where? Near here?"

"No—north county—"

"Can you take us there?"

"Yeah, yeah," Eldon said.

"Good," Grazel said in his papery voice. "We'll go there in the morning, when we can see."

"Mr. G, we've got to get outa here," Chump-Change said.

Grazel shook his head almost languorously. "This is worth waiting for."

"Not to me!"

"It's worth whatever I pay you," Mr. Grazel said. "You leave now, you don't get your per diem."

Mr. Grazel held up the sprig of moss. "I've read your stories, Larkin. You already know most of the story. I'll tell you the rest, to facilitate our search tomorrow."

Eldon tried not to look at Gordon's body. "Got—got a paper and pencil? I'll interview you."

Mr. Grazel chuckled. "What's that Warhol said? 'In the future, everyone will be famous for ten minutes.' I didn't expect to be famous. But you've nearly made me so."

"How's that?" Eldon managed to ask.

"Through my topiary work. I knew you were close on my heels when I read your interview with the gardener, Simon Blood. He already knew too much. This was borne out when Juggy and I went to his nursery. Blood had a file full of material about topiary right on his desk."

Chump-Change puffed out his chest. "I popped him."

"Blood surprised us," Grazel explained. "Then we had to take his office apart to make sure that *he* didn't have the tape."

"You took those topiary clippings," Eldon said.

"Mere weeds," Grazel said.

"We don't have the tape, either," Melissa said.

Grazel lifted her badge case and flipped it open to the identification card. "Melissa Lafky. Quoted extensively in Larkin's stories. And then those other articles—the sports column today and so forth. You two know how to keep the pressure on. . . . Where'd you get the money?"

"From Clete," Melissa said. "It was Archie's."

"What were you going to do with it?"

"Gordon could do anything he wanted with his share," Melissa said. "Eldon and I were going to leave this dump together."

"I wrote stories that would make the card-room owners look bad," Eldon said, "to get more money out of them. Finding you was an accident. We don't care about you."

"That's pretty smart," Chump-Change said admiringly.

"Your lack of back-up tonight almost makes me believe you," Grazel said. "But not quite. You tipped your hand shadowing me in the junk store."

"I didn't—"

"We will settle in for the night. You two will be tied up. Chump-Change will dispose of this corpse—toss it in the woods."

"I get all the dirty jobs," Chump-Change said.

"So you do." Grazel's lips gave a horrible twitch that Eldon realized was supposed to be a smile. "I've been a little hard on you, Chump-Change. So before you tie them up, you can search *her* for weapons."

"Doesn't look like she could have a weapon anywhere," Chump-Change said.

"Why don't you check? It will liven up the evening."

A grin spread across Chump-Change's greenish face. He stepped over to Melissa and yanked her to her feet. "You can start with the blouse."

Jesus Christ, Eldon thought.

Melissa trembled. She stared at Chump-Change and shook her head, forcing it from side to side as if her neck were stiff.

Chump-Change slapped her.

Melissa yelped and cringed, then fumbled with the buttons of her plaid shirt. She worked them open one at a time. She was wearing a lacy black bra. Chump-Change smacked his lips as she slipped off the shirt and dropped it over the back of the chair.

Eldon's stomach roiled.

Grazel was expressionless. Eldon knew he could never spring off the couch fast enough to lunge for Grazel. His knees were too weak to lift him, anyway.

"Oh, man!" Chump-Change said as if it were Christmas. "The skirt next, honey."

Melissa's lips quivered. Chump grinned and raised a hand to strike her again. Melissa flinched and began inching her skirt up her thighs. She was wearing her black garter belt.

Grazel got up and strolled over to stand next to Eldon, as if to get a better view.

Eldon almost turned away, almost missed what happened next.

Melissa's left hand came up with a little pistol in it. The gun went

216

whap! whap! Chump-Change doubled over with a scream, clutching his stomach. *Whap!* Melissa shot Chump-Change between the eyes.

Eldon felt an iron hand clamp his shoulder as Melissa pivoted toward Grazel with her pistol in a two-handed grip—and froze.

Eldon looked to his left and directly down the barrel of Grazel's semiautomatic. Grazel had crouched down swift as a cat, protected by the couch and Eldon's body. He held Eldon's shoulder firmly. The barrel of his pistol seemed so huge to Eldon that it was like looking down a well.

"The Mombasa double-tap!" Grazel said admiringly. "Sister, that was art!"

Chump-Change lay on the floor twitching slightly. Then he grew still. Melissa's face was as white as paper.

"I knew you'd take care of him for me," Grazel said. "Now put the pistol on the table. And get dressed."

Melissa put the pistol down and grabbed her blouse.

"Beretta .22, isn't it?" Grazel stood up.

"Yeah," Melissa said weakly.

"Primo. Loaded with hollow points?"

"Yeah."

"Juggy had to go," Grazel said. "He learned everything the hard way." He watched Melissa finish dressing. "Take a seat with your friend."

Grazel stepped away as Melissa tottered over and sat down next to Eldon. She pulled her legs in so she wouldn't touch Gordon's body.

Grazel returned to his own chair. "Half-naked woman guns down small-time thug. Performance art, nothing more. I don't mean to belittle your achievement—it was suitable for the subject matter. But I'll tell you straight out, since you want to know—I killed Archie Loris. Now, *that* was major. The banjo's going to be my souvenir."

"You've just confessed to a murder," Eldon said.

Grazel shrugged. "I don't expect to get caught."

"You're going to kill us," Melissa said.

"Certainly not before tomorrow," Grazel said. "You have to show me where you got that moss!"

"And if I won't?" Eldon asked.

"Then she dies *slow*. That's why I didn't shoot her just now." Grazel's features became animated; the effect was horrible in the glare and shadows cast by the lantern. "I don't have time to scour the forest. I was here on a job, years ago. If I'd known about the moss then, things would've been very different. So near and yet so far."

"What was the job?" Eldon wanted to keep Grazel talking. He spotted Chump-Change's revolver on the floor in the corner of his vision. Under the table. If he could only dive for it . . .

"I do want to tell you about it," Grazel said. "The unsung artist."

"I pieced it together," Eldon said, nodding. "The Banjo Boy. The shotgun was in the thing's dick. You traced Archie through the mail-order catalogue, when he ordered the Hummel statuettes."

Grazel showed a mouthful of dirty, crooked teeth. "Art's a dangerous thing."

"Why'd you kill him?" Melissa asked.

"Archie had some stuff on bigger boys in Chicago," Mr. Grazel said. "Tried to use it to cut down the size of the kickbacks he had to pay."

"What were they doing for him?" Eldon asked. "He got run out of Chicago—"

"They were letting him *live*," Mr. Grazel said. "He had a fine to pay—for the rest of his life."

"Ah," Melissa said.

"And then he got onto this casino-zone campaign. Loris figured he could set up big-time and legit, cut them out entirely." Grazel slowly shook his head. "Weird politics out here."

"That tore it, eh?" Eldon said. "I can see how."

"Archie was on the lookout for trouble," Grazel said. "He was suspicious when Juggy and I delivered the piece."

"How'd Chump-Change get into the picture?" Eldon asked.

"He wanted to make it big. It didn't cost much to turn him." Grazel sneered down at Chump-Change's corpse. " 'Per diem.' "

"You should've seen Archie when we arrived, rolling his eyes and stuffing spaghetti in his mouth, with that .38 revolver beside his plate—no, Larkin, don't try to jump for the gun; push it over here with your foot."

Eldon obeyed.

"I unveiled the piece!" Grazel said in near-operatic tones. "He saw the banjo and his eyes popped right out. Too fat to move but he *knew!* And then I reached up the Banjo Boy's ass and pulled the trigger! It was my finest hour. Better than the time with the blowtorch."

Eldon's hair stood on end. "The blowtorch?"

"I killed a man here once with a blowtorch. He had also crossed some important people. I vary the M.O. each time."

"The blowtorch murder . . . " Eldon realized he was going to die at the hands of Fiske's favorite war story come horribly true. The knowledge hammered itself into his mind like a railroad spike. He suddenly had a splitting headache, felt his temples pound.

"That made the papers," Grazel said proudly. "You *want* a nice, ugly hit that'll make the papers, as a warning to others." He looked pensive. "My hand hurts. Now that I'm older, I find myself reduced to base trials of strength, such as firing a shotgun one-handed through topiary."

"That seems quite imaginative to me," Melissa said.

"I needed a weapon that would punch through Archie's fat," Grazel said. "My employer won't be pleased, though, if I don't bring back that tape."

"You said this was your last job," Melissa said.

"I'm going to retire," Grazel said. "Or I was. Maybe they won't let me now, if I don't come back with the goods."

"Where's the tape that Chump stole from Gordon?"

"In my car. In the woods. It means nothing. Archie humping away. Gah. We rented that VCR and ran it on a motel TV." Grazel frowned. "I hate to end my career on a downbeat note. Happens to the best of us, though."

"Where are you going to retire to?" Melissa asked.

"I don't know. The whole world's full of foreigners."

"Canada," Melissa said for some reason. "The Gulf Islands."

Grazel said resentfully, "Canadians . . . "

Eldon realized that his jaw was clenched so tightly that the hinges ached. He worked his mouth, trying to relieve the tension. It didn't do any good. "My best interview," he said, "and I'm not going to get to write it."

"Guess not," Grazel said. He might have been discussing laundry. Then he took fire. *"But this is the moss!* The stuff that every topiarist looks for! It's got all the characteristics—"

"Yeah," Eldon said quickly. "That's what Simon told me."

"Show me where you got the moss, and I'll make it quick for you both," Grazel said. "My word on it."

Eldon's bowels churned audibly. He felt his face redden. "I want my hat. I want to die with my hat on."

"You're not going to die just yet," Grazel said. "We've all got to get some rest. You two have to spend the night tied up, but you'll manage."

"Give me my hat," Eldon said.

Grazel pushed the hat across the table. "All right. Reach out and get it."

Eldon slowly reached for the hat. It was now or never. Time slowed down as Eldon estimated the distance to the revolver on the floor, gauged the distance between him and Grazel, watched the man swing the semiautomatic to track him, looked into Grazel's eyes and was for a split-second dazed with their insane brilliance. Eldon knew that Grazel had easily guessed his intentions, that it was all over now and that topiary or no, the assassin was about to pull the trigger.

I hope it doesn't hurt, was Eldon's last panicky thought as he lunged—and slipped on something round.

The eight ball, he realized, and plunged to the floor with a startled yell as Grazel's pistol went off.

Melissa upended the table. The electric lantern flipped over. Grazel fired again. The bullet hit the falling lantern and the room was plunged into darkness. Eldon scrambled for the revolver, didn't find it, and plowed into Grazel. The man's stink filled Eldon's nose as he bear-hugged Grazel's knees and drove forward as hard as he could. Grazel fell and Eldon leaped on top of him, grabbing Grazel's gun hand and trying to lever it away.

Suddenly the lights in the house came on. There was a sound of breaking glass and a man yelled, *"Freeze! Police!"*

Grazel instantly stopped struggling and threw up his hands. Eldon rolled over to see Art Nola in the broken window, covering them with a pump shotgun.

24

Uniformed deputies kicked open the door and piled into the room. Frank Juliano followed them with a camera and popped off a flash picture. "You're on Page One, Eldon!"

Eldon jerked the semiautomatic from Grazel's hand. A deputy instantly took the weapon while another handcuffed Grazel. Nola stepped through the door with his shotgun, rain running off his overcoat.

"You look like Eliot Ness," Eldon said weakly.

The detective ignored him and went immediately to the bodies on the floor. "They're both dead," he said after a moment.

"Chump-Change killed Gordon," Eldon said. "Gordon took a bullet for me. Melissa shot Chump, thanks to a nice little sleight of hand."

That got a grin from Art. "Good shooting, girl."

"Don't 'girl' me, Art." Melissa sat down heavily, her face chalky.

"Sorry," Art said. "You're right."

Eldon found Melissa's Beretta and offered it to her.

"I don't want it," she said.

Eldon handed the gun to Art. "Can't you cover Gordon up?"

One of the deputies snatched a doily and put it over Gordon's face.

Eldon stared at the incongruous piece of lacy cloth, then pulled off his own jacket and laid it over Gordon's head and shoulders. "Poor Gordon. God, he was brave."

It was then that he noticed the bullet hole in the jacket sleeve.

"You can thank Frank you're not lying there, too," Nola said as Eldon stared at the hole. "He told me you'd gone to the Lucky Poke."

"How'd you know to—?"

"Stephanie came to," Nola said. "I talked to her at the hospital and she asked for you. I called your house but you weren't there. Then I tried *her* place—" Art nodded at Melissa "—and no luck again. So I tried the newspaper and Frank answered."

"Fiske had me working late on red tide," Frank said. "Once Art and I got out to the Poke, it wasn't hard to piece together what had happened."

"A couple of loggers named Malcolm and Dewey were very helpful," Nola said.

"I never saw anybody swallow a roach so fast," Frank said.

"Did one of them swallow something?" Nola asked innocently.

"You've got a hell of a first-person story here, Eldon," Frank said.

"Yeah. Great copy." Eldon felt himself running down, as if the adrenaline were leaking out a valve in his foot. "Thanks for being so considerate, Art—about Stephanie, I mean."

"It was what Stephanie told me that was so important," Nola said. "I needed you to interpret the French."

One of the deputies was reading Grazel his Miranda rights. Grazel listened gravely, nodding and biting out, "Yeah," each time the deputy asked if he understood his rights.

"Larkin!" Grazel said.

"What?"

"I've got to have some of that moss. Send me some when I'm in the pen. I'll have a lot of time on my hands."

"It's just ordinary moss, Grazel. I couldn't find the right plant again, anyway."

"That's *Mr.* Grazel. *Je suis artiste!*"

Eldon looked away. He didn't feel like arguing. His gaze fell on the videocassette recorder. Its lights were on and the machine was stuttering over a half-disgorged cassette. Eldon realized that it was attempting to carry out the commands he'd punched in when he'd last visited the house.

He reached down and nudged the tape. The machine swallowed it smoothly and began to hum. A repeating ripple of indicator lights showed that the tape was playing.

"Hit the TV," Nola said.

Eldon found the television's "on" switch. The screen illuminated to an image of Archie Loris, attired in something like a toga with a laurel wreath around his brow. On the wall in the background was a Port Jerome High School football banner.

They watched as Archie, giggling and drooling, pushed his collection of Hummels around a tabletop. He was fumbling with himself behind the table.

Eldon gave a low whistle. "How'd your boys miss this tape, Art?"

Art sighed. "You remember Archie's basket of magazines? It was right in front of the VCR cabinet. When they find the porno, everything comes to a halt. It's a professional hazard of house searches. . . . And by then, the power was off anyway."

Stephanie Hosfelder walked into the picture, stark naked. She carried a tray with a huge goblet on it that looked like a theater prop. Eldon winced at the sight of Stephanie's ravaged body—her ribs showed, there were bruises on her thighs, and her arms were scarred with needle marks.

Loris seized the goblet and swilled from it, then pulled Stephanie onto his knee. He grabbed a statue and began declaiming in a weird language.

"It's French," Eldon said. "He's reading it the way it's spelled . . . off the statue bases."

"There's a code there after all," Nola said. "Stephanie only

223

realized later that she'd stolen the wrong tape and given it to Gordon."

"But she has amnesia," Eldon protested.

"She doesn't remember the beating," Art said. "This happened before that."

"But what's the code?" Eldon asked. "They're just verses of poetry—"

"The English equivalents of the first French word on the base of each statue spell out the name of one of the local banks, when you put 'em in correct order."

"Archie doesn't speak French!"

"Stephanie studied French in high school," Nola said. "And she wrote poetry."

Eldon remembered the pathetic notebook. God knew what had become of it. "Yeah, she did. And Archie liked crossword puzzles. Stephanie used to give Archie crossword puzzle books."

"She came up with the idea of a code to please Archie," Nola said with a nod. "There's a safe-deposit box in the bank—"

"Number *soixante-neuf,* I'll bet," Eldon said.

"You got it," Art said. "And in that safe-deposit box—"

"Is everything they sent me after," Grazel finished. "Stuff on the Chicago boys that oughta be of interest. The key's in my shoe. I took it out of Archie's wallet the day we shot him. All we needed was the bank." He looked at Melissa. "Prosecutor, you look a little green around the gills—but would you like to make a deal?"

"Art, take him out of here, please," Melissa said.

On the tape, Archie was mauling Stephanie. Eldon turned the TV off. "Loris *told* Stephanie what he had?"

"He was an egomaniac," Art said. "A boaster. A football star. You saw the tape."

Frank shot another picture as the deputies hauled Grazel out. "Sounds like this story's going national, Eldon. Congratulations. It'll sure take Jimbo's mind off his troubles."

"His troubles?" Eldon demanded.

"Jimbo thinks he has gout."

"Gout?"

"From overdoing his diet."

"I need some air." Eldon went out onto the porch. The wet instantly soaked through the bottoms of his socks but he didn't care. He stood there enjoying the rain, shivering a little and squinting in the lights of the sheriff's cars as he watched the deputies stuff Mr. Grazel into a rear seat. He'd played for the highest stakes of all tonight; he'd never gamble again.

I need a car—again, he thought. And a vacation.

Melissa came out, too.

"I've won our bet," Eldon said. "Come home with me. We'll sleep like rocks."

"I'm afraid you'll never collect," Melissa said sadly.

I will not say anything, Eldon told himself.

"Conflict of interest," Melissa went on. "We're witnesses together in a murder case."

"But you can't try this case now!" Eldon's eyes burned as the words burst out of him. "What difference does it make?"

"The defense could impugn us in a second if we sleep together," Melissa said. "They'll say we're lying to frame Grazel."

"That's absurd! He's a mob hit man—"

Melissa gripped Eldon's wrist, hard. "And I'm an ambitious deputy district attorney. And you're an ambitious reporter. That's how it'll play."

"Why does anyone have to know?"

"I won't lie under oath. Would you?"

Eldon felt as if he were floating. He knew he had lost the argument—and that he had never really expected to win the bet. "No," he admitted.

"I can't try this case, but I'd sure as hell better be useful," Melissa said. "The D.A.'s not going to be happy about this night's work. I should've told someone where I was going."

"I always figured you'd come up with something like this," Eldon said, trying to keep the bitterness from his voice.

"Eldon, don't you think I want to? *Need to?* I just killed some-one—"

"But you're not going to. I knew it was too good to be true."

"Then why'd you go through it?"

"To get the scoop, of course," Eldon lied. He gave his jungle hat a tug, setting it at what he hoped was a rakish angle. "Anything for a good story."

Melissa touched Eldon's face, her eyes soft. "You had me fooled, then. You're a pretty good bluffer."

"Cards are child's play," Eldon said. "I'm going fishing."